W9-BMP-329

ISBN 0-373-22175-4

9 780373 221752

50279

125112

175
2.79
22175
December

Harlequin Intrigue®

Night Wind

Aimée Thurlo

DBZ588738

**Romance, Suspense and
Adventure . . . At Its Best**

The gorge seemed almost bottomless

"Ready whenever you are," Travis called.

Belara feigned courage she scarcely felt and made a circle with her thumb and forefinger. As she started to attach the safety line, shots rang out from somewhere below. Belara dove to the ground and lay flat against the cold stone. The whine of flying bullets ripped the stillness of the night.

"Come on," Travis yelled. "You've got to cross now."

Belara stared at the rope, realizing that there was no way she'd be able to cross by pulling herself hand over hand. *She'd* be below the line of fire, but Travis would have no cover at all the whole time she was crossing. Her heart constricted. "Change of plans," she yelled back. "We have to do this the fast way."

She cut the safety line and, not giving Travis a chance to protest, broke into the fastest run of her life.

But even as she leapt, she realized she wasn't going to make it.

ABOUT THE AUTHOR

Aimée Thurlo says that *Night Wind* was inspired by memories and discussions at her husband, David's, high school reunion on the Navajo reservation in Shiprock, New Mexico. There, some old friends showed them the value and the tensions of living in two worlds. Aimée and David live in New Mexico. When not working, they enjoy riding their horses, playing with their pack of dogs and practicing their marksmanship.

Books by Aimée Thurlo

HARLEQUIN INTRIGUE
109—EXPIRATION DATE
131—BLACK MESA
141—SUITABLE FOR FRAMING
162—STRANGERS WHO LINGER

HARLEQUIN SUPERROMANCE
312—THE RIGHT COMBINATION

Don't miss any of our special offers. Write to us at the following address for information on our newest releases.

Harlequin Reader Service
P.O. Box 1397, Buffalo, NY 14240
Canadian address: P.O. Box 603,
Fort Erie, Ont. L2A 5X3

Night Wind

Aimée Thurlo

Harlequin Books

TORONTO • NEW YORK • LONDON
AMSTERDAM • PARIS • SYDNEY • HAMBURG
STOCKHOLM • ATHENS • TOKYO • MILAN

To Sue and Mary Elizabeth,
for memories of planes, trains,
taxi cabs and clandestine operations

Acknowledgment
To JB, who can never take credit
but always manages to help when he's needed

Harlequin Intrigue edition published December 1991

ISBN 0-373-22175-4

NIGHT WIND

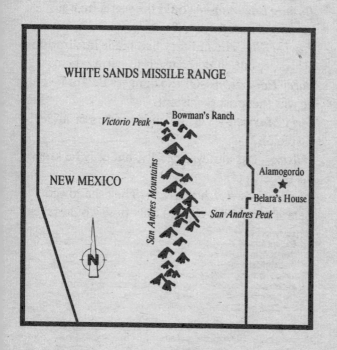

WHITE SANDS MISSILE RANGE

Bowman's Ranch

Victorio Peak

NEW MEXICO

Alamogordo

San Andres Mountains

Belara's House

San Andres Peak

N

CAST OF CHARACTERS

Belara Fuller—Her Navajo uncle had taught her about the desert—and she'd soon find out if she'd learned enough.

Jimmie Bowman—Would the secret he was keeping damn them all?

Travis Hill—The military had made infiltration his trade, but could he use it to betray them?

Barry Robertson—Of the dangers Belara faced, he was the most persistent.

Jerry Maxwell—Was he under orders or under suspicion?

Wilson—His aim was deadly, but only he knew his target.

The Unknown Adversaries—They shadowed Belara's every move, and only time would reveal why.

Chapter One

Belara Fuller walked out of the greenhouse into the noon-day heat. Pensively, she gazed across the shimmering desert countryside that surrounded her nursery. Rows of native southwest plants, ranging from yuccas to mesquite flourished in the harsh environment. Inside, their delicate off-spring required more controlled conditions.

The rocky alluvial plain of the Sacramento Mountains where her property lay seemed covered in shades of gray and sand. The native grasses were withered and short. It had been a dry year. Livestock had gone hungry trying to graze in areas parched by the three-digit summer temperatures. Some ranchers had been forced to truck in hay all the way from Alamosa, Colorado, just to keep their animals alive. Wildlife had suffered, too, competing for a food supply badly diminished by a four-year drought. Without rain, the Circle of Life was interrupted and all suffered. Her mother's brother would have said that Water Sprinkler, the rain bringer and water carrier of the gods, had been slacking off on the job.

Belara selected a potted claret cup cactus for her home, then headed straight for her pickup. Out in the country, this was a girl's best friend. Forget diamonds, the light blue, four-wheel drive Chevy took her wherever she wanted to go. And it even had personality. It groaned when she over-loaded it, and purred when she played her favorite country and western music tapes. Her mechanic had even commented a time or two on the light perfume that seemed to have become a part of the interior. Although his observation hadn't annoyed her, his surprise had. Just because she loved working with soil and sand didn't mean she neglected the little pleasures other women enjoyed.

Belara settled behind the driver's seat and secured the small cactus with the seat belt on the passenger's side. Once she was sure it wouldn't tip over, she started toward her home at the top of the hill. Maybe her uncle would come to visit tonight. He often dropped by for her mutton stew on Wednesdays. It had become their special night, but lately he'd stopped coming so often.

Although she'd asked him about it several times, he'd never really explained. She suspected it had to do with the difficulty he'd had adjusting to retirement. For years, his work at the Range had served as the basis for his day. Now, with hours of inactivity stretching out before him, he lacked direction and his morale had gone steadily downhill. She worried about him, knowing how important it was for a Navajo to feel productive. To the *Dinéh*, the People, it was the road to health and happiness.

Minutes later, Belara pulled into her driveway and walked to her large, barn-shaped mailbox. As usual, it was filled. What had started as a small business six years ago had grown steadily. Orders for her plants came from all over the country. Her inventory, which had expanded to meet the demand, now included everything from ornamental cacti to medicinal plants.

Her nursery's success was due for the most part to the unique service she provided for her customers. Whenever she shipped a plant that traditionally had served some function, she included instructions with the order. People could learn how to make soap from the narrow leaf yucca her people called *tsá'ászi'*, or red dye from Mountain Mahogany. The most popular item in her catalog was what the *Dinéh* called *tsintl'iz*, or the Fendler bush. It never failed to attract interest once people learned that it was considered an aphrodisiac for men.

She flipped through the letters, sorting business correspondence from junk mail, then abruptly stopped. Toward the middle of the stack was a small padded envelope addressed in her uncle's bold, perfectly lettered handwriting. She opened it quickly and found a set of keys, and a note asking her to keep an eye on his home. He'd gone camping and wouldn't be back until after the first of the month.

The first of the month was almost a month away! Something wasn't right, she could feel it. Her uncle could take care of himself out in the desert, he'd done it before. But she couldn't remember him ever going for more than two weeks.

Belara looked pensively at the keys resting in the palm of her hand. She'd better take a look around. It was a short trip.

She was about halfway there on the almost empty highway when the white van behind her caught her attention. It was pulling around into the left lane beside her, as if to pass. But when Belara slowed down to let him go by, the driver stayed even with her, honking his horn. Both he and the man beside him were pointing toward the rear of her truck and shaking their heads.

With a nod, Belara pulled to the side of the road and stopped on the shoulder. Although she hadn't been aware of any trouble, they'd obviously spotted something wrong. As she parked, she glanced in her rearview mirror and saw the van pulling in behind.

The realization that she was alone with strangers on a relatively deserted highway sent a warning to her brain. Maybe she was being overly suspicious, but it was better to be safe than sorry. Leaving the pickup running, she opened the door and leaned out. Everything looked okay on that side. Certainly the tire wasn't flat.

Seeing the driver of the van walking toward her, she evaluated the man quickly. He was dressed in jeans and a sports shirt, and had a black baseball cap pulled down low over dark sunglasses. His passenger was just getting out of the vehicle. He had on sunglasses, too, and was holding a gunnysack and a roll of duct tape in his hands.

Uneasy, she called out to the driver. "Is something wrong with my truck?"

"That's why we signaled you, sweetie. Your spare tire is about to fall onto the road." The man moved closer.

Against her better judgment, Belara slipped out of the driver's seat and started walking to the rear of the truck. Suddenly she stopped in her tracks, remembering the flat she'd had last week. Her spare was in the truck, not underneath. She glanced to her left and saw the tire still lying in the bed. Realizing she'd been tricked, Belara tried to run.

The man with the cap lunged forward with a curse and grabbed her arm roughly. "We're taking you for a ride, beautiful."

"No!" Belara yelled. She kicked out with her work boot, catching him about a foot higher than she'd been aiming.

"Ugh!" The man doubled over, clutching his stomach. "Get that witch!" he shouted to his friend.

Belara was already on the move. Jumping into the driver's seat, she threw the gearshift into low.

But the man had reached the truck, too. Standing on the running board on the passenger side, he leaned through the open window and grabbed her shoulder. "Stop right now before I yank you out of this truck!" he said, a slight Spanish accent evident in his speech.

Reacting quickly, Belara grabbed the cactus pot and shoved the plant right into her attacker's face. With a scream, he jerked back and fell off the running board.

Just as she let out on the clutch, her first attacker leaped onto her side of the truck. With a curse, he grabbed the steering wheel. She caught a brief glimpse of a red-and-blue tattoo extending from beneath his wristwatch, a pointed design in one corner. As a desperate idea flashed into her mind, she shoved the door open with all her might, knocking him to the ground. Fumbling for the gearshift, she slammed the door shut again.

As she struggled to start the engine, a large, old car skidded to a stop right in front of her, dust flying everywhere. Trapped between the two vehicles, she fought a wild surge of panic. Four men shot out of the sedan. With a sinking feeling, she realized she'd never be able to fight them all.

To her surprise, the four rushed past her, chasing her would-be kidnappers. The pair fled to their van, closing their doors a few steps ahead of the men from the car. A heartbeat later, the van whipped around onto the road, scattering her rescuers in all directions as it made its escape.

Everything happened so fast she barely had time to breathe before it was over. Belara leaned out of the window to thank the men who'd come to her aid, but as she got a good look at the first one, she almost pulled back and rolled it up. She normally didn't judge people by appearances, but this man moved with an aggressiveness that bordered on hostility. With apprehension, she noted the large leather knife sheath attached to his belt.

"Are you Belara Fuller?" he asked, his tone brusque.

The fact he knew who she was certainly didn't make her feel any better. "Yes, I am, but how do you know my name?" There was something intelligent, yet oddly reptilian about his eyes and pointed features. It made her feel like a field mouse in front of a rattlesnake.

"We've been looking for you," he said, not really answering her question. He extended his hand. "My name's Robertson, Barry Robertson."

This was one time she wished she lived in a world where Navajo customs prevailed. Touching a stranger came a great deal easier to the whites than to the *Dinéh*. Yet, for the sake of politeness, she shook his hand.

Belara struggled not to show her distaste. His palm was moist and strangely cold despite the heat. "I'd like to thank you and your friends for chasing away those two men," she said. Glancing ahead, she saw the others getting back into the car. "Is there something I can help you with?"

"You're Jimmie Bowman's niece, right?"

Her heart began to beat faster. "Yes. Why do you ask?"

"My friends and I have some business to discuss with your uncle, but we can't seem to locate him. Can you tell us what his schedule is? We've been trying his home for three days."

"Now that he's retired, my uncle comes and goes as he pleases," she answered, reluctant to give this man any specific information. "He shows up at my nursery every once in a while, so if I see him I'll be glad to tell him to contact you. Would you like to leave your telephone number with me?"

His cool, analytical gaze held hers. "No, we're going to be hard to catch, too."

"Okay. I'm sorry I couldn't be more help. Unless there's something else, I should be on my way." Feeing guilty about her suspicious attitude, Belara managed a thin smile. She knew she was being unfair. Just because he resembled a snake didn't mean he was one. And he and his friends had possibly saved her life. "I really do appreciate what you did here today. Things could have gone very badly for me if you hadn't showed up."

"You're a fine-looking woman, and full of fight from what I saw," the man said. "I sure wish you weren't in such a hurry to leave."

Her throat tightened, but she forced herself to remain calm. She couldn't think of anything more repulsive than being found attractive by this man. She glanced at the digital clock on her dashboard. "I really can't stay, but when I see my uncle, I'll let him know you're looking for him."

Robertson nodded, stared at the ground for a few seconds, and spat into the dust. "We'll keep checking at his place. Our paths will cross sooner or later. You can bank on that." Idly he brushed back a lock of light brown hair, then strode back to his car.

Belara watched the vehicle as it pulled out onto the road. She'd call the police about the men in the van later, but right now her uncle was her main concern. Robertson's interest worried her. From the timing of his appearance, he must have been either following her or the pair in the van. Common sense told her there was something going on here that her uncle needed to know about as soon as possible.

Ten minutes later, she drove up the graveled driveway of her uncle's home. Using the key, Belara let herself in through the front door and went directly to the den. The gun rack over the mantel was empty. That meant he'd taken his favorite rifle, a Mossberg .22 with a scope. Also missing was his old, but well-preserved western saddle.

Belara walked to his bedroom and took out the sturdy oak box from under his bed. She hesitated a moment before opening it. It was an invasion of her uncle's privacy, but under the circumstances it seemed necessary. Hoping he would forgive her, she opened the lid.

His prayer stick, the one he used to ward against evil when traveling, was gone. So was his journal. In it were his observations about the San Andres Mountains and details of little known trails, caves and areas where water could be found. They had spent hours with that book during her childhood, her uncle telling story after story, teaching her about nature, the land and survival.

More worried now than ever, she strode to his desk in the den and allowed her gaze to travel over its surface. The notebook with the maps of the area surrounding his old ranch was missing. There was no doubt now where he'd gone. Last month he'd asked for permission to enter what was now White Sands Missile Range in order to visit his old home, and the Army had turned him down. Her blood turned to ice as she pictured her mother's brother disregarding the dangers, both natural and man-made, and making his way back to the place of his birth.

The dry, rugged land that surrounded the old ranch was used by the military for aerial gunnery and bombing practice, adding unexploded shells to the natural hazards of the area. If there were no military exercises going on, a man who knew the desert and was in perfect health would have a good chance of staying alive. Her uncle had one strike against him, however. The main reason he'd retired was because of a heart condition, although he'd kept that a secret from nearly everyone. The mountainous, desert region would tax his body beyond its capacity. *She* hadn't even known about his ailment until he'd hired a *hataalii*, a medicine man, to perform a curing ceremony and asked her to attend.

A month ago he'd become disillusioned with the white man's medicine that treated the body but not the spirit. That's when he'd arranged for a Blessingway Chant to be done for him. His health *had* improved after that, but only for a short time. He'd since become convinced that if he returned to the ranch where he'd been born, he'd be able to make his peace with the gods and restore himself permanently to harmony. It was only at her insistence that he'd continued to take the tiny pills the doctor had given him to control his angina.

She walked to the medicine cabinet over the sink in the bathroom and slid the glass door open. Her body began to tremble as she saw the small amber bottle of nitroglycerin tablets. The prescription was dated ten days ago. She made a quick count. All fifty of the tiny pills still remained in the glass container.

Taking the bottle, Belara rushed out of the house. There was no time to call the police or the military now. They'd only get bogged down with red tape and interfere with what she had to do. Without his medication her uncle wouldn't survive for long. Even his special gifts wouldn't protect him against an ailment like angina. She'd have to trespass onto the range and go after him. She knew she was the only person who stood a chance of finding him. If he saw strangers approach, he'd use his knowledge of that area to successfully evade them.

Belara drove directly to town. She'd begin preparing for the trip at Sy's Place, purchasing the topographical maps she'd need. As she walked into the small shop, she glanced around, waiting for the owner to appear. Within seconds, the rugged-looking sixty-year-old emerged from the stockroom. "Well, hello there! What brings you into town? Ready to go backpacking?"

"I've decided to surprise my uncle with a camping trip into the area east of Caballo Lake." She hated the subterfuge, but it wouldn't do to tell anyone her uncle had decided to trespass on government land. "I'm going to need some topographical maps of the San Andres Mountains and also of the Missile Range. I like to know what I'm looking at, even if it's at a distance." Belara walked over to the wide chart drawers that lined one wall of the modest shop.

Sy brought out the USGS reference book and handed it to her. "Here you go. If you let me know what sectors you need, I'll help you look through our inventory."

Belara checked the listings, then gave him the chart names. "You know, I sure wish there was a fast way to get this trip organized. Some of my gear is too worn-out to use, so I'm going to have to replace it. Depending on what the shops in town have in stock, I might end up having to travel to Las Cruces, over an hour away. Then, after that, I'll still have to buy food supplies. It's going to take two days just to get ready."

"Not if you see Travis Hill. He's reliable and very knowledgeable. He runs a small business guiding people into the wilderness for hunting, fishing, and other expeditions. He rents equipment and packages everything you need."

"Do you think he might be willing to handle the details for me even if I have no need of a guide?"

Sy reached behind the counter and pulled out a card. "Here. You can call him and ask. Use my phone, if you'd like."

Belara dialed, and a man answered almost immediately. His voice was soft yet clear, a quality that held her attention. "I'm in quite a rush to get underway," she explained after a brief introduction.

"I'm on my way out right now to run some errands. If you're worried about time, it might be faster if I met you someplace."

"Could you come to my plant nursery? It's about half an hour from Sy's Place." She gave him the address and quick directions.

"All right. How about two this afternoon?"

His tone possessed an authoritative edge that she found slightly irritating, but there were more important matters at stake than her personal preferences. "That's fine," she replied, glad that he could come so soon.

"I'll look forward to meeting you," he said.

Belara said a quick goodbye to the store owner, collected her maps and then drove to the nursery. While she waited for Travis Hill to show up, she'd switch the nursery plants to a drip irrigation system to ensure their survival during her absence. Thanks to the time this man would save her, details like these would not put off her departure. She made a mental note to send Sy a plant as a special thank-you after her return.

Work kept her hands busy, but her mind continued to drift to uncle. After her parents had died, he'd taken over, becoming both father and mother to her. He'd willingly accepted the responsibility of raising a young girl, giving up much of his bachelor freedom. Now, it was he who needed her, and she intended to be there for him.

Belara was crouching by some potted plants on the floor, when she heard a knock at the door of the greenhouse. She jumped to her feet with a start. Both Charlie and Sam, her employees, were tending the outdoor plants, so she went to answer it.

She smiled at the tall, strikingly handsome Anglo man waiting on the other side of the glass. In his late thirties, he was what a friend of hers would have referred to as a "hunk." His eyes were a clear green, and his hair almost as black as hers. There was a distinctive trace of white around his temples, but on him the effect added to his looks rather than detracted. With his bronzed tan and lean build, he looked like a working rancher.

She saw him turn and wave at one of her employees. "Hello, Sam! How's the wife?"

Sam took off his baseball cap and wiped the perspiration from his brow. "Travis! How are ya doing, you old so and so."

Recognizing the name of her visitor, she unfastened the latch and waited a moment for the men to exchange greetings, then invited him inside. His stance and the way he moved conveyed the impression of strength and power that was being kept in check with effort.

"You must be Belara Fuller," he said, his eyes never leaving hers. Seeing her nod, he added, "I hoped you wouldn't mind moving up the time our meeting. I'm Travis Hill." He extended his hand.

Belara glanced down at her own hands. They were sandy and damp, with bits of vermiculite clinging to the fingers. "I don't think you want me to shake hands with you right now," she said, with a sheepish smile.

He reached for her right hand and pressed it against his own. "I wouldn't have offered if a little sand was going to bother me."

The warmth of the gesture took her by surprise and a tingle of awareness spread through her. "Come in. To be honest, I'm glad you're early. I wanted to get together as soon as possible."

"Good. From what you'd told me on the telephone, I thought you'd feel that way," he said confidently.

She noted his immaculate tan cotton shirt and blue jeans. "I hope you don't mind if I keep working. I'm a little pressed for time."

"No problem." He paused for a moment. "Is it Mrs. Fuller?"

"No, I'm not married. But if you'll use my first name, it'll make everything simpler." She crouched by the length of plastic hose she was extending from pot to pot, and noticed a broken connection. "Excuse me for a minute. I'll be right back. I need to get a replacement from the next room.''

Travis watched her walk away from him. Her waist-length ebony hair and slender hips added to her exotic looks, making her appear almost regal. He couldn't understand why someone in her early thirties and as beautiful as Belara Fuller would have chosen such a lonely business. This far from town, the starkness of the desert seemed almost overwhelming. The nursery wasn't exactly located at the end of the world, but it seemed certain that one could see it from here.

When Belara emerged he noticed that the smudge of soil on her cheek was gone. Dust and planting medium had also been brushed off her sweatshirt.

"Let me know if the heat and humidity inside the green-house bothers you. It can be uncomfortable if you're not used to it,'' she said. "If you need to, we can always step outside.''

He grinned widely. "Don't worry. I won't faint.''

Belara laughed. "Sorry. I wasn't trying to imply that you're too wimpy to stand it. It's just habit. I warn every-one who comes in for more than a few minutes. Young desert plants need a little bit of moisture and lots of heat for comfort. People don't.'' She began to position a water emitter over a section of tiny cacti.

"You know, I was wondering why you called me,'' Travis crouched beside her and lent a hand, holding the black waterline while she attached a plastic connector. "Aren't you Jimmie Bowman's niece?''

"Yes, I am,'' she acknowledged.

"I've heard a great deal about him. He knows the country around here like the palm of his hand. I've very good at what I do, don't mistake me, but no one has as much knowledge of southern New Mexico as Bowman does.''

"I'm trying to surprise my uncle with a week-long camping trip,'' she said, having decided this was a plausi-ble explanation. "Only he's going to guess what I'm up to unless I spring it on him fast. I want to have everything ready for tonight.''

"Surely you don't plan to leave after dark," he questioned puzzled.

"That decision isn't up to me," she said, thinking how true that statement really was. "Jimmy will be running the show."

"You're not giving me very much time. Whether I can help you or not is going to depend on what type of things you're going to need. I have a large inventory of equipment I can sell or rent, but it's not all inclusive."

"My uncle and I have our own backpacks and bedding, but I'm going to need camping gear and food supplies for both of us. I'm also going to need climbing gear." She glanced at Travis, then averted her gaze.

He had a gut feeling that something wasn't quite right about her story, and it wasn't because she avoided looking directly at him. He'd been around long enough to know that was a Navajo custom around strangers.

"My uncle is usually the one who handles the preparations for us," she added when he didn't answer right away. "Since it's not something I'm used to doing, I'm afraid to rush through it on my own and overlook something I might…we might need." She kept her gaze focused on her work. "You could say I'm trying to impress him with my thoroughness as well as surprise him."

One "could" say that, but that didn't make it the truth. He stared absently at the small plants on the bench before her. "Where exactly are you heading?"

"The open country east of Caballo Lake," she answered.

Absently he watched her position a slow-drip soaker hose over a row of seedlings. She was either keeping a great deal back or distorting the facts to mislead him. It was one thing to surprise a person with plans for a camping trip. But you didn't show up on his doorstep fully equipped and expect him to rush right out with you. "That area is tricky," he cautioned with wary suspicion. "Get turned around just once and you're in a restricted zone."

"I'm aware of that," she answered simply. "By the way, I know very little about you," she said, quickly changing the subject. "Why don't you tell me about your qualifications? In your type of work you're taking on the responsibility for people's safety."

He tried not to smile, recognizing the technique. She was trying to divert him by putting him on the defensive. He'd used that same ploy himself many times. "I spent six years in the Special Forces."

"And you learned about desert survival in the Army?"

He nodded. "I even taught it for a while. That, and a few other things," he said with a ghost of a smile.

"How come you quit?" Finished, she checked out the irrigation system once more.

"It was time for me to go on to something else." She'd sidetracked the conversation long enough. Now it was his turn to learn more about her plans. "I'll need to know specifically what areas east of Caballo Lake you're interested in so I can get maps for those quadrangles." If she was planning anything illegal, her answer would give him a clue.

"I've already got maps."

He nodded expressionlessly, having learned absolutely nothing from her answer. "I'll need a more comprehensive list of the items you want me to get for you. Or, if you tell me what you have in terms of gear, I'll fill in the gaps."

"I've written down the things I already have," she said, handing him a sheet of notepaper. "Will this do?"

He glanced down at it and nodded. "This is fine. I should have most of what you need on hand. The other items are things I can get without any problem."

She stood up and brushed the dirt from her jeans. "I'm finished so why don't we go up to my house to discuss your fee? It's just a mile from here and I can guarantee the temperature will be much more comfortable there."

"All right." His questions had made her nervous, yet he had to admit she'd masked it well. Only her nervous mannerisms had betrayed her, like the way she'd continually smoothed her palm over her hip and thigh, as if trying to rub the perspiration away. Actually the gesture was a very sensual one, though he doubted she was aware of it at all.

"I'll follow you in my Jeep," he said, accompanying her outside. As he held the door of her pickup open for her, he caught a whiff of the cologne that lingered inside. The scent reminded him of lilacs. "Just in case I lose you, what's your street address?"

She answered him. "But don't worry. I'll watch out for you. Just keep your eyes on my tail, and I'll get us where we're going." Trying to keep a straight face she added, "I meant the tail of my truck, of course." She reached down and started the truck.

He moved away as she placed the truck in gear, soft laughter shaking his shoulders. Keeping an eye on any part of her anatomy, tail included, would be a pleasure.

Travis went to his Jeep and followed her up the graveled lane. She drove expertly, handling the pickup like someone born in one. He smiled slowly. Her self-confidence and quirky sense of humor appealed to him. Yet, he sensed that there was much more to her than what appeared on the surface.

Travis saw her slow down as they approached a small ranch-style house surrounded by a desert landscaped yard. Belara's isolated home overlooked the city of Alamogordo, away to the northeast.

Travis pulled into the driveway behind her. As he stepped out of his vehicle, he heard the sound of an engine starting close by and a car door being slammed shut.

Belara glanced back at him quickly, her face taut with fear. "No one's supposed to be here!"

An instant later, a dusty green sedan came spinning around the side of her house, sending gravel flying in every direction!

Chapter Two

"Burglars!" Travis said, jumping back into his Jeep. "Come on. Maybe we can get close enough to read their license plate."

He'd started the engine before she could think of a way to warn him that there was another possibility. Suspecting he'd go after them alone if she didn't respond quickly, she climbed in. Images of the man in the cap and his friends hovered at the edge of her mind as Travis sped down the gravel road.

"We have an advantage," he said. "My Jeep is made for this type of terrain, their car isn't. We should be able to catch up," he said, his eyes glued on the sedan fishtailing and bouncing heavily just ahead.

"Be careful. We have no idea how many of them there are, besides the driver. If there're two or three guys in there, and they come after us, we're going to have a problem."

"No, we'll be just fine. I've never come out of a fight in second place," he answered without any particular emphasis. "But to be honest, I doubt it will come to that. Burglars usually aren't looking for a confrontation, or they'd be out mugging someone."

She had no doubt that under ordinary circumstances any woman would have been perfectly safe with Travis at her side. Yet, there were a few facts she hadn't enlightened him on and that put him at a disadvantage.

Travis narrowed the distance. "In another second we'll be able to see the plate despite the dust. Hang on," he said, continuing to accelerate.

Belara saw a man lean out the passenger's side window. He held something in his hand. "Look out!" she yelled.

Two shots rang out in angry succession. The first shattered the windshield about six inches to the right of Travis's head. She only heard the second because by then Travis had shoved her down hard. He cursed loudly, giving the steering wheel a hard twist to the left. As the Jeep began to bounce unevenly, she knew they'd gone off the road.

"Stay the hell down!" he roared as she tried to look up.

She braced herself, expecting another shower of bullets, or a crash, but neither came and they finally rolled to a stop. It was only then that she remembered to breathe and felt her heart begin beating again. Her entire body was shaking.

Travis removed his hand from her back, allowing her to sit up. "Are you all right?" he asked quickly.

"I'm okay," she answered in an unsteady voice.

He cursed violently, then slammed his hand against the wheel. "I'm going to drop you off here for a while and go after them. I think I can still catch up."

She stared at him aghast. "No! Are you crazy? You have no idea what you're up against!"

He watched the dust trail disappearing into the distance, then turned back to her. "Those weren't ordinary burglars. Suppose you tell me what's going on."

"How should I know?" she snapped back. "I never got a look at their faces. All I saw was the gun and the underside of your dashboard!"

His jaw was clenched, but it was his probing, unflinching glare that let her know he wasn't fooled by her evasion. He walked around, examining the sides and front of the open-topped vehicle. "I'll have to replace the windshield, but the rest is still in good shape."

She stared at the two weblike patterns on the glass in front of her and the large holes in each of their centers. If she left the vehicle now her knees would probably buckle. Travis wasn't aware of how kind fate was being to him. At least so far she hadn't become violently ill.

"Are you sure you're okay?" he asked, almost as if he'd read her mind.

She nodded and tried to swallow, but her mouth was drier than the desert air. "I've never been shot at before," she said, realizing how inane that sounded.

He regarded her thoughtfully. "I have, but it's much easier when you can shoot back." Travis slipped behind the driver's seat. "From the hole, I'd say they fired a .45. Unfortunately the angle of the shots was such that there's virtually no chance of finding the slugs."

"Look, I'm sorry about your windshield," she managed, wondering how long it would take for her heart to slow down again. "I'll pay for whatever damage was done."

"No, it's my fault, damn it," he muttered. "I underestimated them, and in the process endangered you." He shifted gears into reverse. "I'll take care of it."

It was a rough ride back to the road, but a picnic in comparison to the one they'd taken going into the brush. "I'll call the sheriff's office and have them come out," she said. "Maybe they'll be able to discover what those men wanted."

He glanced over at her, eyebrows furrowed. "You really don't know?"

She exhaled softly. "I lead a peaceful life. My uncle has, on occasion, even call it boring," she smiled wryly. "But it suits me. I'm doing the things I love, and have enough money to meet my needs and my uncle's, if that should ever become necessary." She paused, shaking her head in bewilderment. "But lately, things have been crazy. I'm not used to threats or having people try to murder me. I wish I *did* understand what was happening. Maybe then I'd know what to expect."

"When things don't make sense, that usually means you're missing information. It's that blind side that can get you killed," he said parking in her driveway. "That's part of S. F. training but I think it applies here, too." His gaze was steely as he met her eyes. "Take my advice and get to the bottom of what's happening fast. Those guys were willing to kill in order to stop us, so you've got a formidable enemy."

She tried to suppress the shudder that ran through her, but didn't quite manage it. Her legs still felt like rubber as she led the way inside her home. The sight that greeted her made her stomach lurch. Her books had been taken off the shelves and her desk had been ransacked. Drawers lay upended, their contents scattered all around the carpet. Her mail had been opened and strewn everywhere. Yet, nothing appeared broken or damaged. Even the little odds and ends that decorated her coffee table and window frame were still intact.

"From this mess, I'd say they were looking for something very specific," Travis said, crouching by a loose pile of mail on the floor.

She glanced down. "Those are plant orders from all over the United States. They're no good to anyone except me." She picked up the receiver from the kitchen wall phone and dialed the sheriff's office. Moments later, she returned to the living room. "I certainly have one major clean-up job ahead of me," she observed exhaling softly.

Travis walked down the hall, then stopped in front of her bedroom. "This is where they got in. The window in here has been broken and opened. They've searched through some papers I figure must have been on the dresser, but nothing else seems to have been touched."

Belara stepped around him and looked into her room. Her thoughts drifted back to Robertson and the others with him. They'd been determined to talk to her uncle. "I wonder if they thought they'd find some answers here in my home," she mumbled under her breath. Perhaps they were hoping to find a letter from Jimmie with a return address.

Travis came up from behind her. "What were their questions?"

Belara felt his gaze on her as she tried desperately to think of a fast explanation.

Hearing a car pull up outside, she almost sighed with relief. "That must be the sheriff." She walked down the hall toward the front door, then stopped and turned her head. "Will you take the job and get the supplies and equipment I'll need for my camping trip? Once you're finished, all you'd have to do is drop everything by the nursery. If I'm not there, Sam will be. He stays until seven in the evening."

He hesitated a fraction of a second before answering. "I'll do it," he replied. "But if I were you, I'd find out exactly what I'm up against before going out into the desert. It's very easy for a gunman to zero in on a target out there."

The words chilled her to the bone, but she forced herself to remain outwardly calm. "I'll be careful, but I'm not going to change my plans." As a loud knock reverberated through the house, she headed toward the door.

TRAVIS LEFT HER fifteen minutes later. The police had taken their statements, but they hadn't held out much hope of catching the intruders. Instinct told him that the trouble Belara was facing was going to get worse. That alone was reason enough to question his sanity in getting involved. Why had he agreed to help her? He didn't need the kind of problems she'd bring into his life. And it wasn't the thought of bullets flying in his direction that worried him, either. It was her subtle sexiness, her need for an ally, and his own inability to turn down someone who needed help that really scared him. The combination spelled disaster.

Walk away. Don't get involved. There probably wasn't much he could do for her anyway, she seemed to want to keep him at arm's length. Besides, the last thing he needed was to keep pushing and end up with more deaths on his hands. He should call and cancel the whole thing. Let her solve her own problems.

His eyes fastened on the bullet holes in the Jeep windshield. One was right across from where she'd been sitting.

Who the hell was he trying to kid? He wouldn't go back on his word now. A woman who spent her days cultivating plants was no match for men like the ones they'd run into. The least he could do was try to even the odds a bit.

As soon as the police left, Belara went to the telephone and dialed her uncle's former office number at the Range. There was one man who might have learned if her uncle's sudden camping trip had been motivated by more than his health. Ernie Yarrow, his best friend, would know if he'd risked going to his old ranch now to avoid Robertson and his friends. She'd avoided mentioning her earlier encounter with Robertson to the police, not wanting to complicate matters even more for her uncle.

A familiar, friendly voice soon greeted her over the line. "I haven't spoken to you in practically forever. How are you doing?"

She exchanged amenities, then quickly explained that she was trying to get hold of her uncle. "I was hoping he might have spoken to you about his trip."

"No, he sure didn't," Yarrow said, his voice suddenly becoming cool. "Didn't he tell you anything about it?"

"No, and I—" She stopped, not wanting to give out any information that might get her uncle into more trouble than he was in. "Well, it's not important."

"Hey, don't worry about Jimmie, okay? He knows how to take care of himself. If I hear from him, I'll have him give you a call."

"I'd appreciate that." She replaced the receiver and stared across the room pensively. She was not finding answers and with each new question, her concern for her uncle grew. Danger was closing in on him and he'd need her help. More than ever, she was determined to go find him.

Travis looked at the list she'd given him. The first thing he'd need to get for her was a compass. He pulled into the parking lot of Sy's store a short time later and walked inside.

The owner greeted him warmly. "I recommended you to a client. Did you ever get together with Belara Fuller?"

"Sure did. I appreciate you sending the business my way," Travis answered. "I accepted the job, and in fact, that's why I'm here. I need to get a compass for her." Familiar with the layout, he took a short cut through the store's map section. A man browsing through the drawers blocked his way to the counter.

As Travis approached, he glanced up. "Well, if it isn't Mr. Green Beret himself. I thought it was you trying to sneak up on me," he spat out.

"Robertson," Travis observed flatly. His eyes dropped casually to the man's waist. Sure enough, he still had that long-bladed fighting knife.

"Checking to see if I'm armed, Mr. Green Beret? Smart move. You wouldn't want to run into my blade accidentally." Robertson spoke out harshly.

Travis noticed Sy standing behind one of the counters trying to figure out what was going on. "It'll take more than a whittling merit badge to get that knife close to me," Travis growled, watching Robertson's eyes. If the man was planning to take action, he'd get his first sign there.

"Consider yourself lucky today, Hill," Robertson said in a soft menacing voice. "Things are a little too public to settle our score now. But the time will come when it'll be just you and me."

"Learn from your mistakes, Robertson. If I have to take your knife away again, I won't be as gentle when I reacquaint your face with New Mexico sand."

Sy came up hesitantly, looking back and forth at the two men. "I hope everyone's finding what they need over here."

"Even some things I don't need!" Robertson muttered, handing Sy a large scale folding map. "I'll take this one."

As Sy and Robertson walked over to the cash register, Travis stayed where he was, watching. The last thing Sy needed was trouble at his store, and Barry Robertson sure as heck wasn't worth it.

When Robertson left, Travis walked over to the counter. Sy met him, a big smile of relief on his face. "I take it you two have met before and aren't exactly blood brothers."

Travis shrugged. "I know him and a few of his friends," Travis said, failing to conceal his disgust. "I took them camping about three weeks ago, and they asked me to teach them desert survival. Once we got near the Missile Range, the boys decided they wanted to take a detour. They thought they'd search for gold on Victorio Peak. Apparently they'd read all about the treasure Doc Noss claimed to have found there in a cave in 1937. I tried explaining that no one's ever proven that story, and that the Peak is on restricted federal land."

"And that made it all the more appealing to them?"

"They wanted to go so badly, Robertson even pulled a knife hoping to intimidate me."

"And he's still walking? Travis, you're getting to be quite forgiving in your old age." Sy teased, back to his usual self now.

"I guess I've mellowed a bit since I got out of the Army. I even gave him his knife back when he woke up. They settled down after that, but I cut the trip short anyway and brought them back in." Travis started to look through the array of compasses in stock.

"Are you going to need any maps?" Sy asked as he waited for Travis to make his selection. "We have a good supply on hand. That is, unless you're looking for quadrants around Victorio Peak. We've had a run on those lately. I think gold fever's in the air again."

"Is the government getting ready to sanction another expedition?"

"Not that I know of, and I would have heard," Sy answered.

"So who's been buying you out then?"

"Well, that guy you just squared off with was one of them. He was in here earlier with some friends and they bought quite a few quadrants. There were also two other men who came by. I've never seen either of them before, but they talked like they'd been around here for years. The strange part was they were both wearing brand-new jeans and shiny boots, like hunters from back east."

"You mean Texas?" Travis baited.

"Maybe even farther east," Sy replied with a grin. "Belara Fuller also bought a set."

Travis glanced up in surprise. "Tell me, how well do you know Jimmie Bowman and his niece?"

"Heck, they've been friends of mine for years. They come in here often. Jimmie loves to talk about the old times. During World War II, he served with the Marines as one of the Navajo Code Talkers."

"I've heard of them. They used their language to communicate, and the Japanese were never able to break the code."

Sy nodded. "Nowadays, Jimmie collects old maps, particularly those of the area around his former ranch. He's got a standing order for any I can dig up. Jimmie lived west of Victorio Peak when he was younger. Then after the war, he was forced to sell to the Army, when they turned almost the whole county into White Sands Missile Range. At the time I didn't think selling the ranch bothered him as much as it did later. Back then, he was looking to make a change in his life. The Army also offered him a good paying job. Since he knew the region so well, they asked him to direct security for that sector. He worked for them right up to last month when he finally retired."

The information only raised more questions in his mind, like why had Belara bought the maps? Her uncle certainly wouldn't need them. "When's the last time you saw Bowman?"

Sy stared across the room, lost in thought. "Let's see. He came by about two weeks ago. Come to think of it, that's unusual for him. He normally drops by at least once a week for coffee and doughnuts. Did you need to talk to him?"

"Yeah, I'd like to, if I got the chance. I know he's the foremost expert on the desert and mountains in our area."

"That he is," Sy agreed. "I'll try to arrange it for you next time he comes in." Sy walked Travis to the door. "By the way, I think you should stay as far away from Robertson and his gang as possible. He's only going to find trouble where he's headed. The map he just took with him shows all the roads leading in and out of the Missile Range."

Travis patted Sy on the shoulder. "Thanks, I'll be careful, but there's no need for you to be concerned."

Thoughts of Robertson were put aside quickly as Travis walked back to his Jeep. He was more convinced now than ever that there was something very odd about Belara's last-minute camping trip. Her uncle was undoubtedly involved somehow, but he was certain it had nothing to do with a surprise she was planning to spring on him.

After gathering the rest of the gear Belara needed, Travis took the items by the nursery and left everything with Sam, according to her instructions. He'd wanted to talk to her in person, but Sam hadn't been able to tell him where she'd gone.

Making a quick stop by the auto shop, Travis had the windshield frame of his Jeep removed so that the glass could be replaced. He was getting tired of the odd looks other drivers were giving him. Then, ten minutes later, with a plan firmly in mind, Travis headed for the Missile Range. He still had a few buddies in the right places and it was time to ask a few discreet questions. After a brief stop at the gate, he was cleared through.

Minutes later, Travis pulled up next to the headquarters building and walked inside. Lieutenant Jerry Maxwell worked in base operations. If anyone could find out about Bowman or his possible whereabouts, it would be Jerry. He had the contacts and would know who to ask. Bowman must have made friends during his years serving at the Range.

Travis noted the increase in security. He hadn't had to sign in and out of the headquarters building on any of his previous visits. Maybe a training exercise was going on or scheduled to start soon.

As he approached Jerry's office, Travis saw him standing near the window, telephone receiver in hand. Noiselessly, he slipped inside.

"Honey, come on," Jerry pleaded gently. "Just because I was a little late doesn't mean I'd forgotten our date."

Travis squelched a laugh. "Maxwell!" he barked.

Jerry dropped the receiver and spun around, bracing to attention instantly, and almost knocking over his chair in the process. When he saw Travis leaning against the wall laughing, he swore softly. "I thought you were Colonel Dumas. You took ten years off my life, you maggot!" He picked up the receiver, mumbled a few quick words, then hung up.

Travis laughed loudly. "Insults, that's all I get for trying to pay my buddy a visit."

Jerry dropped down in his chair and offered Travis half a tuna fish sandwich. "I'm marooned here for the rest of the afternoon. Care to split my lunch?"

Travis stared at the dime-size holes that covered the top slices of bread. "What the heck happened to it?"

"It had a little mold, so I tore those spots off. It won't kill you. Besides, what's left has antibiotic potential. Makes it healthier," he said with a shrug.

"Jerry, your taste buds have all the delicacy of a kitchen grease trap."

"Hmmf," he answered, taking a large bite. "So what brings you here? Don't give me the visiting buddy routine. I can always tell when you've got something on your mind."

"I need some information, unofficially. I'm trying to locate a guy who's supposed to know all about the desert country around here. His name's Jimmie Bowman and until recently he was employed at the Range as a civilian attached to security."

Jerry shrugged. "Never worked with him. I can't help you."

"You could ask those he did work with if they'd—"

Jerry held up his hand, and his tone suddenly changed. "I think this is one subject you'll have to drop, Travis."

For a moment Travis said nothing, rubbing his jaw pensively. "Okay, let's talk in abstracts. Why would three separate civilian groups suddenly become very interested in the Victorio Peak area?"

Jerry sat up abruptly. "What groups? Who are they?"

"So something *is* going on, old buddy." He grinned smugly. "You want to talk trade?"

Jerry challenged Travis with an unblinking stare. "Tell me about these groups, and then we'll deal."

He shook his head. "I've already given you something. What do you have to trade?"

Jerry fingered the groove in his forehead. "I think you're on a fishing expedition, buddy," he said at last. "But I'll tell you what." He stood up and grabbed his hat. "I'll go talk to my boss and see what he says. Give me a few minutes."

"You've got them. But Jerry, don't play games with me."

Jerry nodded, then wordlessly walked out of the office.

Travis stood up and moved toward the door. Casually he leaned against the doorjamb. He didn't care much for surprises. Not that he really thought Jerry would pull anything, but then again, one never knew.

When ten minutes passed and Jerry failed to return, Travis began to get suspicious. Unwilling to wait any longer, Travis walked down the corridor, checking in each office he passed. Everyone he asked said Lieutenant Maxwell had left suddenly and they didn't know when he'd be back.

Annoyed, Travis headed out of the building and went to his Jeep. He was being stonewalled. Jerry had left, knowing he had never been able to keep a secret around him for long. The Army obviously knew where Bowman was, and wasn't about to tell him anything at all.

But where did that leave him? Belara and Robertson's group were both going into the restricted area for reasons of their own. If they ran into each other, there would be trouble, and Belara was no match for them. He couldn't sit by and risk that happening. After all, he was responsible for giving Robertson's group the desert skills they'd needed to go into the Range. To make matters worse, he'd also just provided Belara with the means to make her own trip.

His thoughts drifted back to the intruders at her home. Did that tie in with the military cover-up? If not, exactly how many other groups would he have to contend with? He hated having a blind side.

Well, there was still hope he might be able to catch her before she set out, *if* he moved quickly.

BELARA INSPECTED HER GEAR one final time. Originally she'd planned to wait until nightfall to enter the Range, but intuition told her Travis was getting suspicious. Afraid he'd be back to ask questions about her activities, she'd moved up her schedule. She couldn't afford to let anyone keep her from finding her uncle.

Belara hid her pickup in an arroyo under piles of tumbleweeds, smoothed away the tracks with her boot, then walked up to the fenced area. Beyond that fence lay restricted federal land. Walking down the fence line, she found a spot that had enough clearance to let her crawl under and pull her gear through.

It was 5:00 p.m. and one of the best times to travel across the desert. Even though fall was in the air, daytime temperatures were still high. In the stark expanse of sand and rock before her, she'd find little respite from the sun and heat. Belara strapped on her backpack then checked the map her uncle had sketched for her a year ago as a gift. It listed all the water holes and springs he'd found in the area. It lacked the detail of her USGS charts, but had vital information those didn't. She'd kept it in a frame in her office at the nursery, fortunately, so it had been saved from the men who broke into her home.

She studied the route she intended to take to Lead Camp Canyon. She'd have to make it there before morning. Once she arrived, the high sides of the small valley would provide some shade while she rested. She'd also have water from a spring her uncle had found, and be able to replenish whatever she'd used through the night.

At the spot where her journey was to begin, Belara carefully constructed a cairn of rocks as her uncle had taught her. As she placed a small piece of turquoise at the top, she began chanting in a soft voice.

May a blessing be in my path
Wherever I stand
May a blessing be with those of my family
Wherever they walk.

The ritual finished, she moved away. It was time to go. Searching the area quickly, she found a sturdy, fairly straight branch large enough to serve as a walking stick. Using her hunting knife, she sharpened one end of it to a dull point. The stick would serve to ward off snakes. The only other dangerous predators in the vicinity were the mountain lions, which had been reintroduced recently by scientists. Those animals, however, had grown accustomed to avoiding people in their midst and shouldn't pose a problem. More than likely, they'd do all that was possible to avoid her.

Belara started toward the wash that she could follow uphill until she eventually reached the canyon. The route would enable her to stay out of sight while making steady progress.

As she hiked along the sandy arroyo, she readjusted her pack. It was heavy, filled almost to bursting with supplies and equipment. Trying to anticipate her uncle's needs as well as her own, she'd asked Travis to provide enough food for two people. Although she was certain her uncle would have provided amply for himself, it couldn't hurt to take a few precautions.

As she struggled with the weight balanced on her back, she wished it would have been possible to bring a pack animal. Yet, in the long run, an animal would have become a liability. She wouldn't have been able to take some of the shortcuts she was planning on. Also due to the drought, she might not have been able to find enough water to sustain it throughout the trip. Her uncle was the only person she knew who would have had the knowledge to provide for an animal under the current conditions.

Belara adjusted her pace, making it steady but brisk. All she had to do now was avoid the patrols and use the survival skills her uncle had taught her from childhood. With luck, the journey would be over before she had too much time to dwell on the dangers. As she turned the next bend, she stopped in midstride and gasped. A Jeep, parked across the arroyo, blocked her way.

A tall, lean figure stepped out of the vehicle.

Chapter Three

Belara squinted against the setting sun, then raised her hand to shade her eyes. Slowly her gaze focused on the man before her. Like a giant war god outlined in the reddish glow of sunset, Travis stood his ground silently. His green eyes flashed as he challenged her with a glare.

It took her a moment to collect herself, but then she stepped forward and faced him squarely. "What are you doing here, and how did you find me?" she demanded.

"I'm here to take you back," Travis said. "Once Sy told me about the maps you'd bought, I figured out where you were going. I knew you'd get as close as you could before hiking in, so that narrowed the search. I drove past the last guard post and looked for a spot with plenty of ground cover. Then I saw the arroyo. I was certain you'd follow that route so I decided to trespass long enough to intercept you. It was easy cutting the fence wire, then nailing it back up once I was through."

He'd made it sound so simple. She knew right then that she'd underestimated him badly.

Travis cocked his head toward the passenger seat. "Come on. We should get off the Range as quickly as possible. We're breaking the law and there're stiff jail terms for this type of thing."

"I'm not going anywhere," she said flatly. "I've got a good reason for being here, and I intend to finish what I started."

He clenched his jaw then forced himself to relax. "I've managed to put a few things together, and I don't think you're aware of what you're walking into. I believe your uncle might be out here doing a job for the Army." He told her what had happened when he'd visited the base. "They might be in the middle of maneuvers or some kind of operation, I don't know. What I am absolutely certain of is that your uncle is perfectly able to take care of himself. The last thing he needs is having you interfere with what he's trying to do."

"You misinterpreted what happened at the base. My uncle is *not* working for the military. His reasons for being out here are personal and he's in more danger than you can imagine. Do you think I'd risk trespassing onto a military range if it wasn't absolutely necessary? This is a matter of life and death."

"Yes, your own, if you go on," he countered. "We can find another way to do whatever it is you're trying to accomplish. If you go in, you won't have a chance. If the desert doesn't kill you, then the unexploded bombs and shells scattered all around here probably will."

She exhaled softly. She wasn't going to be able to get rid of him easily. Her best chance was to tell him why she was going after her uncle and hope he'd understand. "You've done some homework on us," she admitted. "Still, there's one important fact you don't know. My uncle is not well."

She patiently explained about his attacks of angina and his current view of the white man's medicine. "He's wanted to go back to the ranch because he believes he can regain his health there. I doubt he's working for the military at all. If your friend did purposely duck you, it was for reasons of his own." She removed her pack and laid it next to her walking stick. "What worries me most is that he left his pills behind, probably deliberately. Without them, he doesn't stand a chance. The angina will incapacitate him and the desert will do the rest."

"Are you certain that he's going back to the ranch? He could have changed his mind and returned home. Or, if I'm right and he's working for the military, he could be anywhere, including behind a desk somewhere.''

''What kind of paperwork requires that he takes his rifle, saddle and maps? No, he's going to the ranch. I'm certain of it.'' Belara studied Travis's solemn expression. She sensed he was weighing the information and trying to decide on the right course of action. ''Let me tell you a bit more about my uncle. Then you'll see why I'm convinced he's going back there.''

Belara glanced at one of the mountain peaks on the eastern horizon. ''Our ancestors belonged to a small band that traveled south to the Sacramento Mountains in the mid-1800s to escape the white soldiers. Kit Carson and his troopers destroyed the crops and livestock of the *Dinéh* up north in Chaco Canyon, forcing most of our tribe to surrender or starve. Approximately eight thousand men, women and children were captured and taken on the 300-mile walk to Fort Sumner. Only a few bands managed to remain free. Some of them, like my ancestors, joined with the Apaches and continued to resist. Then treaties were signed and the Navajo reservation was established. Most returned to their traditional homelands, but our clan chose to remain here.''

''But the Sacramento Mountains are on the other side of the Range.''

''In the early 1900s the Bowmans crossed the Tularosa Basin and settled in the San Andres Mountains. The range land west of Victorio Peak was marginal, so it came cheap. The Bowman clan built their home there and had a few head of cattle and some sheep. Then, during the great drought in the thirties, most of the clan was driven away in search of better land. Only my uncle's mother and father remained. After their deaths many years later, the ranch became my uncle's property. His fondest memories are associated with that place. It's a part of who he is.''

''Military pilots have used this country for years to practice aerial gunnery and bombing. Surely there isn't much left of the old ranch,'' Travis argued.

"My uncle assures me that it has survived because of its inaccessible location."

"Everyone around here who goes camping or backpacking has heard of Jimmie Bowman. He's well respected, and understandably so. If he's decided to go back there, he must feel confident that he's able to make the journey." His gaze softened with sympathy. "Besides, whether you realize it or not, Bowman has a very big advantage over you out here. In addition to his knowledge of the desert, he also has military skills you don't have. There's unexploded ordinance all over the area. When a dud rocket or missile hits, it can lay hidden beneath the sand like an expertly placed booby trap. Risking your own life isn't going to solve anything. I'm going to have to insist you return with me."

Belara shook her head. "I'm doing what I know is right. I'm sorry you don't agree, but it's not up to you to tell me what I can or can't do. You're a trespasser here as much as I am."

"I can't let you stay. By returning without you, I'd be allowing you to commit suicide. You can't ask that of anyone with a conscience. Stop fighting me on this, you'll only make things more difficult. One way or another, I'm taking you back."

She held his gaze, and there was no mistaking his determination. "I'm no match for you in a physical confrontation. I'm very aware of that. If you insist on forcing the issue, I'll have to return with you. But you'll gain nothing." Belara stuck out her chin stubbornly. "I'll return the minute you're not around to stop me."

"I could always tell the people at the Range what you're planning," he replied. "Don't keep pushing this. I'm a lot tougher than you think."

"They can't detain me unless I try something, *then* get caught. Either way, I *will* go."

He stared at the ground, his lips compressed tightly. "Lady, I don't want your death on my conscience. You don't stand a chance alone out there, believe me. If you're determined to do this, then let me go in your place. I'll give your uncle the medication and then head back. Alone, I can make good time and my military training will give me all the advantages I need to get through.''

''Except for one. My uncle will see you coming and avoid you before you ever get near him. He's probably on his guard. He's not going to allow anyone to catch him until he finishes what he has to do. He knows I won't stop him, so he won't avoid me. That's why I have to be the one to go.'' Belara considered her options. ''If you feel you have to help, then come with me,'' she added.

He stared at her in surprise. ''Placing both of our lives on the line is not my idea of a solution.''

''I'm offering you a compromise, that's the best I can do. Help me find my uncle. Then, after I speak to him and give him the medication he needs, I'll come back with you.''

''You're not giving me much of a choice, are you?'' he said resignedly. Belara was so different from the other women he'd met. She didn't raise her voice, nor lose her temper arguing. She just made her points and held her ground. Despite himself, his admiration for her continued to grow.

He glanced down at the sand, then over toward the west where the sun had just set. A breeze was beginning to pick up. Belara just stood there, patiently waiting him out. ''All right. We'll do it your way. Since we're both here, we might as well continue. I keep my gear in a locked box in the back of the Jeep. I also keep an emergency supply of water on hand. I don't have any rations, but I can live off the land. I've done it before.''

''We can share the food I brought and supplement with whatever we can find,'' she said. ''I had you get me extra supplies as an added safety measure.''

He nodded. ''I assume you've charted your course.''

She pulled two maps from her pack, one hand drawn, the other a detailed topographic chart. ''The route I've chosen will take us by as many water holes as possible on our way to the ranch. The USGS maps don't show those locations, but my uncle's information is very reliable.''

"You may be right," he said quietly, "but military survival training recommends taking a more direct route. There's no need for us to waste time searching out marginal water sources. I can make a solar still and collect enough from the plants to take care of both of us. And using the topographic maps you have, I guarantee that I can get us there and back safely and much faster.'' He loaded her pack and walking stick into his Jeep.

"I trust my uncle's experience a lot more than your military survival schools. Finding the water holes he marked will take less time than extracting water from plants. And, for the record, you shouldn't trust the official maps too much, either. Many of the locations are mismarked.''

"These charts are still our best bet.'' He glanced once more at her hand-drawn map, then examined the USGS chart in detail. ''Let's take the Jeep as far as we can get tonight. The route will keep us in the low spots until after dark so we should be able to avoid being seen by ground patrols. And the weather man predicted forty-mile-per-hour winds this evening so there won't be too many flights overhead. Once day breaks, we'll have to leave the vehicle hidden someplace and, from that point on, we'll have to make the rest of the journey on foot, traveling after nightfall as you originally planned.'' Travis went to the passenger's side of the vehicle. ''I'll navigate.'' He tossed her the keys. ''You can do the driving.''

"Fine with me.'' Belara slipped into the driver's seat and put the Jeep into gear. His take-charge attitude was incredibly annoying but at least they were finally getting underway. At the moment, that was the most important thing. ''How come you removed the windshield? I realize it had bullet holes in it, but at least it would have given us some protection from the wind.''

"I took the Jeep by the shop earlier and had the frame removed. By tomorrow they would have fitted it with a new windshield. Unlike you, I hadn't planned on traveling to-night."

They drove without speaking. Gradually, as twilight passed into darkness, the wind increased. As the swirling dust began to obscure the moon, the entire landscape be-came enshrouded in an oppressive gloom. "I can't hear any planes overhead, and I haven't seen any signs of a patrol. Shall we risk using the headlights?"

"Not unless you want to land in the base stockade. The dust would scatter the light and create a glow that could be seen miles away from the air." And on the ground, there was the danger of being spotted by other enemies. Robert-son's group was probably either already in the vicinity or on its way there by now. At least he didn't have to worry about the other gold seekers. They posed no problem since they'd be working hard not to give themselves away.

He glanced at her and wondered if she would have con-tinued had she known about the threat Robertson and his men posed to her. For a moment he considered telling her, but then concluded it wouldn't do any good. Her mind was set on going and Robertson wouldn't change that. Giving her something else to worry about wouldn't serve any pur-pose. "Your eyes will adjust as it gets darker. Keep going. I've got a new trail picked out and we have lots of ground to cover before dawn."

As the winds intensified, powerful gusts slammed sand and gravel into the vehicle. Belara gripped the wheel tightly, keeping them on course. Ducking her head, she struggled to shield her eyes with the brim of her Western hat.

"The wind is a good omen." She had to shout to be heard now. "The *Dinéh* say that the Wind People were given supporting power. They report the truth and act in a way that benefits. Wind helped other *Dinéh* gods by send-ing storms that hid them from their enemies."

"The wind will certainly help us out tonight. As intense as it is, it'll obliterate our tracks." He removed a penlight from a zippered bag in the back of the Jeep, and aimed the small beam at the map. As they traveled across the rocky ground, the beam hopped from one spot to the next despite his efforts to keep it steady. "Surprise me by missing the roughest spots, will you?" he yelled.

"There are no good spots out here. We have 'bad' and 'really bad,'" she shouted back. As the sand flew in great swirls around the vehicle, she decreased her speed. "I remember this stretch," she said, pointing to a wall of boulders ahead. "It's rugged but not impassible by Jeep."

"I'll probably regret asking, but how do you know that? This is a restricted area."

"Twice before, the Range has been open to expeditions searching for the lost treasure of Victorio Peak. Last time, my uncle got permission for me to come along. I rode with a group of reporters. It was interesting, even if nothing was found."

"Were you able to visit the ranch?"

"My uncle took me to the other side of the Peak so I could see the basin where it was located, but I've never been all the way there."

"And you were still willing to try the journey alone?" He shook his head in disapproval.

"When you were in the military I'm sure there were times you were reluctant to do something, but did it anyway," she pointed out. "You, of all people, should know the difference between a matter of duty and a matter of choice."

He said nothing for several long moments as they bounced along. She was right. He understood only too well. But what he'd also learned was that in such situations the wrong choice, however well-meant, could end disastrously.

"The desert can be a very dangerous place, but it doesn't frighten me," she continued. "I know how to find water where there doesn't appear to be any. I know which plants to eat and which will kill you. I'm also capable of trapping animals for food if necessary. As inhospitable as the desert seems, it contains resources and I know how to make use of them."

The winds continued to howl around them, and she leaned forward, trying to see. Sand flew against her face, stinging her skin. Belara concentrated on breathing only through her nose. "It's like trying to look through a window that's frosted over." She stopped the Jeep, then used the bandanna around her neck to cover her mouth and nose.

Travis stared at the compass, then focused the light on the odometer. "Continue for another two miles, then head southeast. We'll save some time going that way because the country's more passable."

"The winds are strong," she yelled coughing. "I'll do the best I can, but help me keep an eye out for hazards." She started the Jeep moving forward again.

Travis tied a handkerchief over the lower half of his face. Leaning forward, he concentrated on the terrain. "It looks clear. Keep going at a steady pace," he said, then glanced at the map. "We shouldn't have any major obstacles in our way if we follow the course I've laid out. At this rate, we should reach our first objective an hour before sunrise." He flashed the light on the odometer. "Okay, start heading southeast. It should be relatively flat now for several miles."

"I'm not familiar with this area," she warned. Belara maneuvered through a rocky stretch of ground filled with foot-high boulders. Cautiously she slowed down to a crawl. "I hope we don't blow a tire. Without headlights we're driving blind. Are you sure of the map? The ground doesn't look quite right...."

As she swerved to avoid a large pile of boulders, the front of the vehicle suddenly dropped rapidly. Belara gripped the wheel, fighting to keep control as they careened down a steep embankment.

Brush and rocks scraped against the Jeep, and the metal sides squealed like a wounded animal in pain as the vehicle bounced violently. Seconds later, they reached the bottom of the arroyo and bounded to a stop.

Belara tried to swallow, but her mouth was completely dry. Switching the engine off, she unbuckled her shoulder belt and turned to look at Travis in the half light. "The map goofed."

Travis had expected and would have understood anger, but Belara had muttered the phrase with perfect composure. He met her gaze, and she stared back at him. Finally, when she didn't turn away, he exhaled softly. "Okay, I admit it. I'll even admit you handled the vehicle better than I navigated." He slapped the back of his hand against the map. "But doggone it, this arroyo just wasn't here!"

"That's why I never trust those 'official' maps completely. Erosion is constantly reshaping the terrain out here, and those charts aren't updated as often as they should be. In a restricted area like this, there isn't even word-of-mouth information from other hikers to go on."

"I was aware of all that and I was expecting some changes in the contours of the land, but nothing this drastic. This channel is twenty feet or so deeper than the map indicates."

She took a deep breath, then let it out slowly. Self-control; harmony could not be attained without it. "We can't change what's already happened. The question is, how do we get out of here? That drop-off was steep."

He sat there in stunned silence. He'd been so adamant about claiming his role as leader that naturally he'd expected a flood of recriminations. Her self-possession threw him. "It's too sandy to push or drive the Jeep out," he said, at last. "We'll have to use the winch," he answered. "Start up the engine."

Travis walked to the front of the vehicle and unwound the cable. He was surprised when Belara came out to help him haul it to the top. Dust whirled in the air and gusts slammed against them as they clambered up the loosely packed sides. Travis scrambled over the embankment moments later, and offered her a hand. She accepted his help with a word of thanks, then stood beside him at the top.

Without the marginal protection the arroyo offered, the wind was merciless in its assault.

"I'm going to have to fasten this to something massive enough to serve as an anchor," he yelled trying to be heard over the roar of the dust storm. "Then, when the winch in front of the Jeep begins to take up the cable, it'll pull the vehicle out."

She stepped away from the embankment and peered into the darkness surrounding them. "There was a boulder near here that was as big as a house," she shouted. "I saw it a second or two before we went over the incline." She squinted, then pointed ahead. "There it is. Will that be enough?"

"It'll be perfect." He looped the cable around it, then attached the hook so it would stay in place. Finished, he started down to the vehicle. "Stay here. I'll steer the Jeep up."

"I weigh less. Wouldn't it make more sense for me to do it? It would put less strain on the winch."

He shook his head. "I'm not sure how well this is going to work. The vehicle could overturn. Besides, I got us into this by trusting that obsolete map. I'll see it through. You can watch the cable. If it looks like it's about to give, or the rock moves, warn me."

Standing at the top of the embankment, Belara monitored Travis's progress. The vehicle inched forward, slowly but steadily. It was almost at the top when she heard the loud rotor slap of an approaching helicopter. As the sound thrummed around her like the pulsating beat of a giant drum, Belara's heart lodged in her throat.

Chapter Four

Belara rushed to the edge of the arroyo to warn Travis. She shouted, but her voice was drowned out by the wind and roar of the Jeep's engine. Close to the top, Travis wasn't watching her anymore. A second later, the vehicle cleared the embankment.

Travis continued for another ten feet, then switched off the ignition, shutting down the winch. He started to work a kink out of his shoulder when he heard a familiar sound over the roar of the wind. Choppers. They seemed to be getting closer. Memories came flooding back and he froze, unable to move.

"They're heading this way," Belara warned, reaching his side. "I don't understand why they'd risk flying in this weather! Do you think they know we're here?"

"No," he managed in a tight voice. "They're probably returning from an aborted mission. It happens. They'll be rushing to get back."

"Will they spot us with their sensors?"

"They could, but my guess is they'll be too busy trying to maintain altitude. They've got to do everything possible to avoid the dust. It can choke up their engines and cause them to crash." He tried, but didn't quite manage to squelch the shudder that ran through him.

"Are you okay?" she asked. "Maybe we should wait here until . . ."

"I'm fine, and no, we can't stop now." He unhooked the cable and walked it back around the boulder. "We're going to have to travel parallel to this arroyo for a few miles. The route will put us much farther south than we wanted to be but we'll still have made better progress than if we'd come in on foot."

"Do you want me to continue doing the driving?" she asked, shouting against the wind.

"Yes, but I'm going to sit on the hood and watch for road hazards. That's the only way to make sure we don't run into any more surprises."

"You're not serious! In this dust storm, I'll be hard-pressed to even see you. What if you fall and I run you over?"

"Try not to," he said with a half grin. "It would ruin my entire evening."

"Wait a minute!" But by the time she'd completed the last syllable, he'd hustled out onto the hood. She saw him seat himself and grab the metal tie-down loops so he wouldn't slide off.

"Drive!" he barked.

Muttering under her breath, she started the ignition. If she lost sight of him, she'd stop the vehicle. This was too dangerous. But she had to admit he was right, they couldn't continue to move in this storm without a spotter.

Her nerves were frazzled as she edged the Jeep forward, her eyes fixed on the figure ahead. Travis was dressed in tan-colored jeans, and was wearing a loose shirt and windbreaker that were approximately the same color. It would be great camouflage in the daytime. Even now it made him barely distinguishable, the fabric being the same color as the sand swirling in the air. Belara's palms were moist with perspiration as she clenched the wheel.

Four very long, bumpy hours later, the storm had finally lost most of its strength. Dust still hung heavily in the air, but the veil it wound around them was penetrable and did not interfere much with visibility. "Get back in. This is almost over," she said.

Travis returned to the passenger's seat, massaging his bruised backside. Seeing the deathlike grip she had on the steering wheel, he gave her an encouraging nod. "Nice job," he said quietly. "It'll be daylight in a few hours, so it's time to start searching for a spot where we can hide the Jeep. We'll need time to hike several miles away from it, just in case."

"I think I know where we are. If I'm right, there are several rocky bluffs about half a mile away. Once the wind dies down more, and the moon comes out from behind the clouds, we should be able to see them."

"We better hope the wind doesn't die down too quickly. Once it does, any tracks not covered over by the drifting sand might give us away. Low-level training missions over the Range are part of the daily routine." *Routine.* His mind recoiled at the word and he tried not to wince. So many memories, and so many regrets...

"Is there something wrong?"

"I'm just trying to stay ahead of the game. The unexpected is what gets you into trouble," he growled.

"You mean like when someone asks you a question you weren't anticipating?"

He turned to look at her. "What makes you say that?" he challenged.

"I know when someone's being evasive." She hesitated for a moment, then continued. "You guard your thoughts well. That takes practice and usually means there's a part of yourself you want to protect."

"What about you? Is your life an open book?"

"For most things, yes, but there are certain matters the *Dinéh* keep within the tribe," she said carefully.

"I thought the Pueblo Indians were the ones who required secrecy as part of their religion."

"Navajos share more willingly than our Pueblo brothers and sisters, I'll admit. Still, we have our own set of beliefs that encompass everything from the way we act, to our view of the world. These are a part of who we are. They're not something that we speak about very often."

"Family loyalty must be a big part of the way you were raised. Being out here, risking your own life..."

"Life is very dangerous anyway. That's why the *Dinéh* have ceremonies. It's our way of controlling the uncontrollable and protecting ourselves." She gestured ahead. "Look, there are the bluffs I was talking about."

"Let's try to find an overhang or cave. If we can camouflage the vehicle well enough, even a patrol passing close by might miss it." He pointed toward a broad expanse of limestone about a quarter of a mile away. "Over there. That projecting cliff will do nicely."

"It's not much of an overhang."

"It's enough to provide a shadow, and that's all we need. Now that the wind's died down and dawn is near, we'll have to work quickly."

Belara parked the Jeep as close to the massive rock formation as she could, then switched off the ignition. As she stepped out of the vehicle, she studied the ground carefully. "It doesn't look like any patrols come this close to the bluffs. Their trails are probably farther out, judging from the absence of tracks here."

He nodded approvingly. "You're very observant."

"I can be when I have to be," she answered simply. "Just like you, I would imagine."

He glanced up quickly and captured her gaze with his own. Her eyes were a shimmering, almost translucent ebony. A man could get lost in those eyes. Heat slithered through him. Muttering under his breath, he forced himself to look at something else. Life was sure getting complicated.

With an unnatural amount of energy, he started pulling his supplies from the back of the Jeep.

"I'll get my gear," she offered, crawling into the rear of the vehicle.

His gaze came to rest on the curve of her buttocks as she wriggled over the seat, and struggled to drag her backpack out. Softness like hers invited a man's touch. He clamped his jaw shut to stifle a frustrated groan. "Let me get that canvas tarp out of the Jeep first."

She gave him a look that left little doubt she feared for his sanity. "You're not planning on carrying that thing along, are you? It must weigh twenty pounds."

"I know, lady, but we can use it to camouflage the Jeep," he replied brusquely. His attraction to the woman spelled danger in more ways than one. When your neck was on the line, distractions were lethal. "I know what I'm doing." He set the tarp on the ground and untied the cords that held it in a tight roll.

Belara removed her backpack and hiking stick from the back of his vehicle. Standing aside, she watched him gather what gear he'd be taking with him. The last item he retrieved was a hunting rifle equipped with a scope and a leather sling.

Wordlessly he handed it to her, then unrolled the tarp and stretched it across the body of the Jeep. Passing a small nylon rope through each grommet, he threaded it beneath the vehicle at key points to keep the canvas in place.

"I see what you're trying to do," she said, carefully setting the rifle on top of his backpack. "Let me help you tie down the rest of it." She started to loop the other end of the rope to a rear bumper support when he reached for her wrist.

"Not that way. We'll attach it to the rear axle. That way the tarp will extend all the way to the ground."

"Everything would have still been covered my way, too," she protested.

"My methods are military tested and proven and that's the way it'll have to be." He felt it coming now. She'd tell him he was an insufferable pig, and the arguments would start. At least it would make things easier. Contending with an angry woman would keep his thoughts busy and the attraction at bay. As it was now, just looking at her made his insides ache. Passion was one thing, but this other feeling was different. It went deeper. He found it extremely annoying.

Belara watched him in silence for a moment. Then with a nod, glanced around. "I'm assuming you'll want to attach some brush to that to make it look more natural. I'll gather some."

He watched her go, stunned. Was she just trying to irritate him by not reacting? By the time she returned, he couldn't resist trying to goad her. "I'm glad you realize I was right about the tarp. Frankly I expected you to put up a fuss."

"You're very inflexible," she commented, "but it doesn't matter. Living in this area, I've learned to ignore the military mentality whenever possible."

Her comment made him glance up quickly, but she continued before he could say anything.

"Besides, you aren't really infringing on anything I want to do."

"And if I was?"

She smiled, a playful, taunting smile that surprised him. "I'd do things the way I saw fit, and let you do the same. I have no right to impose my ways on you and vice versa."

He realized with sudden clarity that she was more than a match for him. She wouldn't obey him without thinking like most of the people he usually escorted out into the desert. At first he wasn't sure whether to be annoyed or pleased. Annoyance won. "The only reason I'm here is because you didn't give me much of a choice. The least you can do is cooperate with me."

"I agree we should try to work together. Only that's going to take a considerable amount of effort from both of us."

She was calm, but inflexible. Swearing under his breath, Travis finished covering the tarp with brush. "You've got extra supplies in your pack, and there's no need for you to shoulder all that extra weight. Let's split the load up between us so it's more even, then we'll get going. We have a lot of ground to cover."

Once finished rearranging the supplies, Travis slipped his backpack on. As he slung the rifle over his shoulder, he saw

Belara waiting for him. Taken aback, he stared at her for a second. He hadn't been slow. What was the woman trying to prove?

With deliberate intent, he started hiking across the rocky ground at a brisk pace.

To his growing irritation, she kept up easily. She moved gracefully with scarcely a sound. A few times he had to turn to make sure she was still there behind him. Finally, after about four miles, she began to slow down.

He stopped and waited for her to catch up. To his surprise, she didn't ask him to alter his pace. He started forward again, his rapid strides as strong as before. Five minutes later, seeing her fall behind, he stopped and waited for her again. As she drew near, he braced himself for complaints about his pace. Instead, she walked past him silently and continued on.

Frustrated, he caught up with her easily and retook the lead. A few moments later, realizing he was outdistancing her again, he stopped. "Would you like me to wait for you?" he growled as she caught up.

"You've already been doing that. Your jackrabbit starts and stops seem like a waste of energy to me."

Travis saw the smile that touched the corners of her mouth and realized he'd been had. Shaking his head, he fell into step with her. This woman was definitely going to drive him crazy.

An hour later, they'd almost reached the goal he'd set for them on the map. He was about to break the silence that stretched between them, when he heard a sound back the way they'd come. Gesturing for Belara to wait behind cover, he turned and crept downhill. In the dim predawn light, he made a methodical sweep of the area below him using a small pair of binoculars.

Unable to spot any signs of another party, he returned to Belara's side. "Sorry. False alarm."

"No problem." She adjusted her backpack, then glanced at the sky. "We'll have to stop soon."

"We're almost there," Travis said, remaining alert to any hazards. Now that they were well up the slopes of the rocky San Andres Mountain range, the brush was marginally thicker, providing better cover for them. Still, there were areas that were as stark as the lowlands they'd traveled across. He'd have to make sure they didn't get caught in the open by either the military or other trespassers.

An hour later, as the sun peered over the horizon, they stopped in a steep, narrow wash, cut by runoff water. "Let's hole up in the deepest shadows. We'll be sheltered from patrols here, and since it's not too rocky we should be able to sleep fairly comfortably."

"It's a good choice," she answered with an approving nod.

With a few short words, she'd managed to let him know that she was agreeing only because she concurred. "So glad you like it," he muttered.

"It was a compliment," she said quietly. "Relax. You're very tense and that uses too much of your energy."

Not enough of it, he thought. Out of the corner of his eye, Travis watched her unroll her thin sleeping bag. The climb had been a long one and the pace brisk. She should have been dead tired, yet she still looked beautiful. Her cheeks were flushed, and her long black hair, now loose, shone in the faint rays of dawn. A flash of desire snaked through him and he turned away from it and her.

With effort, he forced this thoughts to Barry Robertson and his group. They were potential trouble, but if they got in his way, he knew he could handle it quickly and decisively. Still, he hoped a confrontation wouldn't take place while he had Belara along. As he stole a long furtive glance at her, he realized just how complex his reasons were. It was true that he didn't want her endangered, but there was more to it than that. He was also afraid that she'd see a side of him that would frighten and maybe even repulse her.

"Do you want the first watch or shall I take it? We shouldn't both go to sleep at the same time," Belara asked, interrupting his thoughts.

"I was planning to let you sleep first. I'm too keyed up right now anyway."

"Wake me when you start getting sleepy. We'll spell each other throughout the day. It's going to be rough until we get used to the pace and strange hours."

He nodded and stared off into the valley to the west. He'd have to keep his attention focused away from her. That was the only way he could guarantee that he'd remain alert. Minutes passed and he heard her breathing deepen. He smiled, thinking that it hadn't taken her long to fall asleep.

As the sun rose and the temperature began to climb, he stripped off his windbreaker. He doubted it would reach ninety today. The temperature didn't often go that high in early September, but today it would be close. He glanced down at Belara, making sure that she still rested in the shade, then looked away.

With his eyes focused on the horizon, he listened for any unusual sounds. He didn't think they'd been followed. But if Robertson's group had gotten into the area before them, it was possible they'd meet somewhere on the trail. Their routes would coincide much of the way. But, at least so far, he hadn't noticed any signs of them.

His gaze moved back to Belara. She was stubborn and headstrong, and impossible to control. Yet she drew him with her subtle challenges. He admired her ability to make decisions and act on them. Unfortunately that also made her a wild card, impossible to second-guess. Remembering that his commanding officer had said almost the same thing about him years ago, he smiled.

Perspiration began to cover his body. Opening his shirt, he left it hanging outside his pants. A breeze coming up from the north felt cool against his moist skin. As he turned around to pull a bag of trail mix out of his windbreaker, he saw Belara's eyes open. Her gaze drifted down his open shirt and focused on the scar that outlined a section of his rib cage. Feeling self-conscious, he reached down and buttoned his shirt again.

"What happened to you?" she asked quietly.

He shook his head. That portion of his life was off limits. "It's not important anymore. It happened a very long time ago."

She sat up and braided her hair loosely, allowing it to drape down her back. "It's the things that happened to us a long time ago that sometimes matter the most," she countered softly.

"Don't your people prefer to concentrate on things that bring harmony?" he countered. "There's no harmony or beauty in my story."

"The *Dinéh* don't try to hide from reality," she explained, surprised by his distorted view of her culture. "We learn to find harmony by understanding the balance between the good and evil. Everything exists in two parts and, together they complete the whole. Being able to see the order in that is 'walking in beauty.' Shall I tell you one of our tales of origin? It might help you get a better grasp of what I mean."

He sat cross-legged on top of his bedroll and gave her a nod.

"The war god of the *Dinéh* is named Slayer," she said. "In the beginning, Slayer went out and killed all the monsters that preyed on the land." Her voice became measured and she intoned the tale with a strange rhythmic cadence that drew him into it. "Slayer thought his job was finished when suddenly he came across four frightening strangers. They identified themselves as Cold, Hunger, Poverty and Death, so Slayer decided to destroy them immediately to protect the land. Cold, an old woman who was freezing, warned Slayer that if he killed her, there would never be any snow. Without it, streams would run dry in the summer and the people and land would know thirst. Slayer saw that it was better to let her live, and that's why we still have cold."

Her compelling words reached out, luring him back to a time when the power of the ancients ruled. "Then Slayer went to Hunger to strike him down. Hunger warned that if he was killed, the people would lose their appetites and there would be no more pleasure in feasting or eating."

"So Slayer let him live," Travis whispered. Tension washed out of him as her words held him gently spellbound.

"Poverty was an old man in dirty rags," she continued in the stillness. "He told Slayer to go ahead and kill him. He wanted to be put out of his misery. If he was destroyed, however, Slayer would have to face the consequences. Old clothes would never wear out, so the people wouldn't make new ones. Everyone would be ragged and filthy like him."

Images formed in his thoughts and leaped to life with a driving power of their own. Through her, he could glimpse another reality, patterned out of the fabric of her tribe's beliefs. "So that's why Poverty was spared," he verified softly.

"Last of all Slayer faced Death, who warned him that if he was destroyed the old would not die and make way for the young. Death asked that Slayer let it live so that the young could marry and have children. Death claimed to be Slayer's friend, though Slayer didn't know it." Her voice was hushed and reverent.

"So we still have death," he finished for her. Visions of people and events he'd never even imagined before played before his mind's eye.

"Can you understand our ways a little better now?"

He stared at the camping gear beside him, and tried to force his thoughts back to the present. "Yes, I think I do." His gaze drifted off into the distance and he remained silent for a long time. "It's very difficult for me to talk about the scar on my side, but if you like I will tell you about it someday when we have more time. Right now, it's more important to rest. Are you ready to watch? We have a long journey ahead of us tonight, and I won't be of much use if I'm too exhausted to think straight."

"I'll keep a careful watch. Rest easy."

"If you even *think* you hear someone approaching, wake me up," he warned, his voice hard. "We might have to move in a hurry."

"I'll stay alert. Relax and go to sleep."

Travis lay on his side and closed his eyes. "If I'm not up in a few hours, wake me."

Belara stood up and stretched. The man must have been practically ready to drop, though he masked it well. As she stared absently at the mountains to the north, she thought of her uncle. Concern and love mingled within her, making the uncertainty unbearable.

Finally, with a quiet sigh, she turned away. It was time to search for the desert plants that would augment the provisions they'd brought along. Walking stick in hand, she traveled over the shadowed rocky ground looking around. Before long, she found a patch of prickly pear cactus. With care, she extracted the red fruit nestled on top of the beavertail-shaped leaves.

Belara studied the surrounding vegetation, searching for another plant she knew would be in the area. She found it a few feet away, beside a small rock. The dry, long stalks of the *cañutillo* plant grew wild, and steeped in hot water made a very good tea. Beside it, she saw a plant she recognized immediately. Gathering seeds from the hardy Fendler Bush her people called *tsintl'iz*, she placed them in a small pouch to take back to the nursery. These wild plants looked hardy and would produce good offspring.

As the breeze swept across the desert, Belara stopped in her tracks. She was sure she'd heard voices, but as she strained to listen, there was only silence. She smiled, thinking her uncle would have said it was the whispers of the Wind People.

She had nearly reached camp when a twig snapped beneath her feet. Travis bolted to a crouch with a wicked looking, serrated fighting knife in hand. As he recognized her, his face lost its harshness and his body relaxed. "Don't do that," he said roughly.

It took her a moment to catch her breath. "Who did you expect?"

He looked away. "How the heck do I know? Don't surprise me, for both our sakes."

As he settled back down on the sleeping bag, he noticed what she was carrying. "Prickly pears," he said with a nod. "Good. They're nutritious and moist. As long as we keep finding those we won't need as much water."

"That's why I picked them for us. Now go back to sleep while you still have time." She saw him lay on his side, facing away from her.

Belara poured two cups of water from the canteen into large aluminum mugs, and then broke a few *cañutillo* stalks over each of them. After a short while, they'd be able to share a very pleasant drink. She was careful to make it weak, however. If it was too strong, it made you thirsty again. Noiselessly she walked to the shade and sat down.

"I can't sleep," Travis said, rolling over and facing her. "You want to try and rest some more?"

"I'd rather eat. I'm starving." She pulled a package of freeze-dried chicken stew from her pack, then called his attention to the mugs. "In a few minutes we should be able to have some Mormon tea."

"That's great. I've always liked the taste. It reminds me of almonds." Travis selected a packet of freeze-dried beans, added water to it, and began to eat. "Who taught you about plants?" he asked, picking up one of the prickly pears she'd brought along.

"My uncle. He's very knowledgeable about things like that." She retrieved their cups from the sun.

"I'm curious. I've noticed you never actually use his name. Is there a reason for that?"

"It's our custom," she explained, finishing her food. "To the *Dinéh*, a name contains power. If you use it too often, you wear it out. On the other hand, if you guard it, just whispering it might get you out of a tight spot sometime. That's the reason so many of us also have secret names." She glanced at Travis, who raised his eyebrows in a silent question. "Oh, no," she answered with a chuckle. "When you start telling me more about yourself, then, *maybe*, I'll share that with you."

"Fair enough," he answered, standing up. "Let's start breaking camp."

She started to pick up her cup and the discarded food pouches, but he interrupted. "Put away the large things first, then take care of the smaller items."

She took a deep breath and struggled to remain calm. "Are you this methodical about *everything* you do?" She'd meant it only as a mild rebuff, but his rakish grin made it obvious he'd taken it differently.

"There are times when thoroughness is appreciated," he drawled, his voice a husky whisper.

His words slid around her, enveloping her in a hazy cloud of heat. Trying to collect her scattered thoughts, she reached into her backpack and pulled out a clean shirt. "Before I put anything else away, I'm going to go change. I'll be back in a minute."

Belara walked behind some boulders, glad for a chance to be alone. Her attraction to Travis was a complication she didn't need to indulge. It would only make a difficult situation worse. Yet his protectiveness and caring nature, despite his attempts to mask them with gruffness, had touched her heart.

Logic, however, warned her to be cautious. The man was surrounded by mystery. Her compulsion to find out all she could about him was bound to be ill fated. The last thing she needed was to risk getting involved with a man who'd find her ways as strange and as alien as an arctic wilderness would seem to her.

She shook herself mentally. Her mother's brother had taught her the value of self-control. They had a job to do here, and duty to family had to take precedence in her thoughts.

She had begun to unbutton her blouse when she heard a faint rustle of branches in the sparse brush to her left. As she glanced back, a figure burst out from cover. Belara started to run but a sweaty arm jerked her furiously back. Her scream died before it began as a hand was clamped firmly over her mouth.

Chapter Five

She couldn't breathe. Desperately she slammed her heel down onto the man's instep and jabbed her elbow into his stomach. As the man doubled over in pain, his iron grip loosened. Twisting free, she gulped a lung full of air then yelled out a warning to Travis. As she darted out of her attacker's reach, a second, familiar-looking man appeared suddenly, blocking her path of escape. Belara ducked and hooked one foot around his ankle, sweeping his legs out from under him.

She heard Travis running toward them at the same time the two men did. Wordlessly the taller one yanked the man on the ground to his feet and pushed him through the brush. By the time Travis appeared from around a boulder, rifle in hand, they'd disappeared down the hillside.

"Are you okay?" he asked, rushing to her side. His voice broke with emotion. "If they hurt you, I swear I'll even the score in spades." Travis glanced in the direction they'd escaped, his rifle ready.

Belara leaned back against a large boulder, trying to steady her breathing. "I'm fine," she assured him, explaining what happened.

His gaze traveled over her methodically. For a moment, he had to fight the urge to hug her and try to erase the fear he could still see in her eyes. Yet, even if she had been frightened, she'd showed an admirable amount of courage and quick thinking. "You handled yourself well against two men," he said gently.

"My advantage wouldn't have lasted and they knew it," she admitted. "They only took off because they heard you coming. My bet is that they knew you'd be armed, and they didn't want that kind of confrontation. It's obvious they've been watching us, since they knew just when to strike."

"I should have paid more attention to my instincts. I was almost sure I'd heard someone behind us, but I didn't follow up on it as well as I should have. This is my fault."

She shook her head. "I'm as much to blame as you are. While you were sleeping I thought I heard the faint sound of voices. I stopped to listen, but nothing seemed out of place, so I dismissed it as my imagination."

He had no doubt that Robertson's group had been responsible for the attack on Belara. He regretted having taught those men well. Now his own knowledge was being used against him.

He said nothing as they returned to camp, but continued to watch their surroundings carefully. "Did you recognize either of the men who attacked you?"

"I only saw them briefly," she replied. "It's possible I might have seen one of the men before somewhere. I'm just not sure. Things were happening so fast."

She was keeping something from him. He felt it right down to his bones. Remembering the break-in at her home, he began to wonder if the situation was more complex than he'd first suspected. He watched her as she shifted nervously. "Since we're not exactly sure what these guys want, that means they're even more dangerous to us. They might try to ambush us again unless we lose them now. We're going to have to change our plans, then push on hard to put distance between us."

"What do you have in mind?"

"We'll take a more circuitous route to your uncle's ranch and make up the time by making fewer stops," he answered, quickly gathering their gear and eradicating the

signs of their presence there. "I already have an alternate
route picked out in case of unexpected problems."

Belara followed Travis down a rocky slope, picking her
way slowly. One slip on a loose rock could send her tum-
bling quite a distance. "So what's next?"

"As soon as it's completely dark, we'll double back.
We'll look and listen for signs of the men, and then circle
around behind them. Then, once we're certain they're
ahead of us, we'll continue to the ranch."

"Do you think it's possible they've already given up on
us?"

"It's possible, but not likely. My guess is they're still
tracking us." He gave her a long, hard look. "Don't you
think it's time you told me everything? Keeping things back
at this stage is only going to tip the scales against us." He
allowed several seconds of silence to stretch out between
them. Forcing the issue wasn't exactly the way to go about
winning someone's confidence, but he had no choice. She
had to trust him. That was the only way he'd be able to
protect either of them. "You can start by telling me why
people are after you. This is at least the second time you've
been attacked."

Belara chewed her bottom lip pensively. "Third, but
who's counting?" she said wryly. She took a deep breath,
then let it out again. "I don't have the answers you're
looking for. But you're right. You deserve to know the little I do." She fell into step beside him as they turned north,
paralleling a long ridge. "I only caught a quick glimpse of
the man who grabbed me from behind, near our camp. I
saw him when I tore free, but by then I had his buddy to
contend with. Despite that, I'm almost certain it was a guy
by the name of Barry Robertson."

Travis gave her a quick look. "How do you know Robertson?"

"I've only met him once, but if I'm right and it was him,
then this makes absolutely no sense at all." She told him
about the kidnapping attempt made on her. "Without

Robertson and his friends, the other two guys would have hauled me off with them, one way or another.''

Her story took him by surprise. To see Robertson as a Good Samaritan, even briefly, took a giant stretch of the imagination. ''And you think both groups were looking for your uncle?''

''Robertson's group was, and it's likely the others were, too. I'm not sure why they would be, though I can make a guess. The only real fortune my uncle possesses is his intimate knowledge of this area. It has to be something connected to that.'' She zipped up her jacket as the cold night breeze blew up from the lowlands below them. The temperature had already dropped over twenty-five degrees. With the wind chill, it would get even colder before morning.

''I've dealt with Robertson in the past. He's interested in finding the cache of gold that's supposed to be hidden on Victorio Peak. If he's gone after your uncle and now you, it's probably because he's realized he's going to need a guide to find it. The other two are a different story. Sy mentioned something about a pair of hunters in the area,'' he said, then told her what he'd found out.

''But why are they picking on me? I can't help them. My uncle's the one who was raised in this area.''

''Maybe they're assuming that your uncle passed his knowledge on to you. Or Robertson might have decided to try to use you to get to your uncle. I'm not sure.''

Belara glanced at the thick clusters of sage that shimmered with a silvery hue in the moonlight. ''I wonder what created this renewed interest in the gold at the Peak. Something must have triggered it. You mentioned that the base had increased their security measures. You think they're conducting another search, and that's what your friend was trying to keep from you?''

Travis considered it as they moved along a sloping bed of sandstone. ''It could be, but it's also possible that they've heard gold fever is in the air again. That means they know they'll have trespassers to deal with. It's easy for intruders to avoid the guards' outposts because their locations are well-known. Perhaps the base thought it was necessary to send someone out who could maintain a low profile while keeping a watch for any illegal activities. Your uncle would have been the ideal man for the job. He knows the area better than anyone else and, since he's retired, they wouldn't have to reassign any of their personnel.''

"He would have been tempted to take a job that allowed him to go into the Range legally," she admitted. "But I'm still not convinced."

As darkness descended, Travis began to backtrack. The hard surface they'd crossed had tapered into a jumble of loose stones and brush. "Be careful with the walking stick. You don't want to poke through the rocks and leave a trail they'll find."

"I'm not using it for support," she said. "When you move across terrain like this at night, the chances of coming across a rattler are good. With the stick, I can push a snake away without having to harm it, or letting it harm us."

"Good thought." He stopped and pressed the release lever on his rifle. Four cartridges dropped into his hand. "From this point it's going to get more dangerous. I want you to learn how to operate my rifle, just in case."

Belara nodded. "It looks similar to my uncle's .22 caliber rifle. Only his is a bolt action that loads from a clip."

"I'm glad you've seen a bolt action before, but there are a few major differences." He demonstrated how to load and unload the rifle and operate the safety. "This is a Ruger M-77. It's very accurate even at long range. It has a healthy kick to it, so hold it firmly against your shoulder when firing. If you had to, could you use it in an emergency?"

"Yes, but I don't know how well I'd do. I've never handled a hunting rifle that powerful before."

"Just aim and fire in their direction. They'll get the message."

As they moved along, Belara helped Travis by studying the ground carefully for signs of the men who'd attacked her. The sooner they could circle around and leave them far behind, the better. Yet, exploring only by moonlight, the search was difficult.

Travis finally slowed his demanding pace. "So far I haven't seen anything to indicate they're still in the area," he whispered. "If we don't find something soon, we'll travel back about a mile, then start on that alternate route to the ranch."

As the wind blew against her face, she stiffened. "Do you smell it?" She turned to look at Travis. His muscles were taut and he held his rifle in an iron fisted grip.

He remained motionless trying to determine the location of the scent. "It's faint, but unless I miss my guess, it's insect repellant." Something out of the recent past triggered his memory. One of the men in Robertson's group had insisted on dousing himself with the chemical nightly. All the others had complained about the stench, but Mike Halliday had pointedly ignored them.

Belara gestured with her chin, calling his attention to a gum wrapper on the ground. Travis picked it up, noting that the scent of spearmint was still fresh on the foil. He checked the fluorescent dial on his compass, then cocked his head, signaling her to follow.

Travis led the way up a small hillside dotted with thick clusters of rabbitbrush. Although his pace was brisk as they headed away from the area, Belara didn't have any difficulty keeping up. Her desire to avoid another encounter with those men gave her all the added energy she needed.

Thirty minutes later, after a strenuous march, Travis crouched on the ground studying the map. His penlight illuminated only a small section, so he traced a path with the small beam, verifying their route. Finally he stood and returned the map to his rucksack. "Robertson and the others will try to trail us, but they'll be looking in the wrong direction. For the time being, we don't have to worry about them."

Belara watched him stare pensively at the rocky sand beneath his feet. "What's on your mind? Please don't keep things from me."

"There is something I haven't told you," he admitted slowly. "It's about Robertson," he said, leading the way down the path he'd selected. "I had a real strong suspicion he was on his way here to the Range," he told her about his experience with them. "He's the kind who doesn't let anything stand in the way of what he wants. I should have warned you about him from the start, but I didn't want to alarm you."

"So you came with me because you were afraid I'd need protection against Robertson and his group," she observed. His caring filled her with a rush of warmth, but as she met his eyes, she saw something else reflected there. Was he apologizing for wanting to keep her safe?

"That was one of the reasons I came," he admitted. "I also didn't think you had much of a chance out here alone, even if Robertson hadn't been involved." He paused for a minute, the lines of his face deepening. "But I really blew it by not telling you about him right from the start. If I had, I'm sure he wouldn't have taken you by surprise."

He captured her gaze with his own. "I can't change what's happened," he said, his voice vibrating with the emotions that fueled his words. "But I'll do everything in my power to make sure you never even see him again. You have my word on that. Robertson is smart and dangerous, but so am I."

His tone and the fire in his eyes made a believer out of her. "We'll protect each other, my friend," she answered quietly. "Neither one of us is in this alone."

Travis gave her a startled look as if that fact had temporarily escaped him. Lost in thought, he climbed the sloping hillside, working his way toward the next high spot. He wanted to use his binoculars as soon as possible. Not knowing the exact position of Robertson and his men put him at a disadvantage and he didn't intend to allow that to continue. His adversary was highly resourceful and would be quick to turn the tables on him, if he could.

As soon as they reached the summit, he pulled his field glasses from the pack. Carefully he scanned the moonlit area around them. "I don't think Robertson is wise to us yet," he said at last, "but now we'll have to make up for lost time."

"That's okay. Not leading him to my uncle is worth any price we might have to pay," Belara answered.

Travis studied the rock formations around them, checking the elevations against the map of the sector he'd pulled from his pack. "This quadrant seems to be charted accurately, from what I can tell. With that in mind, there's an option I want to discuss with you." He paused, placing the binoculars back inside his pack. "Would you be willing to risk climbing across to the other side of the mountain range at night? So far we've been paralleling the higher elevations, and although the going's been tough, the terrain has been manageable. Scaling the mountain and then descending partway down the other side at night will be extremely difficult. The advantage is that it might help throw the others off our trail, even after they discover we double-backed." He stared at the ground, then back up at her. "But I want to warn you, the steep terrain and the lack of light are a very bad combination."

She considered it for a moment. "In his current state of health, my uncle is no match for men like Robertson. I'd be willing to try anything to make sure we lose them."

"Have you ever been in the mountains this far south before?"

She shook her head, then shrugged. "Weren't you the one who preferred to trust maps?" she smiled slowly. "This is one case where we're going to have to."

As they climbed up a long, steep incline, Travis was forced to slow down. "We're going to have to pick our way carefully. There isn't enough rocky ground here to hide our trail completely."

"I remember my uncle telling me about the different tricks our ancestors used to evade the cavalry. Once a patrol of foot soldiers was tracking a Navajo raiding party. The warriors decided to go off in different directions and later meet at a prearranged point. The soldiers, under orders to stay together, tried to follow one of the warriors, but ended up getting lost. The raiding party got away clean."

"Well, we're not going to split up, so that won't work for us," Travis answered flatly. The last thing he needed now was to worry about Belara alone with Robertson's men trailing her.

"There were also times when the *Dinéh* would walk in the previous person's tracks. The last person in line would gently rub out the marks with a leafy branch." She chuckled softly. "Only there's a trick to that. My uncle and I used to make a game of trying to track each other. He taught me that it never pays to erase footprints with anything that's too stalky or stiff. Unless you have just the right touch, you end up *creating* a trail."

"I know. We were taught that, too, in the..." He decided not to mention the Army again for a while. He still carried too many memories of the way he'd failed others then. "The point in our favor is that it's darned difficult to track anything by moonlight. By dawn, small animals and rodents will have obscured much of what's left of our trail anyway. Keep in mind, too, that, like us, Robertson and the others will have to hole up to rest and hide when the sun rises."

As they continued up the mountain in a southeasterly climb, Belara looked behind them frequently. Travis was doing a good job of obscuring the trail. Yet the knowledge that sooner or later Robertson would realize he'd been tricked preyed on her mind. If he came back for her, he'd come better prepared. Fear traveled up her spine. She knew they needed her alive, but what would happen to the man with her? He'd risked his life to protect her and she'd do the same for him. Yet, she couldn't deny that the prospect left her quaking right down to her knees.

Travis stopped and took their bearings, studying the maps and the terrain around them. San Andres Peak, close to where they stood, was about 8,200 feet above sea level. It would be quite cold at night, even this time of year. If they went another mile to a small saddle located between San Andres and the next unnamed peak to the south, they might have an easier time crossing over.

"That's right," he said, seeing her check behind them again. "Help me listen and watch for them. Four men will make more noise than the two of us and the wind carries sounds."

"Both Wind and Darkness have been Navajo mentors before and they're working for us now," she said trying to reassure him the best way she knew how. "The breeze is coming toward us bringing information about them, not vice versa."

"We can use all the help we can get," he replied. As they reached a rocky stretch of ground, he slipped the branch he'd been using to obscure their tracks into the middle of another bush of the same species. Pulling the map from his pack, he checked for landmarks, trying to reorient himself. The bare ridge to his left contained a long, narrow limestone shelf that ran parallel to their direction of travel. "It's not very clear on the map, but I think if we head for that shelf, and follow it around, we'll be able to save several hours of hard climbing. It'll be like walking around the ledge of a building instead of climbing over it to get to the other side. The going should be relatively easy, too, because it's flat and hard."

"Good idea. We can get there by going straight uphill. We'll have to work a little harder, but the distance will be shorter, and we'll save time."

Their ascent up the rock face was more difficult than she'd anticipated. The shelf he was aiming for was part of the steepest section of the mountain. Belara leaned forward against the incline, careful to avoid a dangerous slip. It was getting more difficult to keep up with Travis who was always pushing forward. Her limbs ached from the exertion and thin air, but she focused on her uncle and what she was trying to do. This was no time to listen to her body's complaints. Forcing herself to endure the aches, she tried to maintain a steady pace.

Travis continually glanced back, checking her progress. The admiration that shone in his face made it easier. At least she was slowly proving to him that her word was good and could be trusted. She'd assured him that she'd be able to make the journey, and so far she'd been able to match his skills and efforts.

Travis stopped a few minutes later, and gave her a long, speculative look. "You're really breathing hard," he said, gulping for air.

She smiled at him, trying to catch her breath. "So are you. Big deal. It's the roughest climbing we've done."

"Between Robertson, the Army patrols and the time constraint we're under, we're going to have to push ourselves to the limit," he warned. "And even if we do our best, there's no guarantee we'll succeed. There's a large number of things that could go wrong before we ever reach the ranch."

"They won't," she said flatly, her breathing labored from the strain of matching his pace. "You better start thinking positive." She struggled to keep her own thoughts focused on the good she wanted to accomplish. Her uncle had taught her about the power of thought. The Holy People had created the world with it.

"There's a big difference between being negative and being a realist. You've got to consider these things."

"I already know what the risks are. Dwelling on them isn't going to change anything," she explained as she hauled herself upward, step by rugged step. "Most Anglos are taught to prepare themselves for the worst. They plan for it, just in case it happens." As they reached the rocky shelf, she clambered up onto it and sighed with relief. "The *Dinéh*'s way is exactly the opposite, and if you don't mind my saying so, infinitely healthier. It's dangerous to dwell on all the bad things that *could* happen. You'll bring them into your life for sure that way. Think of it in terms of a self-fulfilling prophecy. And it's not just the *Dinéh* who feel that way, either. Almost every religion has a theory of origin, and it all comes down to the same thing. *Thought* brought the world into being.''

He nodded slowly. ''I follow your reasoning, but I'm not sure I agree. Preparation can be everything in certain cases.''

''It's one thing to prepare, and another to expect the worst. You remind me of someone who buys a big life insurance policy. You bet you die, the company bets you live. What kind of deal is that to make?''

He chuckled softly. ''I see we're not going to get anywhere on this,'' he said, starting to make his way across the shelf. ''Stay low. We don't want to be outlined against the skyline. Fortunately, with the full moon out, crossing to the other side won't be too difficult from this point. Just make sure you stay away from the edge. It's starting to crumble.''

Belara followed him easily. It was like the game she'd played as a child. Despite her uncle's warnings, she'd amused herself by walking along the top of the cinder-block wall that bordered his property. Her thoughts drifted momentarily and by the time she glanced up, she was almost on top of Travis. ''Why did you stop like that?'' she demanded, taken by surprise.

''There's a gap in the shelf that's about eight feet wide and about fifty feet deep. As usual, it wasn't on the map.'' He pressed his back against the wall of the mountain, allowing her to see past him.

Belara exhaled softly. ''We'll have to turn back. There's no way I can jump that, particularly at night.''

''If we do, we're taking the chance of meeting Robertson again. By now he's seen our little trick and is looking around trying to pick up our trail. Remember that if I learned the general area of your uncle's ranch, it's possible he might have, too. That'll give him an advantage, even if we've covered our tracks. Depending on how thorough he is in his search, he could even spot us up here."

"We could climb down and walk parallel to the shelf until we can find a way to get across."

"As steep as it is, that would be extremely dangerous. We'd also be leaving tracks everywhere. I have another idea. Let me sink a piton into a crack in the rock, attach a rope to it, then make the jump. Once I'm set up over there, I'll control the rope while you cross hand over hand using a safety line."

"That gap is extremely wide for an unsupported jump, and the ledge is narrow. Are you absolutely certain you can make it? If you have *any* reservations about it, you shouldn't try. The slightest hesitation could increase the odds against you." The way of the *Dinéh* had taught her to respect an individual's right to make his own decisions, but Travis was talking about taking a very big chance. Even though his words were filled with logic, her heart compelled her to try to get him to change his mind.

Travis studied the gap for a moment, then nodded. "I'm certain I can do it, but I don't think I'll try with my gear strapped on. Once I get to the other side we'll run my backpack and yours across the line. Consider it a test run for the system."

As a mountain breeze blew down and across her face, she listened to the sounds of the night. The Wind People were unusually silent.

"You'll have to trust my judgment on this," he said quietly. "I'll have one end of the rope tied securely to myself and the other will be held by the piton. I wouldn't endanger you by placing myself at risk unnecessarily. I've committed myself to help you as much as I can, and my word is good. How about showing a little faith in me?"

"You have it," she said, swallowing back her fear.

"That's the spirit." He gave her a confident grin. Travis used a hammer to sink a sturdy piton into a small crack in the limestone shelf. "I know the sound will carry, but maybe they're making so much noise they won't hear us.

And the wind is in our favor." Working with methodical precision, he knotted one end of the rope around the metal spike. Yanking it roughly a few times, he made sure it was secure.

"Now for your safety line." He cut a length of rope off with his knife then tied a metal, heavy-duty clasp at one end of it. "Fasten the rope securely to your waist, then attach the clasp to the main rope that will be strung over the gap. Then if you lose your grip, you still won't fall." He grinned at her and lowered his voice to a provocative whisper. "If you come closer to me, I'll be glad to help you wrap it around your waist and show you what you need to do."

His velvety voice caressed her and left her tingling all over. "I can manage all by myself when the time comes, thank you." She knew he'd been trying to distract her, hoping to ease the tension, and it had certainly worked. Without even touching her, he'd made her feel warn and relaxed. Yet, they were facing too much danger for her to allow herself to become sidetracked for long. Without thinking, she glanced up at him and sighed.

He gave her a quirky, sympathetic grin. "My sentiments exactly."

She felt her face burning with embarrassment. "We better hurry. We don't want Robertson and the others to have too much time to think about the clanking noise your hammer made."

He nodded somberly, then moved his rucksack out of their way. "You're going to have to stay back a bit. I'm going to need a running start."

Belara stepped farther away from him. With the safety line he'd fashioned for himself, he wouldn't fall far. Yet, he could miss and slam against the side of the rock face on the other side. Her stomach tightened and for a moment she thought she might be sick.

Belara closed her eyes for a second then opened them again. It was time to focus on success, not failure. She took a deep breath and forced herself to appear calm. She wouldn't undermine his efforts by letting him see her fear.

She had to support him by showing confidence in his judgment and ability. That was the only way she could help him now.

Giving him a thumbs-up, she went to the end of the rocky shelf. Travis walked to a point about twenty feet behind the drop-off, then turned and broke into a fast run. She saw him hurtle the gap and land upright on the other side. Suddenly the edge of the shelf wobbled beneath him, parts crumbling into the crevice below. Travis slipped backward, stumbling toward the precipice.

She held her breath and watched him fight to remain on his feet. As he hovered between success and disaster, she reached out to him instinctively, despite the futility of the gesture. After a few heart-wrenching seconds, she saw him dig his fingers into the limestone wall. He must have found something to hold on to because he recaptured his balance with the sudden agility of a cat and hurried away from the edge. Belara stepped forward, standing as close to him as the gap would allow. Then he turned and smiled at her and, for a moment, that simple gesture did strange things to her knees.

"I made it," he said shakily.

"Never doubted it for a minute," she answered, hoping he hadn't heard her voice crack.

As their eyes met, they both burst out laughing. The tension of the past few minutes washed out of them as they contemplated each other from opposite sides of the gap. "I'll hold the rope," he said at last. "Use the safety line to send my backpack over. I'll need to sink another piton into the rock here before it'll be secure enough for you to cross."

Belara followed his instructions. Seconds later, he was busy hammering another piton into a solid mass of rock farther away from the edge of the vertical drop. "Okay," he said, as he finished. "Send over the rest. We'll test things out."

Belara tied his rifle and her walking stick securely to her backpack, then sent them and their other gear over. That part was easy. When her own turn came, her mouth began to feel as if she'd swallowed a bottle of glue. The gorge below, in the darkness, seemed almost bottomless. Depending on one's point of view, it was a spectacular sight or a horrifying nightmare.

"You can make it across safely," he assured her, sensing her trepidation.

She made a circle with her thumb and forefinger, feigning courage she scarcely felt. Fastening the safety line in a bowline knot around her waist, she glanced up. Travis sat on the ground, anchored against the back of the shelf. Clasped tightly in his hands was the section of rope he'd threaded around the piton. "Ready whenever you are," he called.

"I'm coming over now." As she started to attach the safety-line clip on the rope, three rapid shots rang out from somewhere below. Belara dived to the ground, her arms folding over her head as she anticipated another volley. She didn't have to wait long. As she lay flat against the cold stone, the whine of bullets ripped apart the stillness of the night.

"Come on," Travis yelled, longing to reach for his rifle. "You've got to cross now. They'll be right on top of us in fifteen minutes."

Belara stared at the rope, realizing that there was no way she'd be able to cross by pulling herself hand over hand now. She'd be below the line of fire, but Travis would be sitting with no cover at all the whole time she was crossing. Her heart constricted as she pictured it in her mind. "Change of plans," she yelled back. "We have to do this the fast way."

Her hands were shaking as she pulled out her sheath knife and cut the end of the rope Travis had fastened to the piton. Bullets continued to ricochet above her, spraying her with fragments of rock. Ignoring Travis's protests for the moment, she cut the safety line off her waist and replaced it with the rope. She tied it securely around herself using the bowline knot she knew would hold. He'd made it across.

She would, too. There was no time for rituals to invoke aid, or for doubts.

"Don't try to jump. You won't make it!" he shouted at her, on his feet now, oblivious to the harassing gunfire.

"You better hold on to that rope, mister. I'm counting on you!" Not giving him a chance to say more, she moved farther back on the shelf and broke into the fastest run of her life. Her momentum would have to carry her forward.

She felt herself soaring through the air, but even as she leaped, she realized she wasn't going to make it.

Chapter Six

Travis swore roughly as he gripped the rope with all his strength. Shivers were running down his spine like raindrops trickling down a windowpane. He saw her leap, but knew she'd fall short of her mark, particularly since the edge of the ledge was unstable. As her body lost momentum and began to fall, he braced himself against the limestone surface. Ignoring the sporadic gunfire, he tensed for the abrupt jerk that would signal her body had stopped its descent.

It came almost immediately, dragging him forward a foot before he managed to regain control. He went cold as he pictured her body broken by the impact against the rock. The fear that clawed at his gut went far deeper than any memories called up from the nightmarish scene in his past. It wasn't just the possibility of having failed again that made him feel as if his heart had been packed in ice. It was the knowledge that he might have lost Belara.

A faint spark of hope helped him hold back the chilling numbness creeping over him. Forcing his legs and hands to function, he secured the rope to the piton, grasped the end of it, and inched toward the edge. The bullets impacting above him seemed more of an annoyance than a danger now. He hardened himself before looking down.

"What in the heck are you waiting for? Pull me up, will ya?"

Relief washed over Travis making him feel almost giddy. "You scared me half to death, lady! Don't you *ever* do that to me again. Can't you follow directions?" He started to pull her up hand over hand.

"Will you try to get me up there a little faster? Something about bullets flying all around me makes me nervous." Belara scrambled up the rope as he hauled in the line. Seconds later, she dragged herself up onto the narrow shelf. She crawled over to her backpack. "Let's get out of here," she said, grabbing her walking stick while he crouched, collecting the rope.

"I'm assuming that you fended off the rock face with your legs. At the speed you were traveling you're lucky you didn't break anything."

"I know enough to bend my knees," she retorted as he grabbed his gear and hurried along the shelf with her. "I'm sore, but I'll worry about it later."

"We should start jogging if you can manage it," he urged. "I don't want to take a chance of them catching up."

"Do you think they'll risk jumping that gap to come after us?"

"They might, but in my opinion none of those guys is in good enough shape to make it across. If they try, my bet is we'll be hearing some screams real soon."

They moved as quickly as they dared for about a half a mile before Travis finally slowed down. "We're out of rifle range now. Let's conserve our energy," he said. "We've traveled a klick in ten minutes over hazardous and rugged territory. I haven't done that since my days in the Special Forces. You're in extremely good shape," he said, stretching and taking several deep breaths.

"I told you that I was," she answered with a smile. "Now tell me something I don't know, like what's a klick?"

"Slang for a kilometer, about six-tenths of a mile," he answered. As he started to catch his breath, his caring anger returned. He should have harangued her unmercifully for taking ten years off his life! What on earth had possessed her to try that leap? Looking at her leaning against the mountainside casually he decided to cool his temper before bringing up the subject. As it was, he couldn't decide between wanting to shake her and wanting to kiss her until they were both too weak to stand.

As they started walking again, he set his pace considerably slower. Finally the limestone shelf tapered off. They emerged at the windswept saddle between the San Andres Peak and the unnamed point farther south of them.

"Do you think we've lost them for good this time?" Belara asked after several minutes of silent travel.

He would have liked to reassure her, but she deserved more from him then a few placating lies. "I doubt it. They're very determined. I have a feeling Robertson's looking at this as some kind of contest between us. He's out to prove he's the better man, and he's pretty sharp, as much as I hate to admit it."

"Pride is a powerful incentive," she said quietly.

"Yes, but without experience, it won't give him much of an advantage over us in the long run. In fact, the angrier he gets, the less clearly he'll be thinking." He shot her an icy look. "And speaking of muddled thinking," he added, unable to hold back any longer. "What made you decide to jump that gap at the last minute? You took me completely off guard!"

"I didn't have much choice. Their shooting was inaccurate because of the distance between us, but that would have changed fast. I couldn't let you sit there holding the rope, making the perfect target for them, while I crossed."

"You knew you couldn't make that jump. Putting *your* life on the line wasn't a very good solution." He tried to keep his temper in check, but she was being so logical and cool about the whole thing, it incensed him even more. "Damn it, woman, you scared the hell out of me!"

His reaction was quite unexpected. This wasn't the cool, professional he always tried to be with her, but a man whose anger stemmed from his feelings for her. The knowledge pleased her. But after seeing the stricken look on his face, she thought better of it. "The rope was sturdy and

I was certain you could pull me up." She placed one hand on his arm. "You asked me to have faith in you. Now you're upset because I did?"

"That's not it," he started to protest, then clamped his mouth shut. He wasn't going to get trapped into a verbal battle of wits. This was a serious situation and he had to find some way of maintaining control.

Unable to think of a solution, he lapsed into silence as they continued moving rapidly along the crest of the mountain range. He'd always thought of women as an added responsibility for a man, companions who needed to be cared for. Yet, by taking that jump, Belara had taken care of him. Few men would have shown the courage she had in trying to leap a distance she'd believed too great for her, just to protect him. No one had ever done such a thing for him before. The thought of what she'd done filled him with such a sweet ache he wasn't sure how to handle it. His feelings for her were growing with each hour and this was exactly the kind of complication he'd hoped to avoid. He wasn't ready to share his life with anyone. The last thing he needed was full-time responsibility for another person's happiness and welfare. He'd let enough people down already.

He set his jaw and stared off into the distance. He'd known she would be trouble, and now he had his hands full.

He'd have to stay sharp and avoid thinking of her as anything except *major* trouble. And he wouldn't be too far off, either.

SHORTLY AFTER MIDNIGHT they finally began to descend the mountain range on the east side. Going downhill made it easier, but her legs still hurt from when she'd struck the side of the cliff. Travis had expressed concern a few times when her pace lagged, but something in his eyes had stopped her from admitting that she needed to stop and rest. She'd sensed his anger, and had concluded that he blamed their predicament on her.

As her thoughts focused on him, she entertained a few choice adjectives, all having to do with the circumstances of his birth. She hadn't asked for his help. In fact, she'd done everything possible to get him not to interfere. Still, she couldn't deny that she was glad he'd come, and even gladder he was still here.

There was much to like about this man. From what she'd seen, he had a strong sense of duty, and he cared enough to do what he felt was right despite the risks. It was that, and the intensity of the feelings he evoked in her, that worried her. She couldn't allow herself to get involved with an Anglo man. Her mother had tried it, and failed. Sooner or later, their ways of looking at life would come to a head-on collision. In theory, there was no reason why it should, but she'd seen what happened when the theory confronted reality.

They were about a third of the way down the mountainside when Belara's gaze drifted over the ridge directly ahead. In the moonlight, she could see the shattered remnant of a wooden shack ahead. Several swimming-pool-size craters ran in a jagged line, straddling the shack.

Travis glanced back at her, then followed her line of vision. "The Air Force was here," he muttered. "This is the result of one of their more accurate practice bombing runs. Thorough, aren't they?" he asked, not really expecting an answer. "We should detour and avoid that, even if it does cost us time."

"Why can't we just keep our eyes open for unexploded bombs and walk parallel to the holes? It wouldn't be for any great distance." She saw the exasperated look he flashed her, but ignored it. "We both took quite a risk jumping over that gap so we could save time. Let's not make it pointless by detouring before we even check and make sure there's a need," she reasoned. "I don't know anything about military ordinance, but aren't bombs quite large and heavy? Even if they didn't explode, they'd dig a big hole in the ground wherever they landed, right?"

"Yeah, but depending on where the bombs hit, it's possible wind-blown sand could have drifted over some of the holes and buried them completely."

"But surely not enough to eliminate all traces of them."

"Probably not," he conceded. "I suppose we can try to cross it, since time is working against us and your uncle, but we'll have to stay sharp. I'll lead us on a course that keeps us out of the bombing pattern. If we spot signs of unexploded ordinance, we'll move back up the slope. I want to keep a wide margin between us and the duds."

"All right." She followed him closely for several minutes, staying on his tracks. Hearing the soft rustle of an animal moving through the brush, she glanced around. Snakes were out this time of night, and the last thing they needed right now was an encounter with a rattler.

As she studied the rugged hillside, she saw a woodrat darting into its hole. It was a good omen. The woodrat, *lé'étso,* had warned Rainboy, one of the Navajo heroes, and helped him avoid danger. She smiled, half doubting the small creature could do much for them. Suddenly her eyes came to rest on a foreign-looking object and she froze in midstride. "By the way, Travis, what would one of these unexploded bombs look like after it hit the ground?"

He groaned. "*Now* you ask?"

"Well, I *think* I'd know one, but I'm not sure. Look to your left."

Travis glanced into the large depression beside him. "There's nothing there."

"Look about three feet beyond the hole, just by the side of the boulder. There's something metal sticking up. Whatever it is, it has fins."

Travis moved a few feet forward and then saw what she was looking at. "How did you spot it? In the moonlight it's almost the same color as the ground."

"The woodrat told me," she answered, then explained.

"I'm not going to get any closer, but from the stenciled marking and the size, I believe that's a five-hundred-pound bomb. It's still intact, and that means trouble. Let's go back. There might be others around us. Depending on how long they've been out here, the explosives could be unstable. Someone our size kicking a loose stone against them might be all it takes to set them off."

Moving along slowly and carefully, they retraced their steps until they reached the slope that had led them there. Travis checked his maps, then glanced back at her. "We don't have to go far out of our way. We can maintain our course by climbing up a bit higher. The ground's more uneven up there, but we shouldn't lose more than an hour if we force ourselves to increase the pace."

"All right." She'd pushed herself constantly for several hours, and her muscles ached from the strain. But she'd seen matching lines of weariness etching Travis's face, yet he never let up. He was driving himself and her constantly to do better than their best. "Just remember that we'll be able to maintain a more rapid pace in the long run, if we don't exhaust ourselves, now."

"We can't ease up yet," he replied flatly. "So far we've managed to stay on top of things, but that can change."

His tone surprised her, but there was truth in what he'd said. "All I meant was the *right* pacing will insure we last the distance."

"I know," he answered, his tone losing some of its harshness. "But I've got to make sure I don't let you or myself down," he said, then shook his head as if he hadn't meant to disclose so much. "Let's keep moving."

She gazed at him curiously, wondering more than ever about him. There was pain behind his jade-green eyes. Her heart responded to it, wanting to comfort and soothe, but there was nothing she could do. He was a man determined to stay locked safely inside himself.

Travis led them up onto a rocky outcropping covered with twisted, stunted junipers that stood less than three feet tall. "Listen for sounds of aircraft. We're exposed up here, so it would be easy for a low-flying pilot to see us. If they fly over, we'll have to try to hide from their sensors by staying still so they don't pick us up as a human form, or else by ducking under something." He glanced back at her as they moved quickly past a barren, exposed area. "We'll slow down right after we cross this section."

"It's okay. I can keep up, and any time we save can only end up helping us."

He nodded slowly. "We'll keep it brisk, but steady. It's easier that way. If we slow down too much, you'll have time to be more aware of your body and you'll probably feel even more tired."

As they crossed an area of massive rocks beneath a vertical cliff, Travis instinctively moved to the shadows. Belara followed his lead automatically, her thoughts miles away with her uncle. With every delay, her fear for his safety increased. Some connection to him had turned Robertson and his men into their deadly adversaries. It was clear to her now that her uncle would be needing her help in more than one way, and she was determined not to fail him.

Pulling her thoughts back to the task before her, she studied the moonlit landscape. Her gaze came to rest on a curiously shaped mound at the base of a car-size boulder. She took a few steps up the slope, straining to get a closer look. There was something about it that didn't seem quite right.

Moving silently, she advanced another few feet and saw that it was the fresh carcass of a small mountain sheep. She looked away automatically. Death was inevitable, and as a Navajo she didn't fear it. Corpses and objects associated with the dead were an entirely different matter, however. Even looking upon the body of a dead animal, except one killed for food, was dangerous.

She started to walk back down the way she'd come when a low, deep growl brought her to a sudden standstill. She turned her head slowly toward the chilling sound. Crouched on the rock above her, ready to spring, was a cougar. Its fangs gleamed yellow in the faint moonlight.

Moving only her eyes, she searched the shadows for Travis. He was not within her field of vision. Afraid to call out to him, she remained as still as possible. After a moment, the animal shifted slightly, inching forward.

Belara's legs felt weak as she tried to prepare for the evasive jump she'd have to make if the cat leaped. Slipping her hand down slowly, almost imperceptibly, she reached for the small hunting knife inside the leather sheath on her belt. Her attention was focused on the cougar as she thumbed off the snap holding the blade down. The sound made the cat crouch even lower and step to the edge of the rock, all four feet together, poised to spring.

She had no desire to injure such a beautiful animal, particularly since she'd been the trespasser, intruding on his kill. Still, she would do her best to defend herself. Angling her walking stick toward the predator, she silently invoked the help of Earth Woman, the holy person most known for aiding and sustaining. The beast watched her, but made no new move to attack. Its growls had a strange, alien quality that made her skin prickle. To most Native Americans the mountain lion was respected as mysterious and powerful, offering protection to one who carried its fetish. Yet right now, all she could think of was the lion's reputation as a hunter.

She started to take a step back when she heard a click behind her. The cougar turned its head slowly and looked past her. The animal's deep, guttural snarl was an affirmation of confidence in his ability to defend his territory.

"I've got you covered," Travis told her, his voice a gentle whisper that blended with the breeze. "Move away from the kill slowly."

Belara's feet felt as if they were encased in concrete instead of comfortable hiking boots. With an influx of willpower, she forced her limbs to work. Her heart thudded painfully as she edged backward, her eyes on the cougar. He seemed to relax with every inch of ground she relinquished to him, but perhaps it was only her imagination.

An eternity later, she reached Travis's side. His rifle was still pointed unwaveringly at the animal. Her stomach was churning and she felt dizzy with relief as the cougar watched them retreat, but remained in place.

Careful not to break into a run, they worked their way down the slope until they lost sight of it. Travis leaned back against a stand of boulders, closed his eyes, then opened them again.

"What on earth possessed you to go up and look at the cougar?"

"I didn't see it until it was too late. I'd spotted an odd shape on the ground, so I thought I'd go check it out. It was inert, like a bundle of old rags, so I never expected any trouble."

"Let's get out of here," he said, engaging the safety on his rifle. "And please, don't make anymore side trips without saying something first, okay? I've never thought of myself as high-strung or nervous, but if you keep doing things like that, I'm probably going to give new meaning to both."

"I haven't..." She exhaled softly. "Okay," she conceded. "Whatever you say. You're the boss."

He glanced up at her quickly. "Can I get that in writing?"

She grinned at him. "Naw, it's just something I said to make you feel better."

The sudden shriek of the mountain lion penetrated her flesh and pierced her to the marrow. Its almost human quality gave the eerie, primitive sound a disturbing, flesh-crawling intensity. The beast's primal challenge to the night vibrated in the air, shattering the stillness. She tried to suppress a shiver, but didn't quite manage it. "It's a victory cry," she whispered. "It knows it's safe with its prey."

They left the area hastily and trudged forward in a ragged line that strung them out against the desert sky. By morning, they were halfway down the northeastern side of San Andres Peak.

Travis stopped by a cavernous opening in the midst of a rocky expanse of limestone. It seemed to lead right into the mountain. Cobwebs were strung across it like fine linen.

Individual strands hung in streamers from his shirt sleeve as he brushed against it. "I don't think there're any large animals using this as a den. The entrance is practically void of tracks and covered with old spiderwebs."

Belara crouched beside him, peering into the darkness. "You're thinking of going inside?"

"I wouldn't normally recommend it, but it will keep us out of the sun and prevent anyone from spotting us." He led the way into the dark interior. "The first thing I'd like to do is check to see if there's a second opening somewhere. Keep alert. If there is, we might have company in here."

Using a small flashlight, they made their way into the pitch-black tunnel. The first chamber they encountered wasn't very large, but the gloom in the back recesses of the cave was oppressive. Belara fought the feeling of being buried alive. "I've never been comfortable inside caves."

"Claustrophobia?" he asked. His voice, though muted, echoed in the stone confines.

"Maybe a touch." She glanced at another tunnel that appeared to wind into the heart of the mountain itself. "The *Dinéh* believe that each mountain is a person. It has an inner form we call the *bi· yistí· n* that gives it life and makes it able to think and feel."

"Is it a violation of your beliefs to use this place as shelter? If it is, we can find someplace else."

"No, that's not necessary. There are no special taboos about caves." She gave him a sheepish smile. "It's just me. I find it difficult to be comfortable in them."

"We can keep hiking for a while until we find another suitable place to make camp. We're bound to come across another spot, sooner or later."

Belara shook her head adamantly. "No way. I'll welcome the mountain's hospitality, particularly since it means I don't have to walk anywhere else."

He chuckled softly. "I'm with you on that." As they approached the side tunnel, he shut off the flashlight. "So, it does have another exit." He made his way to the opening and checked for tracks. "I don't think anything larger than a rabbit has been in this cave for years," he said at last. "We can set up camp here. It's perfect since we won't be right at the face of the cave and this section is inaccessible from outside. We're also sheltered by another rock overhang, so we can't be seen by low-flying helicopters."

"Then let's get something to eat and roll out our sleeping bags. We need to get some rest." Belara reached into her backpack and brought out a packet of freeze-dried macaroni and cheese. "In some ways this trip must be harder on you than on me. My reasons for coming give me all the incentive I need to keep going. You're here under duress."

"That's true," he said with a soft chuckle, "but making sure Robertson is not in a position to become a serious problem for either of us is all the incentive I need." He reached for his canteen and took a long swallow of water. "By the way, how long do we have before people start worrying about you? I assume you told your parents or some friends what you were planning to do."

"I didn't tell any friends because I felt that secrecy was far more important in this case. I would have told my parents this, but they're no longer alive. They'd both passed on by the time I was eight." She stared off into the darkness of the cave, her mind drifting back through the events that had shaped her life. "My uncle was the one who raised me after they were gone. Without him, I might have never come to know myself as a Navajo. I would have been raised by my father's mother and she knew nothing about the ways of our tribe. She, like my father, is *bilagáana,* white."

"So you're only half Navajo?" he questioned.

"By Navajo law, I'm considered Navajo," she answered. "And my appearance makes me a Navajo in the eyes of the whites."

"Tell me about your family," he asked gently. "Do you remember much about your parents?"

"I recall events and images more than things in general. My uncle was the one who filled in the gaps for me. Over the years he's told me much about them and their life together. Theirs wasn't exactly a match made in heaven," she said sadly. "My father was a building contractor who worked very hard to keep his small company in business. Socializing was important to his trade since it helped him make new contacts and meet potential clients.

"Unfortunately the people in the community never accepted my mother. Her race made her too different in their eyes. My mother was a very sensitive woman and their attitudes hurt her deeply. She couldn't quite shut her eyes to their prejudice, so instead, she chose to keep to herself. She argued that the way the others felt about her made her more of a detriment to him than an asset."

"She might have had a point," Travis observed. "Prejudice is hard to fight."

"My father never understood that. He blamed my mother for allowing them to make her feel inferior. He saw her reluctance to mingle with the others as a sign of her lack of ambition. He couldn't understand why the *Dinéh* culture didn't emphasize personal success, in the sense used by the *bilagáanas*. My mother, on the other hand, figured that we had enough to meet our needs. To her, enjoying life was far more important than amassing wealth. Their different views led to continual arguments which I *do* remember.

"My father felt betrayed by what he saw as her lack of support. By the same token, his inability to understand her ways broke my mother's heart. Eventually this split them up. My mother just packed my stuff and hers one day and we went to live with relatives in northern Arizona."

"Did you understand what was going on?"

"Yes, I was old enough," Belara said in a faraway tone. "I was also very aware of my mother's sadness. She loved my father. And you know, I believe he loved her, too. That's what made it even worse for both of them. Then, after we'd been in Arizona a month, a tribal policeman came to tell us my father had been killed in a plane crash. He'd been flying over to sign the divorce papers when his private plane went down."

"I'm so sorry," he said softly.

She put her cup down, lost in thought, and leaned back against the rock wall. "My mother and I returned to New Mexico shortly after that. Father, as it turned out, hadn't been as much of a businessman as he wanted folks to think. His debts forced her to sell the company, and she had to work two jobs to support us. Even so, there was very little money. She got sick the following winter, but kept working because she didn't have any sick leave benefits. Finally, pneumonia with complications killed her. A year and a half after I lost my dad, my mother was dead, too."

"It must have been a very frightening time for you."

She nodded. "It would have been even worse if it hadn't been for my uncle. He asked for custody of me right away. Since then, I've wondered if he actually realized what he was getting into." She smiled ruefully.

"Was he a bachelor back then, too?"

She nodded. "I'm sure he had considered the matter from an abstract point of view. How difficult could it be to take care of an eight-year-old girl? At that age, it wouldn't have been as demanding as caring for an infant who was totally helpless, or a teenager with a mind of her own."

"Maybe he needed you as much as you needed him," Travis said quietly. "The bachelor life-style can wear on you after a while."

She gave a curious look, but he didn't elaborate.

"Did you adjust to the changes in your life easily?" he asked, urging her to continue.

"Not really. I was a difficult kid," she answered. Memories flooded over her with a vividness that surprised her. She'd never forgotten the pain that had clouded her past, although time had helped her deal with it. "I'd wake up in the middle of the night in a panic, wondering what would happen to me if my uncle was killed or hurt. If he was a little late coming home, I'd go half-crazy worrying, or go out looking for him."

Her throat tightened, and she had to take a deep breath before she could continue. "As time went by, I learned to stop being so fearful. I had a new life and a place where I belonged. My uncle was Navajo and so was I, so our close-ness seemed to go even deeper than regular family ties. The *Dinéh* had a history that made me part of an even larger whole. I learned to be proud of who and what I am, and to value myself. From that came independence.''

''He did a fine job of raising you. You're a very special woman,'' he said, capturing her eyes openly. ''I'm glad I came with you because it's given us a chance to get to know each other. We might not have, otherwise,'' he said, then with a smile he added, ''even though I would have tried to.''

''I'd have been disappointed if you hadn't,'' she an-swered honestly, though her spirits felt leaden. She would not repeat her mother's mistakes. She would choose a mate from her own tribe and give her children the gift of a home united by the harmony that came from shared beliefs. They wouldn't know the conflict that invariably came of trying to blend two different cultures.

Still, despite all the arguments against it, this man was claiming a part of her heart. Although she wasn't sure what his story was, she recognized the pain thinly veiled in his eyes. She ached with the need to soothe and heal it. Per-haps it was easier to empathize when you'd been there yourself. She'd had her uncle, but Travis had shut himself off. He needed someone, whether or not he knew it, and she cared too much about him not to try to help.

Travis was about to say something when the sound of aircraft approaching reached the confines of the cave. ''Several jets are coming this way. I better go take a look and make sure there's no foot patrol heading right toward us, too.''

He walked to the entrance carrying his binoculars. Standing in the shadows, he searched the skies. ''It's a squadron of A-7's and a KC 135 tanker about to rendez-vous. They're practicing in-flight refueling.''

Belara came up to the entrance and stood to one side of him, staring east toward the Tularosa Basin and White Sands National Monument. ''How do they do that?''

"There's a boom that extends from the rear of the tanker. It's a matter of aligning it with the A-7." Travis switched from watching the aircraft, now out of their view, to the area below. "There's a group of men approaching from the west. They're on this side of the ridge. It could be a military patrol responding to the shooting last night. Or maybe Robertson and the others managed to pick up our trail."

"Should we keep going? I don't want to run into any more trouble if we can help it. I'd just as soon give up some sleep."

He shook his head. "Even if they find the few tracks we may have left and don't take breaks, they won't get here before nightfall. We'll be okay in the cave. No one's going to sneak up on us here." Travis gestured for her to move farther away from the entrance.

Belara watched the airplanes that had circled back overhead cluster around the tanker like birds of prey. She hesitated, wishing she could watch a bit longer. The gloom of the cave seemed a poor substitute to the free-flying planes. Reluctantly she turned and started back, blinking to get her eyes to adjust to the darkness that greeted her.

Travis strode to where they'd left their gear and made a quick check of their water supply. With an opened canteen in hand, he stepped toward her. "Have a swallow?" he asked.

There was a sharp crack and suddenly the ground seemed to open up beneath his feet. Travis uttered a single expletive as he reached out in a futile attempt to grab on to something solid.

Belara made a lunge forward, but was a second too late. Wood snapped and splintered and dust flew into the air as Travis spiraled downward into an abyss of impenetrable darkness.

Chapter Seven

Travis reached out, trying to grab hold of something that would stop his descent. The sides of the pit were rough, scraping his flesh away, but there was nothing there to hold on to.

His body smashed viciously against one side of the shaft, then bounced in the opposite direction. Finally he came to an abrupt stop, landing on his backside with a bone-jarring thud. The impact knocked the wind out of him.

He looked around, gasping for air and trying to make out shapes in the darkness. He wasn't at the bottom. Somehow he'd managed to land on a sandy ledge. An empty black hole yawned below him. Yet even in the dim light he could tell that the shaft wasn't completely vertical. That one factor had probably saved his life. He checked his arms and legs, but nothing seemed broken. Bouncing off the side had slowed his fall. He ached, but he could still move.

Looking up, he realized Belara was yelling down at him from about twenty feet higher up.

"Travis, can you hear me?" she cried out. "Are you okay?"

"I need some light," he answered, his voice shaky.

A strong beam, made hazy by the dust he'd stirred up, pierced the blackness of the tunnel. "Are you hurt?"

"Bruised mostly," he managed, "and sore as hell."

"I can't figure out where you're at. From up here you look as if you're suspended in midair."

"I'm on a tiny ledge about a third of the way down this mine shaft, from what I can tell." He glanced below him. "I can't see the bottom clearly."

"Don't worry. It's down there."

"Get my pack and find the rope, okay?"

"I've got it," she yelled back a moment later. "Let me tie it to something secure first. Stay put."

"Where would I go?" he muttered in reply.

"Here it comes," she said, throwing the rope down. "Only don't try to climb up by yourself. Maybe I can help haul you up."

He chuckled softly. "I appreciate the thought, but don't try. I'm too heavy. You'll just get pulled down on top of me. I've secured myself to the line. I'll come up hand over hand."

"Wait. I've got an idea," Belara yelled back.

He heard some muffled sounds, and within five minutes she called back down. "Come on up, slowly," she called.

Nothing had changed, so he couldn't figure out what she'd been up to. Deciding to wait to ask questions until after he reached the top, Travis began to climb the rope. He traveled a few feet then stopped to rest. As he took a deep breath, he felt a tug on the rope and suddenly realized he was still ascending in small increments. Somehow, she *was* pulling him up!

When he finally made it to the top she held out her hands and helped him climb onto the floor of the cave. Travis buckled to the ground, exhausted. He started to thank her, and saw that she was almost ready to collapse. Her breathing was hard and her face was flushed with exertion.

"How did you manage to help me get up here?"

She gave him a wide smile, and pointed to the rucksack over her shoulder. "I filled it with large rocks until I equaled your weight. Then, with my feet against the rock lip on the cave floor, I faced the mine shaft, leaned back, and slowly fell to the ground. My body weight and the rocks did all the actual pulling. After each sequence I'd wrap the rope I'd accumulated around the boulder that served as an anchor and repeat the process."

He crawled over to her, freeing himself of the rope as he moved. "Smart lady." His eyes moved over her tenderly. "You look like a soldier who has seen too many battles."

"Gee, thanks," she replied with a half smile. "You better hold back on the sweet talk. You might turn my head." She gave him a long, thorough look, her face filled with concern. "Did you break anything?"

"I've got a bunch of cuts and scrapes, but that's all."

She hesitated for a moment. "I could clean those for you."

"Let me guess," he said with a grin. "You brave unexploded bombs, and guys trying to shoot you without batting an eyelash. Yet when it's time to get the iodine out, you're squeamish."

"No, that's not it. Normally, it wouldn't bother me. But when the person hurt is someone I..." She clamped her mouth shut. Letting him believe she was squeamish was probably much safer than the truth—that she couldn't stand seeing someone she cared about injured.

His eyes captured hers. "Go on," he prodded gently.

She thought fast. "When the person hurt is someone...who's not acquainted with our remedies, it's a bit awkward. You'd probably prefer iodine or antiseptic, but I have a salve made from special plants that would be wonderful for those cuts and even better than iodine. It really promotes healing and doesn't sting nearly as much."

He looked deeply into her eyes letting the warmth of his feelings flow into that gaze. "If you trust it, so will I," he said, his voice a gentle, caressing whisper.

A rush of tenderness left her feeling vibrant and weak all at the same time. As she brushed away a lock of hair that had fallen over his forehead, her palm grazed his face.

He sucked in his breath, his eyes aglow with a strong inner fire. "I'm in your hands," he murmured, unbuttoning his shirt.

His words made her pulse quicken and heightened the yearning she felt for the comfort of his arms. She picked up a small leather pouch she'd removed from her pack in haste earlier. As she turned toward him, the sight of him practically tore her breath away. His tanned chest shone with a light sheen of perspiration that accentuated the contours of his muscles. Dark masculine hair dusted his upper body, angling downward provocatively and disappearing beneath the waistband of his pants. She forced herself to concentrate on the small container with the healing salve.

"What's in that?"

"It's a mixture of Caltrop root, and Summer Fearing plant."

She kept her touch gentle as she covered each cut on his upper arms with the herbal medicine. In a barely audible voice, she chanted a Good Medicine Song to Beautiful Flowers, the chief of all the Medicine Spirits.

Shifting, she knelt before Travis and began to apply the salve to his scraped hands. Finishing that she turned her attention to a cut on his chest. His muscles quivered beneath her touch, yet he kept his body turned slightly so she couldn't see his scar. For a brief second their eyes met and his gaze seared through her.

She looked away, desire making her body tingle with awareness. The warmth of his body near hers and the light contact between them had teased her imagination. Longing turned into a languorous heaviness she could barely disguise. Keeping her gaze averted, she closed the pouch. "That will help you, you'll see."

"Thanks," Travis managed in a raw voice. "Get some rest now." He stood. "I'll take the first watch. I need time to unwind and to think."

She nodded, then carefully lowered her sore body onto her sleeping bag. At first, images of what might have been flashed unbidden into her mind and she tossed and turned, too restless to sleep. Using what was left of her willpower, she forced her mind to go blank. Weariness did the rest. She

drifted off to sleep, dreaming of this man whose green eyes
flashed with fire and life.

HOURS PASSED SLOWLY. Travis watched her, wondering if
his life would ever be simple again. The more he got to
know Belara, the more special she became to him. When
they'd started on this journey, he'd honestly believed that
she would be completely dependent on him. Along the way,
she'd proven that she didn't need him to take care of her.
But even then he'd never dreamed he'd be able to depend
on her to help him. Something stirred deep inside him as he
savored the feeling of partnership he'd found with her. She
was his match in every way that counted, except one. If she
really got to know him, would her gentle soul be able to
accept him? His past was filled with dark clouds that would
haunt him for as long as he lived.

Once before he'd lost someone who'd been unable to love
him for what he was. His thoughts drifted back to his ex-
girlfriend Nancy. When he'd refused to speak about his
past, she'd thought he was rejecting the military life-style
and philosophy she abhorred. When Nancy had learned
that he was a natural soldier and would always retain the
traits of a fighter, she'd rejected him totally. He remembered the incident that had triggered the breakup quite well.

Nancy had been waiting for him in a nightclub when a
guy had tried to pick her up. She'd told him to get lost, so
the man had decided to grab her car keys from the table.
He'd refused to give them back unless she agreed to have a
drink with him.

Nancy had still been trying to get her keys back when
he'd arrived. He'd solved the problem right away. First,
he'd asked the troublemaker to return the keys to her.
When the man had refused, he'd pinned the guy to the wall,
ripped off his pocket and taken the keys. Then, he'd thrown
the guy out of the club.

Instead of being grateful, Nancy had been angry at his
overreaction, as she'd called it. She'd argued that he was
incapable of tolerance and too willing to fight if another

man challenged what he felt was his. She'd been partly right. He wasn't incapable of tolerance, but he would not allow someone he cared about to be victimized. In that respect, nothing had changed. If Robertson or the others threatened Belara, he'd do whatever was necessary to protect her.

He glanced back at her, thinking that in the process he'd probably lose her forever. She'd see the lethal side of him, and what he could become when the need arose, and she'd never look at him the same way again.

He stared off into the darkness. It didn't matter. If he had to lose Belara in order to keep her safe, he'd pay that price.

Aware of the constant need for vigilance, Travis stepped over to the entrance of the cave. He studied the area below with his binoculars. It didn't take long for him to locate two men moving far off, on one of the low canyons. They had what appeared to be metal detectors and were obviously searching for something. He watched for some time, but couldn't imagine what they could be looking for this far from Victorio Peak.

Farther back, on a ridge at least two miles away, he could see another man sitting on a rock. Either Robertson's men had really scattered, or that was a member of the other group Sy had told him about. He considered the matter, then finally decided not to concern himself with them as long as they stayed far behind.

After keeping watch ten minutes without the men coming any nearer, he went back into the cave. Belara was still asleep. He watched her for a moment, wishing he could lay himself beside her and gather her into his arms. He stood rock still, trying to tell himself that just being able to look at her was enough. Her hair cascaded across her shoulders and down her back in long, jet-black strands. He imagined what it would be like to undress her slowly and kiss every spot her hair touched now.

A long shudder traveled down the length of him and he turned away. This was not the time to let himself get distracted. Her life, and his own, depended on keeping alert.

All throughout the day, they took turns sleeping and keeping an eye on their distant pursuers. By the time it was finally dark outside, Travis was even more puzzled about Robertson's activities.

"I sure wish I knew what those men are doing. They seem to be looking really hard for something."

"Probably us, don't you think?" she asked, putting on her backpack.

"With metal detectors? I don't know what they're hoping to find."

"Well, with any luck, we'll never see any of them again," she said with an air of finality.

"We can't count on luck," he snapped tersely. "Even if they're hours behind us, we have to keep moving."

"Are you always this testy when you've had trouble sleeping?"

He turned his head slowly and looked at her. "How do you know I didn't sleep well?" He shouldered his rifle without waiting for an answer, and they started across the slope leading away from the cave.

"I saw you tossing and turning all day long," she replied with a shrug. "You didn't seem to be having a nightmare, though, or I would have awakened you."

He quickened his pace. Had she guessed? A man's body could do more to betray him than any traitor. "I slept just fine," he said sharply.

Ten minutes later, he came to a stop and studied the soft expanse of sand that lay ahead. "There's no way to avoid going through that stretch. The sides of the canyon are too steep to climb around it. We're going to have to work overtime to keep from leaving a trail a blind man could follow."

"Maybe not," she answered thoughtfully. "I remember something I heard once. In the old times, the soldiers used to have a difficult time tracking Indians who were on foot.

Indian moccasins had no heels, so they left a very soft impression on the ground. We can achieve the same effect by taking off our shoes and crossing this stretch wearing only our socks. Just a little wave of the branches should remove the impression that's left.''

Travis shook his head. ''Bad idea. This is snake country and we're moving at a time when they're out hunting. Sidewinders in particular are tough to spot. They bury their bodies in the sand until only their eyes show. You can be almost on top of them before you know they're there.''

''My ancestors didn't have boots,'' she answered with a trace of a smile. ''They learned to watch and listen and spot the wavelike patterns the snakes make. We'll be okay as long as we keep our eyes and ears open.'' She started removing her hiking shoes. ''Let me lead the way, I was raised in the desert. I may not be an expert in military ordinance, but I can keep us from stepping on snakes. I guarantee it.''

Travis said nothing as he considered the matter. ''That's not necessary. I can see as well as you can.''

''Yes, but are you as skilled at spotting as you are at looking? When I was a kid, my uncle and I used to go out into the desert and make a game out of tracking. He was always concerned about snakes, so he taught me how to watch for the signs that would indicate they were nearby. After a while, I got darn good at finding them before they could ever be a danger to me.''

He gave her a long, speculative look. He was used to being the expert. This plan of hers, however, made him feel definitely at a loss. Snake hunting barefooted wasn't his idea of a good time. ''Okay, but try not to miss anything important, like fangs for instance.''

''I'll make a special point of it,'' she answered with a soft chuckle. She led the way across the sandy ground, her gaze shifting as she searched for telltale marks.

Travis noted gratefully that the moon was out and shining brightly across the desert floor. At least that would make it easier for her to spot any tracks. Though he was certain she wouldn't have overstated her ability deliberately, he still felt uneasy about padding around the desert in his socks.

"Oops! I think I missed something," she whispered, then turned and laughed, seeing the wide-eyed look on his face. "Just teasing. Relax."

He muttered something vile under his breath. And to think he'd been beginning to like her. "You have a very black sense of humor, lady."

"We're okay. I'm not going to get careless and risk either of us being injured." She lapsed into a somber silence that lasted for several minutes. "I just wish there was a way for us to move across the desert faster. I don't like to dwell on negative thoughts, but I can't stop thinking about my uncle's health. It scares me to think of him alone out here."

"We're making better time than I thought we would," he said quietly. "You're very adept climbing and you've got more heart than anyone I've ever met." He saw her turn to look at him, and scowled. "Don't look at *me*. Keep your mind on snakes, will ya? A bite from a rattler is supposed to hurt like the devil."

"Yes, and it begins immediately. But as long as you stay still afterward, you're not in much danger. Of course in our situation that might be a bit difficult," she said, unable to resist teasing him a bit. "But you don't really have to worry. Very few people actually die from a snake bite. As you probably know, a quick trip to an emergency room is all it takes to make sure all's well. Then again, that might pose a problem for us, too."

"Thanks so much for that enlightening information," he growled acerbically.

"You're very welcome," she said, her shoulders shaking with laughter. "Ease up, okay? We're in this together, and I'm not about to let you down."

He'd enjoyed teamwork of this kind with his military buddies, but never before with a civilian, particularly a woman. "I have to admit, you certainly carry your share of the load."

"Why do you sound so surprised?"

"I guess I am. You're as good a partner as any man could be on a cross-country march like this." This wasn't coming out right. He struggled to find a better way to say it, but felt awkward. "Not that I would have minded looking after you, but it's easier like this." He shook his head. "Forget it. The way this is coming out, I'll be lucky if you don't *throw* a snake at me."

She chuckled. "Try again. I think there's a compliment in there someplace."

"There was supposed to be." He took a deep breath then let it out again. He would have enjoyed the chance to hold her close and tell her all those sweet, wonderful things women always wanted to hear. The problem was he'd never been able to get those things right. He always ended up sounding just plain dumb, so he said exactly what he thought. "For what it's worth, you're a great person to have along when someone's trying to shoot your... butt off."

She turned her head, then laughed softly. "You've been a learning experience for me, too." As they left the area of soft sand Belara stopped and began lacing up her boots. "Well, that didn't go so badly, did it?"

Travis studied their trail and nodded. "Our tracks are barely there. The breeze will cover them in no time at all. Nice work," he said. "Your knowledge of the desert is a definite asset. I've got to admit it's nice sharing the responsibility, even if I'm not used to it." He leaned against a large rock, and slipped his hiking boots back on.

"It's probably your military training," she said with a grin. "There are leaders and followers and the two aren't as interchangeable there as they are in civilian life."

"Maybe," he said with a shrug. Her point, though valid, bothered him. He couldn't tell whether she was just trying to tease him, or whether she was taking a shot at his former career. If she was the kind of person who disliked the "military mentality" then he was destined to live through a repeat of what had happened between Nancy and him.

"We have a darned good partnership," she said, misunderstanding his sudden change of mood. "Don't think for a minute that I'm minimizing your contribution. I have my knowledge to offer, but your physical strength and tactical knowledge has been a big benefit to us, too. I haven't forgotten how you helped me back up to the trail when I missed that jump. Had I tried to climb up by myself, I might not have made it."

"You've handled yourself like a pro out here. I'm glad I was in a position to help you. A guy likes to feel needed." He smoothed his hand across her cheek in a gentle caress.

She leaned into his touch like a kitten, and desire coiled in his gut. With iron-willed discipline he forced himself to move away. "We better get back to business. It's not exactly healthy to stand still out here." Travis saw what he hoped was a flicker of disappointment in her eyes. Of course, it could have been something else, from mild indigestion to boredom, but those explanations didn't give him half the pleasure the other one did. "I'm going up on that ridge. I want to check out the trails behind us."

"I'll go with you. Then, we can continue from there. The canteens are getting light, which means we'll need water fairly soon. One of the springs marked on my map is only about forty-five minutes from here. We should go directly there next."

Travis led her up the bluff, then crawled out onto a rock overhang on his stomach. Using his binoculars, he surveyed the area below him. "They're closing in on us," he said after a moment. "I can see Robertson in the lead. I think they've skipped all rest periods trying to catch up to us. I'm almost certain now that they know the general area of your uncle's ranch. Undoubtedly, in addition to that, their tracker Wilson is probably finding enough of our trail to be able to be certain they haven't lost us."

"He must be exceptionally skilled," she observed.

Travis nodded. "When I took them across the desert, Wilson gave me the impression that he knew much more than he was letting on. For instance, he could find his way around with or without the maps. Once, when Robertson left on a small, practice orientation hike, I noticed Wilson following his trail from out of sight. It was like he was stalking the man just for fun. I didn't say anything then because I didn't want to create any more problems than there already were. But, in my opinion, Wilson is a far more dangerous opponent than Robertson.''

"I have an idea. Why don't we head for the limestone outcropping just above the rubble from the cliff. We can hide out there and let them go past us. Then, while they're going off in the wrong direction, we'll have a chance to get to the spring and replenish our water.''

He nodded. "They'll figure out what we've done pretty quickly, but it will buy us some time. Since that spring your uncle found is out of our way, and doesn't appear on the maps, we might just be able to pull this off.

"You take the lead, and go as fast as you think you can,'' he said quietly. "I want to hang back in case they send a scout ahead. Since I won't be able to monitor their progress once we move away from here, I want to make sure no one sneaks up on us.'' Seeing the concerned look on her face, he gave her a quick smile. "Don't worry, I excel at this. I've had the best training there is.''

They started uphill again, Travis stopping every few minutes to listen. His body was relaxed as he adopted the casual attitude men going into battle often used. It was for reassurance, a way of telling yourself that *you* were in control and it was the other poor slob who should be worried. It usually worked, but as his eyes focused on Belara, he felt his stomach tighten. Nothing had ever prepared him for the intensity of feeling that came when things became personal. As usual, he had lousy timing.

He shut his mind to that, and focused on the smells of the stunted desert pines and the movements of birds and animals around him. Instinct took over again and he felt the old reflexes returning. He planned his escape route, should they have to make a run for it. He noted areas where a scout might hide if he wanted to keep them under surveillance.

Silently he moved toward Belara and placed a hand on her shoulder. "We need to start looking for a place to hide. It'll have to have enough room for two because I'm not leaving your side."

"We'll make do with whatever we find," she countered firmly. "This isn't the time to quibble over details."

"Exactly. So we'll do this my way." He took his bearings with one long glance. "There're several boulders ahead. Let's see if we can find anything among them that'll suit our needs."

Belara moved quickly, avoiding the obvious paths and easy routes, yet not allowing the rough terrain to slow her down. "If not, maybe we can find a spot farther below, near the arroyo," she suggested.

"It won't be necessary," Travis said, gesturing to his left. "Here. Squeeze in between these two boulders, and get down in the shadows. I'll cover the front with some tumbleweeds and whatever else I can gather."

"This gap is barely two feet wide. We won't be able to maneuver at all. If they catch us, we'll be trapped for sure."

"No. They won't be able to do much except get shot. We'll hear and see them before they can approach."

She edged in carefully, then waited as he came in behind her. Placing himself between her and danger, he blocked the crevice with some scrub brush.

"This must be what they mean when they say stuck between a rock and a hard place," she muttered.

He heard her voice crack and felt his heart go out to her. She was scared, but she had her emotions under tight rein. He reached back and touched her hand. "We'll make it. We've come too far to let these guys stop us now."

Chapter Eight

Belara's gaze remained on Travis. He was so still, he scarcely seemed to breathe. He kept the stock of his rifle against his shoulder, the barrel pointed outward at the enemies. If the men did find them, there was no way he could win a fight against four of them. Not alone. But then, he wasn't alone. She'd be right there beside him.

She reached down to her hip and unsnapped the strap that kept her knife sheathed in place. As she brought the blade forward, Travis turned his head. Seeing the surprised look on his face, she gave him a thin smile. "If there is trouble, I'm not just going to sit there," she whispered. "I'll make it as difficult for them as I can."

Travis gave her a silent nod, then focused back on the opening before them.

Belara heard the sound of someone approaching. Her heart hammered as faint footsteps drew near and increased in volume. Low voices, indistinct at first, became clearer with each passing second.

"Barry, we're taking five right now," a Hispanic man said flatly.

"Come on, Frank, just a little farther. We're going to catch up to them soon, I can feel it."

"I'm glad *you* can," another growled, "but not me. Listen, I've kept you on the right trail for hours now, but I'm with Perea. Dropping from exhaustion isn't going to help us much. Keep in mind that once we catch up to them, we're still going to have to deal with Hill. He's not going to let the woman out of his sight after what happened before."

"Look, Wilson, I've already told you. Hill might be tough when he's riled, but he bleeds like everyone else. If he gets in our way again, he'll be a dead man."

"Oh, yeah, right. I'm sure Hill's going to cooperate and stay still while you take him out. Wise up, man. It'll be one hell of a firefight. You can count on him knowing how to use that rifle. Our best chance is to make sure we get to the woman first. He'll hold back then long enough for us to neutralize him."

"We're going to have to be careful with her. If anything happens to her, it could be all over for us, too. I'd bet my last dime that she's on her way to warn her uncle about us and the two jokers behind us who wanted to snatch her. I just wish we'd moved faster trying to find the old man. As it was, the Army got to him first, probably with some patriotism pitch," Perea said.

"It doesn't matter. Once we have her, Bowman will cooperate with us. With his knowledge of the area, we'll find what we came for in no time at all," Robertson assured them.

"That is if the guys following *us* don't manage to find it before we do," Wilson said in a sour tone. "I keep telling you not to ignore them."

"I doubt they're after anything we're interested in. If they were, they would have made a move before now. We've got more immediate matters to worry about. The woman's got to be holding Hill back. He's probably carrying her by now, so he'll be giving out soon. Start tracking, Wilson."

"You've got tunnel vision, man. That's your biggest problem," Wilson muttered.

Belara heard their footsteps grow faint as they began moving away. She started to shift, but Travis sensed her movement, reached back and placed one hand on her arm. Belara waited as time ticked by slowly. Fifteen minutes later, Travis's shoulders finally relaxed and he turned to look at her. "Stay here. Let me make sure they're gone first," he said softly.

She watched him move the brush away from the front, then step out and replace it. For several moments she did nothing except listen for sounds, but then curiosity overcame her. She moved forward noiselessly and peered out. Travis was nowhere to be seen.

Her body tensed. Was it a trick? She stared at the knife in her hands. It wouldn't be much of a weapon against a gun. Yet, if Travis was in trouble, she had no other choice. Gathering her courage, she stepped out of the enclosure.

She'd taken only a few steps in the dark when a hand clamped down hard over her wrist. Unable to use the knife, she reacted instantly. Kicking backward and up, she hit her adversary at his most vulnerable point. She heard the man's breath come out in one shuddering gasp. As he released his hold, she spun around, knife ready to strike.

The instant her gaze locked on his face, she cringed. "Oh-oh."

"I told you to stay put!" Travis groaned, then fell to his knees. "Lady, I think you've done some serious damage to the future Hill family."

She crouched beside him and placed one hand on his shoulder. "I didn't know it was you," she managed weakly. "Will you be able to walk?"

"Sure," he struggled to even his breathing. "In another century or two. Next time I approach you, I'll be on my guard."

"What can I do to help?" she asked, desperate to make things right again. Dealing with a humongous attack of guilt was not one of the things she did best.

To her surprise, he scrambled to his feet and rushed away from her. Feeling at a complete loss, she stood there wondering what was going on. Belara took a hesitant step forward, then came to an abrupt stop as she heard the unmistakable sounds of someone being violently ill. She wished she could find a rock to crawl under. "Are you sick?" she said, trying to be sympathetic.

"No, I'm doing this for fun," came the surly reply a moment later.

It was several more minutes before he emerged, looking shaken, but otherwise okay. "Let's get going."

"Maybe you should rest."

"Please, out of pity or remorse, will you just do what I tell you for once?"

"Whatever you say," she replied, feeling chagrined.

"I intended to come along and act as your bodyguard. I never thought I'd be the one who needed protection!" he muttered darkly. He gathered his gear once more, then glanced up. "Go ahead and take the lead since you know where the water hole is. Only stay diagonal to the direction Robertson took. Once we're well past the area they're in, we'll cut across to our original route."

"No problem." She adjusted her pack and went forward at a brisk pace. "Let me know if I should slow down."

"Humph."

She trudged northwest in a more or less straight line, crisscrossing over a ridge and canyon covered with loose rocks. Concerned about him, she stole furtive backward glances, making sure he was okay, but he seemed to have recovered completely. Instinct told her that it would be a mistake to bring up the subject or try to fuss over him. Long minutes passed before she spoke again. "It's over the next rise and halfway down the reverse slope."

"Good. We'll replenish our water supply and get going. My guess is that Wilson is beginning to get suspicious about now. Soon he's going to realize that the reason he's not finding our tracks is that they're not there. Then, he's going to start circling to find signs of us."

"What about the others, the group behind Robertson? Should we start worrying about them, too?"

"This time I have to agree with Robertson. We shouldn't concern ourselves with them unless they become a threat to us."

"I keep remembering what the man named Perea said. Like you, he thinks my uncle is working for the military."

"You still don't believe it, do you?"

She shrugged. "Not really, but I'm not as willing to discount it as I once was." As they started downhill, Belara pointed to a large rock surrounded by clumps of wild grass. "It's over there, under the edge of the rock. It's a very tiny spring, but it'll give us more than enough water."

TRAVIS CROUCHED by the cold, shallow pool and filled his second canteen. After Belara had refilled hers, he placed one hand in the water then brought it up to his face. "They'll find us soon," he said, expelling the air from his lungs. "What we did may have gained us a few hours, but nothing more and possibly less."

"If they do catch us, we'll have to fight," she said quietly. "I won't be used as leverage against my uncle, nor allow you to get killed for me," she added, her voice vibrating with conviction.

The determination in her tone took him off guard. He'd heard it before in soldiers who were willing to put everything on the line. "Just what were you prepared to do with that knife of yours?" His green eyes searched hers intently.

"Whatever it took to defend myself, and you. I'm no trained soldier, but I've learned a few things from my uncle. I could make it very difficult for them to take either of us anywhere." She met his gaze, and did not look away. "When you decided to come and help me find my uncle, you became involved with my family. We value friendship and loyalty, and repay those in kind."

"If there is a confrontation, I'll keep them at bay. But you have to do your part. I want you to take off and go as far and as fast as you can."

"I can't do that," she answered simply, "anymore than you could with me."

"I am a soldier, a trained fighter. By your own admission, you're not. You have to be prepared to make a run for it."

She smiled sadly. "I'm not as helpless as you seem to think I am." Wordlessly she allowed her eyes to drop down the length of him, then glanced up again. "You should know that by now."

Travis winced at the memory. "Yeah, maybe you've got a point. But you had me at a disadvantage. *I* knew it was you." Not wanting to discuss the matter in any more detail, he placed his rucksack on the ground. "I'm going to bobby-trap this water hole," he said, reaching inside the pack.

She stared at the object he held in his hand. "With a grenade? That's a little much, don't you think?"

He gave her a quick sideways glance. "Give me some credit, okay? I know how to fight and I've had some specialized training, but that doesn't make me a bloodthirsty killer." He saw the surprised look on her face and cursed himself for letting her know what a sensitive nerve she'd hit. "It's a pepper gas grenade," he explained after a moment. "The chemical it releases will sting, but it's harmless and won't contaminate the spring." He stood and began to gather some brush.

"How can I help?" she asked, crouching beside him.

"Get some of that sturdy cord out of my pack. I'll need a two-foot length, no more. Then *very* carefully tie one end around the ring."

By the time she finished, he'd placed several tumbleweeds around the hole at random. Surprised by his carelessness covering the spring, she gave him a long look. Maybe she'd hit him so hard he'd only appeared to have recovered. "That isn't going to hide that water hole from anyone except a blind man," she said quietly.

He looked at her, then grinned. "It wasn't meant to." With care, he positioned the grenade beneath the brush, then fastened the loose end of string to the tumbleweed. "The idea is for them to know it's there, lift the brush aside, then get pepper gas all over them. It'll take all the water in there and then some for all four of them to wash the stuff off. Then they'll be forced to waste time waiting for the pool to refill naturally before they can replenish their water and go after us."

"Good plan," she conceded admiringly.

"Military training, particularly guerilla warfare tactics, does make me handy to have around the neighborhood, wouldn't you say?" He watched her reaction carefully, wanting to know once and for all if she was antimilitary.

"One compliment's all you're getting, buster. Now hurry it up."

He still didn't know. Cursing his luck, he finished the booby trap and set out again. The normal buzzing and chirping of the night insects filled the air around them as they continued across the rugged terrain. They'd traveled about two miles when there was a deep *thud*. The noise reverberated through the air, silencing even the most persistent insects that had kept them company.

Travis stopped for a moment. "It looks like our trap worked. The bad news is that I didn't expect them to be able to pick up our trail again so quickly. Wilson's skills are improving with use."

"We'll be safe for a while, at least," Belara said.

Travis said nothing, allowing the silence to stretch out between them. "We're going to have to speed up," he said at last. "There's one possibility I hadn't suggested earlier."

"That maybe not all four men approached the hole at the same time?"

"Some big secret." He gave her a quirky half smile. "The grenade's radius should have insured that everyone would get some of the chemical on them, but you never know." He stared off into the distance, lost in thought. "I'll continue to guard the rear. Now let's get going."

Belara called up all her energy reserves. Her legs ached and she had a stitch in her side, but she forced herself to concentrate on her uncle. Robertson and the others seemed to think he was working for the Army again. If she was wrong, and he had accepted a job from them, that meant he was under even more stress than she'd originally thought. Without his medication the results could be disastrous. Fear for his safety helped her push herself with the relentless determination she needed to keep going at the brutal pace she'd set.

Without looking, she could feel the man behind her. His presence communicated itself to her senses. Once again, he'd placed himself between her and danger. Fear for his safety reached through her, touching every nerve ending. She glanced back, looking over his shoulder into the desert beyond.

"There's no sign of anyone approaching," Travis's voice was nothing more than a harsh whisper.

"It's like being in a crazy nightmare. You know the kind, where someone's chasing you and you can't get away."

"But we are getting away. Take it as a win, lady, because it definitely is."

As the sun began to peer over the horizon, Belara's body ached for a rest, but she was determined not to complain. She'd seen the area he'd marked on the map as their goal, and they were almost there. She glanced back to see if he was searching for a campsite yet. Instead, she saw his eyes were focused on a rugged hillside.

Before she could say anything, he pulled her into a crouch beside him, and signaled her to remain quiet. She followed his line of vision. There was something moving in the rocks behind them. That outcropping would make an ideal refuge for someone who wanted to monitor their progress. And from there, a person skilled with a rifle would have found them easy targets. She broke out in a sweat.

"I think we're being tailed, but I want to make sure. I'm going to move off alone." He gave her hand a squeeze and shook his head to stem her protests. "You'll be okay. They're too far away right now to make their move, and besides I won't go far." He grasped his rifle in his hand. "Let me get busy doing what I do best. I'm an old hand at turning an ambush into a trap for the hunter, when necessary."

"Where are you going?"

"Up to those rocks to take a look around with my binoculars. This time, stay put." Without turning to look at her, he moved uphill in a crouch.

Belara leaned against a boulder trying to revitalize her dwindling energies. She'd never been so exhausted in her life. Even the thought of having to pick up the pace again made her cringe inwardly.

Travis returned a few minutes later. "He's there alright. It's Wilson, but I don't think he's found our trail yet. Let's keep moving."

They carefully traversed an expanse of rocky desert soil. Belara felt the energy that had returned to her limbs. It was strange how fear could recharge the human system. Survival reflexes were deeply ingrained and the body responded when the need for flight arose. "It'll be daylight soon."

"We'll have to keep going after dawn. We can't let up now."

"They'll have to stop after the sun comes up. They won't catch up to us," Belara said. "There's a limit to how far people can push themselves in the desert. From the conversation we overheard, they've pursued us all night without stopping to rest. The heat and the sun will sap whatever energy they've got left."

He nodded. "I think you're right, but we have to maintain our advantage. Robertson made a wise decision when he sent Wilson up ahead as a scout. He's in better shape and more skilled than any of the others. I want to make sure I don't underestimate his endurance. He's the type to press on, out of sheer stubbornness."

"Gee, that almost sounds like someone else I know," she muttered under her breath.

"I heard that. Just remember if I'm pushing you it's for your own good."

They pressed on for several more hours. Finally, as the morning temperature began to climb, Belara, still in the lead, paused and glanced back at Travis. "We'll have to stop soon. The area ahead has some open stretches and any aircraft that flies overhead is bound to spot us. Do you want to try to find someplace to hide near the peak of that ridge up ahead?"

"Let's see if we can find someplace that's protected. Maybe in the shadow of a rock where we can have a good perspective of the ground below us."

"I never thought it was possible to be this tired and still keep moving," she admitted wearily. "I guess what you said about me slowing you down is finally coming true. I think you could keep going at least a while longer."

"You've done a terrific job, lady. I have no complaints. Keeping this pace over rough terrain is no easy feat. Remember Robertson saying that I was probably carrying you by now? He'd sure be surprised to see how capable you really are."

"I've tried to do what has to be done, but make no mistake about it. I'd much rather be back at my nursery tending plants."

"I've known a few women in my time," he said gently, "but never one like you."

She couldn't pass up a line like that. Besides, baiting him would help keep her mind off her sore legs. "Are we talking 'known' in the biblical sense? I'd like to find out if I'm being propositioned."

He matched her grin. "You can consider it one, if you think you'd be interested," he answered back.

There was no way she could answer. If she denied it, her nose would grow a mile. "You're a very eligible bachelor. I would imagine you're absolutely swamped with applicants," she said, hedging the question.

"No, not really. And as for my being an eligible bachelor, that depends on your definition. There was a woman in my life once, but it didn't work out." He moved up to walk beside her as they started the climb up the ridge. "She thought I'd always have a problem because of my specialized training. She claimed it brought out the violence in a man and that became a part of him forever."

"We're all capable of violence. Training makes you a more deadly adversary, but that's all it can do."

Her answer surprised him. He hadn't expected her to take that particular viewpoint. "I thought you hated the military, too. You've been taking little shots at it all along."

"Just in fun. I never meant for you to take it seriously. I'm sorry if I gave you the wrong impression."

"That's okay." He couldn't deny the relief that flooded over him. Not that it really changed anything. There was still so much she didn't know about him. If she thought of him in gentle terms, that was only because it was more in keeping with her own nature. What would she really think if she knew him as he knew himself? There were so many memories he'd fought to push out of his mind. They stayed there on the edge of his mind, circling like hungry sharks. He'd never be free of them. At best he'd confine them to the darkest corners of his soul for the rest of his life.

"We'll make camp there," he said, pointing ahead to a barren, sloping hillside covered with massive rocks.

They reached it minutes later. Belara wearily slipped her pack off her shoulders and moved into the shade. Wordlessly she sat on the ground.

"You mentioned that there had been a woman in your life," she said hesitantly, then saw him nod in agreement. "Were you very much in love with her?" she asked at last, as if the question had never gone far from her mind.

"I thought so for a time. But, looking back, I don't think I was. I guess I needed something to compare it to." His eyes strayed over her tenderly. "You're dead tired. Why don't you get some sleep? I'll take the first watch."

He'd changed the conversation too quickly, cutting off the opportunity to follow up on what he'd meant by "something to compare it to." Forty minutes ago, she could have sworn she was practically ready to pass out from exhaustion. Now her mind was racing, and the last thing she could do was rest.

Seeing him move away, she lay down and reluctantly closed her eyes. She wasn't certain how much time had elapsed when the sound of Travis tearing open a food package woke her.

He smiled at her. "It's time for you to eat something and for me to get some sleep. I've checked the area, and there's no one out there. Maybe we really did lose them this time."

"We can hope," she said, sitting up and selecting her own food as he lay down. It wasn't long before he was sound asleep.

Belara watched the lines of tension ease from his face as his breathing deepened. There was so much she wanted to know about Travis. Yet, he seemed determined to hide behind layers of images, from gruff to dictatorial. Only none of the images really revealed the man within. And in the center of all the camouflage was a secret he was determined not to share with anyone.

As he rolled over, his shirt came open revealing the scar on his side. Her heart constricted.

"You look so serious," he said. His eyes opened and he fastened his gaze on her. "What are you thinking about?" Realizing his shirt was open, revealing the scrapes from his earlier fall and the scars on his side, he reached down with surprising shyness and began to button it.

She saw him avert his eyes. The scar on his flesh was an outward sign of the wound that had touched his soul. Yet he had to be the one who broached the subject. Resisting the temptation to ask, she retrieved the binoculars from on top of his pack. "Let me take a look around, this is still my watch. You should try to get some more sleep."

When she returned several minutes later, his eyes were wide open. He'd moved off the sleeping bag to a patch of sand cooled by the shade. He lay on his side, trying to use his backpack as a pillow. "We're still all alone," she said.

"They might be holed up somewhere out of the sun. It's quite hot, in case you hadn't noticed. Even lying on the sleeping bag is uncomfortable."

Belara took her jacket out of her pack, then rolled it up and walked to where he was. "Here you go. This'll be softer than what you're using." Crouching by one side of him, she slipped her hand beneath his head, moved the pack aside and slipped her jacket beneath him.

Before she could move away, Travis turned his head slightly. His warm breath caressed her throat and drifted down the opening of her collar. A long shiver traveled down the length of her.

"I like the way you respond to me," he murmured. Curling his fingers beneath the curtain of her hair, he pulled her down toward his mouth. His kiss was soft and gentle, only hinting at the intensity of feelings that lay behind it.

He drew back slightly and gazed at her, the fire in his eyes leaving her breathless. She didn't resist as he positioned her body over him, her palms flat on his chest. With a gentleness that was practically her undoing, he pulled her mouth to his. His kiss deepened slowly, inevitably, demanding a response.

An intense flash of heat sizzled down the length of her. As his tongue pushed through to touch hers, yearnings more powerful than any she'd ever known shot through her. His body was warm and hard. She could feel his heart beneath her palm racing in a tempo that matched hers. With a soft cry, she pressed herself into the kiss, tasting him with a greediness that she could no longer hold in check.

Her sudden aggression ignited his. His breathing turned harsh. "Honey, don't. It feels too good. I won't be able to..." As she tore her mouth from his, the temptation the bare column of her neck posed was too much to resist.

His tongue was warm as he rained small moist kisses into the hollow of her throat. Her hands curled into the folds of his shirt, then hastily pushed the cloth barrier aside. His chuckle was husky, sending its vibrations rippling through her. "So, there are times when you *do* get impatient."

He cupped the back of her neck, his grasp strong, but his tongue seductively soft as he kissed her again deeply. When he broke the kiss, taking a long ragged breath, she felt utterly alone, separated from the vital force that completed her.

She moaned as he pushed her upward until she rested on her forearms. "Shh," he soothed. "We're not through, not by far."

His fingers worked the buttons of her blouse open. Her soft breasts were hidden by the nearly transparent lacy bra she wore, yet that partial concealment seemed to fuel the fire in him even more.

She felt his hardness pressing intimately against her as he wound one arm around her and unclasped her bra. He pulled her garments away, baring her from the waist up. His hungry gaze seared over her as if he were trying to memorize every detail. She shivered with anticipation.

"Lay down over me, honey. Let me feel you against me," he said, urging her toward him.

She whimpered softly as his hair-roughened chest abraded her nipples and brought her to a fever pitch of desire. She sought his mouth, needing the taste of him to fill her. Her tongue danced seductively around his until his breathing turned harsh.

With a groan that seemed to come from the depths of his soul, he rolled her onto her back, positioning himself on top of her. Her breasts tantalized him with their sweetness. As he lowered his mouth to one, he caught a flicker of movement to his right.

Chapter Nine

Travis swore softly, struggling to clear his thinking. "Don't move, sweetheart."

His abrupt change of mood made a cold chill run down her. "What's wrong?" she whispered, her voice taut.

"There's a rattlesnake moving toward us," he said in an ominously calm voice.

She tensed, fear and alertness making her muscles tense. "How close it it?" she asked, her eyes searching the ground to her side. Without turning her head, all she could see was a vague motion.

"It's less than six feet away. Hang on. I'm going to roll us both to your right very quickly. Then, we can jump up."

She nodded. "I'm ready."

He held his breath, every survival instinct he possessed coming to the fore. With catlike grace and speed, he swung to one side, pushing Belara up and away from him as she came around on top. A heartbeat later he was on his feet beside her.

The dry shaking of the snake's rattle drew her attention immediately. A three-foot-long diamondback had coiled less than a dozen feet away, its tongue flicking out as it sensed their presence.

Travis picked up Belara's hiking stick and cautiously moved toward the snake.

"Don't kill it," she said.

"I wasn't going to," he snapped. "I was only going to move it out of our 'living room.'" Using the stick, Travis picked up the snake as he would a strip of garden hose.

In silent approval Belara watched him take it down the slope before releasing it. As he turned around, Belara saw that his jaw was clenched in anger. She knew that her warning against killing the snake had really upset him, but she couldn't understand why. She wondered if it had more to do with his past than with her words. There was so much he kept hidden! She bent down to retrieve her shirt and bra and quickly slipped them back on.

He waited at the base of the slope for a few minutes, then started to rejoin her. "Why did you naturally assume I was going to kill it?" he challenged harshly, when he reached her.

"I didn't, it was only a warning," Belara protested in confusion. "It might be superstition to you, but the *Dinéh* are taught never to kill a snake. It brings illness and troubles. We don't want the former and have more than enough of the latter."

"I see," he muttered, looking somewhat mollified.

Belara watched Travis's expression. Perhaps she'd misinterpreted the reason for his sour mood. They *had* been interrupted rather abruptly. "Actually we've been lucky not to have encountered more snakes so far. They thrive on rocky ground like this."

"I should have checked the area more carefully. Had I stayed alert, I would have seen the snake before it came so close to us."

"You insist on shouldering the responsibility for everything. You're not exclusively to blame for what happened. It was my watch, not yours. I let *you* distract *me,* not the other way around. It was at least a fifty-fifty proposition." She saw the flicker that crossed his eyes. "Okay, maybe proposition was a bad word."

He started to smile, but quickly grew serious again. "Don't make light of this. The way things turned out, we were extraordinarily lucky. It could have been Wilson, holding a gun.''

"True," she conceded, then added. "If it had been, what would you have done?"

He stood stiffly, his green eyes as hard and cold as jade. "There's a side of me you haven't seen, and I hope to hell you never do," he muttered, quickly gathering their things. "But just so you know, I intend to do whatever is necessary to insure we come out of this alive."

Belara looked at him, lost in thought. She could feel his tension as he waited for a reply from her. "Do whatever you have to. I trust your judgment because I trust you."

He gave her a strange look, then shrugged as if he'd decided that she really hadn't understood the import of his words. "I hope you'll remember that if we ever have to fight."

Belara followed him as they crossed to higher ground. "I have no doubt that you can be profoundly dangerous," she said softly. "Are you afraid I won't be able to handle it if I actually see proof of that?"

"The thought had occurred to me," he said, deliberately understating it to mask his apprehension.

"You're forgetting that I've also seen the gentle side of you," she answered in a whisper-soft voice. "No matter how you try to hide it, that's a part of you, too. The dark side of your nature will never frighten me because I know that the good in you is stronger."

"I've seen too much of life to ever take things like that for granted," he muttered.

They continued without speaking for another forty minutes. Tension hung heavy between them, though it seemed to her that they were both determined to hide it from each other.

"I'm going to look over the canyon rim and check the progress of the others behind us," Travis said at last. "There's very little cover up there, so it'll be better if I go up alone. I'll leave my gear here with you, since I'll have to move fast." Travis set his pack down beside her, carefully placing his rifle against a bush. "I've got some trail mix in the side pouch. You're welcome to some, if you like. I'll be back in a few minutes."

"Thanks," she said, reaching for the pack.

She watched him jog away from her and was surprised by his energy and speed. At the moment, a brisk walk was almost all she could manage. She sat on the ground, leaned against a boulder, and closed her eyes, intending to rest them for just a second or two. As her body relaxed, she began to nod off.

A hand suddenly jerked her up to her feet. She came abruptly awake to find herself pinned against a man's sweaty chest. She tried to scream but the arm that was wound around her neck, tightened. She tried to kick backwards, but her foot bounced harmlessly off her attacker's thigh.

"Where's your boyfriend?" the man asked in a bored, casual tone. When she wriggled, trying to get free, the man's grip on her neck increased to an almost complete stranglehold. "Keep in mind that I can kill you right now. If you cooperate, I'll settle for having you pass out. The choice is yours."

"I'm no good to you dead. You're not about to kill me," she managed in a choked whisper. If only she could reach her knife or Travis's rifle!

"Listen, lady, not even the Marines could tell me what to do. Spending five years in the Brig didn't do much to change me, either." He shook her like a rag doll, suspending her by the neck in midair for a brief second. "Now where's your boyfriend?" he asked again, caressing her face with the barrel of his pistol.

"You looking for me, Wilson?"

She heard Travis's voice from somewhere behind the man, but as her air supply was depleted, everything started to spin. Darkness was closing in.

The man man pivoted in the sand, hurling her limp body around effortlessly. With a chuckle, he released his hold on her and she tumbled to the ground with a thud. "Don't worry. I haven't damaged her much. Yet."

She wanted to reassure Travis that she was all right, but nothing worked when she tried to speak. The black veil that had enshrouded her was just beginning to clear, but she couldn't stop coughing long enough to get a good breath. Her neck felt as if she'd been caught in a vise.

"We don't have any use for you, Hill, so kiss your butt goodbye." The man pointed his pistol at Travis's chest.

Belara tried to clear her vision, but everything still seemed slightly out of focus. Forcing herself to concentrate on just one thing, she kicked, catching Wilson behind the knee.

As the man staggered, Travis kicked the gun out of Wilson's hand. "Way to go, babe," Travis said.

She fell back onto her side, her heart pounding like a runaway freight train, and fought to clear the stars away from her eyes. At least now Travis had a chance.

"I don't need a gun to finish off an ex-officer," Wilson said, scrambling to his feet in a balanced stance. In one fluid motion, he unsheathed the long bladed combat knife in his boot and held it defiantly. The blade was sharpened on both sides and tapered inward to a jagged, serrated edge.

Travis moved his eyes to the knife, then back to his opponent. That particular blade was a killing instrument, and the marks of wear on it attested to its use.

As his adversary lunged, Travis stepped aside and grabbed Wilson's forearm. Yanking him forward, he used the man's momentum to throw him off balance and force him to release the blade. Wilson recovered quickly and spun around, renewing his attack bare-handed.

Travis blocked Wilson's fast vicious kick with a sweep of his forearm and spun inside his guard. A high kick to Wilson's chest sent him flying to the ground, stunned.

Hauling Wilson up by his collar, Travis used the same arm hold that Wilson had used on Belara. "You don't like it much, do you? I don't think the lady did, either," he said, his voice hard.

"Travis," Belara managed in a shaky voice. "I'm okay." In the confusion, she'd managed to reach Travis's rifle.

Without a word, he swung his hip against Wilson's back, and began to bend the man's body backward, using the weight of Wilson's body to cut off the blood supply to his brain. Finally Travis released Wilson's limp body and bent to retrieve the man's knife.

As he approached Belara, his body felt charged from the fight and his senses were alive. He crouched beside her and noticed she was shaking. Her eyes were wide and her face was ghastly pale. "Honey, are you all right?" He took the rifle from her, clicked on the safety and propped it back against a bush.

"My throat," she gasped.

He reached for the canteen and held it up to her mouth. She took several swallows then pushed it away. "Can you move?"

She nodded. "Sore, that's all," she said, her voice a little stronger. "Did he hurt you?"

The question took him completely off guard. She was more worried about *him* than anything else. "I'm fine. I told you I could handle a fight, if it came to that."

"How long before he wakes up?"

Travis's mouth fell open. "What makes you so sure I didn't kill him?"

"Believe it or not—" She coughed, then continued, "I think I know you better than you know yourself. Besides, you wouldn't have bothered picking up his knife if he was dead."

He chuckled softly, then shook his head. "You're right, he's not dead. All I did to him was what he was going to do to you. He'll be out cold for a while, then wake up with one whale of a headache."

She stood with his help and tried to ignore the way her hip hurt. When Wilson had tossed her on the ground, she must have landed squarely on a rock. "What are we going to do with him? If we leave him, he'll follow us again. But if we tie him up, he'll probably die of dehydration."

Travis glanced around. "I've got to find his pack. It must be around here someplace." He walked a few feet away into a mass of sagebrush, then grinned back at her. "It's here. Now we've got him." Travis pulled out Wilson's canteen and poured the water out on the ground. Tossing it aside, he reached back into the pack and extracted several clips of ammunition and a length of rope.

"I know you wouldn't leave him tied up without water or supplies," she narrowed her eyes speculatively, "so what are you up to?"

Travis gave her a quirky half grin. "I'm going to tie his hands, that's all. I'll do it loosely enough so that in an hour or so, if he's agile, he'll be able to get out of it. In the meantime, he can walk back to his friends. It's going to take him a few hours to backtrack and find them, and by then we'll be long gone. This time we'll make sure they have the devil of a time finding us. Now that we're getting closer to your uncle's ranch, they'll have to rely solely on tracking to find the exact location. I want to make this as difficult for them as possible." He gestured toward the binoculars. "Go see where the others are. I'll finish this."

Belara hurried uphill. It didn't take long to spot Robertson and his men. They'd made camp near a shallow arroyo. The second group was farther west, resting on the side of a steep incline. She focused on their faces but was unable to see their features. Yet from their baseball caps and general appearance, she was certain Perea had been right. They were the same men who tried to kidnap her.

By the time she returned, Travis had Wilson lying on his side, hands bound behind his back. "Were you able to locate them?" Travis asked, gathering his gear.

Belara gave him a quick rundown while she removed Wilson's boot laces. He wouldn't be able to move fast now without "throwing a shoe."

They walked away from the area quickly, leaving Wilson behind. As they crossed the sloped landscape, he stripped bullets out of the clips and threw them randomly into the brush. "His pistol's useless or I would have taken it with us. I think it must have struck a rock. The slide was so dented I couldn't feed a cartridge into the chamber. As a precaution, I also broke off the trigger with my mountaineering hammer. That way I know they don't even have a hope of fixing it.''

She watched as he took the empty clips and bent them so they were no longer of any use. Stopping for a moment, Travis dropped the clips into a narrow crevice in the rocks.

"So what now?"

"From your map, I'd say we're still about a day and a half from your uncle's ranch. Only it's going to be rough hiking there, particularly in the heat of the day. Despite that, I'd like to push on if you think you can stand it.''

"I'll be fine," she said with conviction. "My throat took the worst of it.''

Travis gave her a long admiring look. "We make one heck of a team. I'm too mean to go easy on you, and you're too stubborn to give up.''

She chuckled softly, then reached up to touch her throat. "Don't make me laugh. It hurts.''

"It's going to be sore for a few hours, but after that, you'll hardly notice it.''

"How do you know?"

"I had it done to me in training a few times," he answered. "Drill sergeants enjoy that type of thing.''

"By the way, how you dealt with Wilson proved that I was right. You fight as if you took lessons from Slayer, the *Dinéh* war god. But you're also compassionate and that tempers the rest.''

"Were you so sure of that while we were fighting?"

She nodded. "I've seen men, particularly military men from the base, tangle with each other before. They come alive in the heat of the battle. You're that way, too, but I knew that even then you wanted to defeat, not kill him.''

He said nothing for a long time. "I would have killed him if I had had to," he said, his words measured and resonant.

"I'm aware of that," she replied with a long sigh. "There's something I just don't understand about you. Why are you so determined to have me see you in the worst possible light? You're the one who passes the harshest judgments on yourself."

"I've disappointed many people. I don't want you to be one of them," he answered, his voice taut.

"No," she observed pensively, "I think the real problem is that you've disappointed yourself."

His head snapped up and he glared at her. "You don't know a thing about it!"

"You haven't chosen to tell me anything," she countered calmly.

He grunted, not knowing what to say. She was right. But damnation, her opinion mattered to him! He had the blood of many people on his hands, and that was not something a woman like Belara would be able to overlook. He studied her in quick glimpses as they walked. Or would she understand? "Someday."

"I can wait," she answered simply.

Maybe that was what he loved most about her. She allowed things to unfold at their own rate. Her tranquillity soothed his own troubled mind. "You're good for me," he said at last.

"I've known that all along," she answered, a smile tugging playfully at the corners of her mouth.

He groaned. "Don't rub it in."

Their breaks were few, and by late afternoon she felt an immense weariness beginning to spread through her. It was a good thing they had plenty of water, the heat was intense. "We're going to have to stop soon. Let's try to find someplace where we'll be relatively sheltered."

"Let's hike past that wrecked farmhouse first. The map shows there's an area just beyond it where some tall pines and—" He didn't finish. His body tensed. He stood immobile, his senses alert as he listened.

Hearing a faint sound behind them, Belara turned her head. She looked into the distance, and spotted a line of dust that heralded the approach of a vehicle.

As the deep rumbling of its engine reached them, Travis pulled her behind a clump of brush. "A patrol, coming this way. We've got to find a place to hide." He looked around. There was nothing that would provide the substantial cover they'd need if the jeep happened to pass close by. "Let's head for the farmhouse. That's our best chance."

Chapter Ten

They jogged the half mile to the farmhouse, keeping low behind a small ridge. As they reached the tumbled-down-wood and sheet-metal building, Travis muttered an oath. "We can't go inside. The walls are so full of holes they'd have to be blind not to spot us."

"We've got less than five minutes before they get here, judging from the dust." She looked around quickly. "Over there." She pointed to a low, stone structure a few yards from the building. "It's a root cellar."

Travis nodded. "It'll have to do." He rushed over, then struggled to pry the heavy wooden doors open. Someone had nailed a sheet of plywood over the entrance. The safety measure had probably been intended to protect a hapless soldier from falling in, particularly at night.

Belara moved beside him and tried to help him loosen the board from its nails. Finally a partially rotted section gave way and the opening came into full view.

"Let me go first," he said. "There's no telling what we're going to find there."

"Don't give it a thought. It beats getting caught by a patrol after we've come this far," she replied.

He glanced off into the distance. "We still have time." He started down the steps, then offered her a hand. "It's dark and musty, but otherwise okay. Just watch yourself as you climb down. There seems to be something slippery on the steps."

She grimaced but entered the low-roofed interior muttering. "I don't understand why all the dark, confined places seem to be calling out to me on this journey."

"Be thankful you spotted it, or this might have been the end of the road for us." He lifted her by the waist and set her down in front of him on the bottom landing. Working quickly, he lowered the door back down, sealing them off from above. "Besides, you've got me. With such wonderful company along, why worry?"

He was so near she felt his breath caress her lips. "It's hard to think of an answer when you're this close to me," she whispered in a tremulous voice.

He'd meant to distract her, only he hadn't counted on how tempting she'd be, standing this close to him. Hesitantly he ran one finger down her jawline, and felt her hold her breath.

Even though he could hear the vehicle approaching, in the dark safety of their haven, she was all that mattered. A man could tell when a woman needed and wanted his touch. He took her face in his hands and, with his thumbs, smoothed away some of the stray ebony locks. For a moment, he was content to just gaze at the luminous eyes that were fastened on his.

He didn't see her hands come up, but felt her fingers lace behind his neck. Her touch sent a tremor through him. "If we keep this up, I'm not going to care about the jeep or the patrol. I'll take you right here," he said, his voice raw and vibrantly sensual.

She shivered in his arms. "There's no harm in a kiss. You were hoping to distract me, weren't you?"

His laughter was like a soft rumble that came from the center of his chest. "You guessed that, did you?" he said, his voice a husky murmur. "Well, as I'm sure you've realized, it didn't exactly work the way I planned. I meant to keep you from worrying, not fill my head with things I shouldn't be wishing for."

"Sometime I'd like you to tell me about those wishes. Then we'll see how closely they match my own." She turned her head and tenderly placed a kiss on the center of his palm.

Something gave inside him. He knew that this was no time to divert his attention, but he needed her, and the knowledge that she wanted him was making him half-crazy.

He lowered his mouth to hers, aware he'd have to keep the kiss light. It wouldn't take much to push him over the edge.

Then she parted her lips, asking him without words to take more. It was an invitation he couldn't refuse. He slid his tongue forward, seeking hers and mating with it. She trembled and moaned as he slid his arms down her sides and pulled her to him.

Belara turned to fire in his arms. Everything male in him made him want to take her until her surrender was total. He cupped her buttocks in his palms, pulling her upward and holding her intimately against him. She moaned softly, and the tiny sound sent a blast of heat spiraling through his body.

Unexpectedly the sounds of hammering and loud male voices nearby filtered through to their hiding place. She stiffened in his arms and groaned softly with frustration.

"Shh." Pressing his lips to her ear, he added, "I want to love you, but even more, I want to keep you safe." He eased his hold, and allowed her to step out of his embrace. "I didn't think I could do that," he admitted, his voice barely audible.

"I didn't think I'd let you," she answered softly.

The sounds continued, and raucous laughter echoed above them. "At least, *they're* having fun," he said sourly.

"What do you think they're doing?" She started to edge toward a small opening to take a peek when he grasped her arm, restraining her. "Don't. This is no time to take chances. They don't know we're here, and with a bit of luck they'll leave soon."

She nodded, and returned to the landing.

Minutes later, the sounds of hammering stopped. They heard a few noises neither of them could identify, then that of an engine being started. As they drove away, the desert stillness claimed the area once more.

Travis held rock still and listened. Only the distant rumbling of the vehicle marred the silence outside. He waited, his senses sharp. He tuned in to the sound of the breeze, and the songs of the birds. Out of the corner of his eye he studied Belara's expression. It was one of alert caution, her patience and wariness matching his own.

Minutes ticked by. Finally he edged toward the cellar opening. "I think they're gone, but just in case they left behind a sentry, let me go out and reconnoiter first." Seeing her nod, he slipped out into the soft light of the fading day.

Belara stood peering out a small hole in the wood. Her eyes remained on him until he turned the corner of the house. If they got caught by a military patrol their prospects at least would be better than they would have been in the hands of Robertson. Still, she wasn't sure how she'd cope if anything happened to her uncle because she'd been unable to reach him in time.

Travis returned less than five minutes later. "We're okay. They're gone. I can see them off in the distance, just below this hill. They're constructing something else down there. The good news is that no one is going to want to go past them to get to us. So, for the time being we're safe."

She stepped out of the root cellar, glad to be outdoors again. "What were they hammering?"

"I'm not sure. Maybe they were sealing up well openings or entrances to mine shafts. They've got some lumber stacked by their jeep, but not enough to build anything very big." He took the binoculars from his pack and passed them to her. "Take a look, but make sure the sun doesn't reflect off the field glasses. Go around the building, then stay low with your back to the sun. It'll be setting soon so it's at an odd angle."

She returned a moment later. "I saw them working a few miles away from us," she commented. "All I can say is that

I hope they stay there for a long time. We could sure use a break.''

He nodded slowly. "We'll hang around until the jeep is long gone. I'd hate for them to circle around and spot us as we're trying to climb the next ridge."

Belara pulled a small package of beef Stroganoff out of her pack. "I sure wish I had some fresh fruit or vegetables. After this outing is over I may never be able to look at anything that has egg noodles in it again." She added water and started kneading the package to mix the food.

He offered her the package he'd just prepared. "Try this. It isn't exactly gourmet cuisine, but it's good."

She looked at it and tried to figure out what it was without reading the label, one of her own personal tests. "It's Italian something," she said, at last, peeking at the label. "Lasagna?"

"Try it and quit being such a skeptic."

"Hey, not bad," she said after one spoonful. She glanced at the food she'd given him. "You got gypped on that deal."

He grinned. "Naw, when you take into account the big picture, I'm doing just fine. Look at the company I got in exchange." He took a swallow of water. "Do you still have any of the herbs for tea that you picked?"

She nodded. "They're in the rucksack, wrapped in cellophane. Help yourself. After that wonderful compliment, you deserve a treat," she teased.

He put the herbs into two cups, poured water on top of them, then set one before her. "We'll give them a few minutes to steep."

She finished her food as Travis reached for his cup. "Is it ready?" Seeing him nod, she picked it up by the handle, then glanced casually at the tea. "Wait! Don't drink that! You put the seeds that were mixed in with the *cañutillo* in here!"

He froze, then placed the cup back on the ground. "You didn't mix anything poisonous with those stalks, did you?"

"Worse," she muttered, then started to laugh. "Forget it. Just don't drink it. It wouldn't hurt you, but you don't need it."

He gave her a puzzled look. "What *are* those?"

"They're seeds from the Fendler Bush. It's one of my nursery's most popular plants." She met his eyes, barely able to keep a straight face. "Legend has it that they're an aphrodisiac for men."

His mouth fell open, then he dumped the tea he'd made out. "You're right. I don't need any help in that department," he muttered. "Being near you is enough to make me half-crazy."

"You have such a wonderful way with words," she said laughing. "You really know how to turn a woman's head."

"I can do better without words," Travis said, his voice a seductive whisper. He smiled as she quivered in response. She wasn't the helpless type, not by far, but around him she could be exquisitely vulnerable. It made him feel more powerfully male than he'd ever felt in his life.

Searching for a distraction, he stood up and walked over to his backpack. He wanted her, but not here, and not now. There would only be one first time for them, and he wanted that to be perfect. He'd take her so thoroughly that there would never be room in her mind or heart for anyone but him. The intensity of that desire took him by surprise. He clenched his fists in a struggle for control.

He forced himself to relax. He felt her eyes on him as he stripped off his shirt and pulled a fresh one from his pack. For a brief moment much to his own surprise, he wanted her to see him as he was. He turned around and looked at her, leaving his scarred side unprotected.

Her gaze traveled over him and came to rest on the scar that outlined his rib cage. "I know much about you," she whispered. "Things you haven't even discovered in yourself. But there's still a great deal you've kept back. How do I earn your trust?"

Slipping into a clean shirt, he went to where she was sitting. He stretched out on his side, one arm propping his head. Lost in thought, he traced indeterminate patterns on the sand. "I do trust you, but there are things in my past I've never spoken about to anyone. They're difficult for me to deal with." He struggled to find the right words. "What you think of me matters and that makes it harder. I know you're not going to like the story I've got to tell. There's nothing redeeming about it."

"I like the man you are now. What came before, molded you into who you are today. Liking or not liking the events that shaped your life doesn't really come into it. But knowing what happened will help me understand you, and that is important to me."

He was still unsure, and that was a feeling he didn't deal with often or well. He couldn't say he cared much for it, either. It made him feel uncomfortable. He was exposing the part of him that felt, and cared, and risking rejection that could shred him to ribbons. "After I'd spent quite a few years with the Special Forces, I was given the job of teaching new trainees," he began at last. "I enjoyed the challenge. New teams were embarrassingly graceless out on a mission. It would take time to mold them into a solid A team, a detachment of twelve soldiers who could live and work effectively behind enemy lines." Silence stretched between them. His throat was dry and his chest ached. He'd started this. Now it was time to finish it.

"After their training reached a certain point, it was my job to test them. The night of the operation we had the perfect weather we'd hoped for. The trainees were scheduled to rappel from a helicopter in the dark for the first time. The procedure called for them to get to the ground on the double, only it's tricky because at night, it's hard to gauge the distance. The exercise started off fine. I went down first to make sure the helicopter was at the correct hover altitude. If it wasn't right, the men could have ended up with broken ankles or worse, due to their inexperience. Once I reached the ground, I stepped to the edge of the landing zone where I could spot for them, and gave the order for the men to descend."

Travis felt physically ill, but he forced himself to continue. "Seconds after my men started coming down the
ropes, the helicopter's rotor blade failed, flying off in
pieces. With its lift gone, the chopper spun to the ground.
All I could do was stand by and wait until the helicopter finally hit. The three who'd been on their way down at the
time were trapped beneath the wreckage. Then the 'copter
burst into flames, igniting the thick ground cover around
us."

Belara held one hand over her heart, her eyes narrowed
with horror. "There was nothing you could have done,"
she managed, her voice thin as she visualized the nightmarish scene. "These things happen..."

In his mind, he could still see the corpses and smell the
stench of burning flesh. "I ran to the wreckage," he continued, his voice strangled, "and pulled man after man out
of the machine. My clothing caught fire during one of the
trips, but I rolled around and managed to smother the
flames. Two of the men I'd rescued helped me out and we
continued to haul those we could reach out of the chopper.
Finally the smoke was so thick, I couldn't breathe. It felt as
if I was burning up from the inside out. I passed out just as
more help arrived."

"How many were saved?"

"All but four of the men," he said. "The three who'd
been crushed beneath the 'copter, and the pilot." He took
a deep breath to steady himself. "The scar you've seen is a
skin graft, a reminder of that night."

"You have nothing to fault yourself for," she said, her
heart going out to him. "You showed leadership and a great
deal of courage by going back and saving the men you
could."

"You don't understand," he observed quietly. "A commander is responsible for his men. I should have required
the helicopter crew to double check everything with me
standing by. Maybe if I'd done that, they would have spotted the stressed rotor blade on their second inspection.

There were things I could have done *before* the accident that might have made all the difference in the world.''

''The military must have had some type of investigation or hearing on the incident,'' Belara commented. ''What were their findings?''

A deep scowl etched his features. ''They grounded the choppers for testing and pinned a medal on me.'' His tone was hard and grim. ''I couldn't deal with that. I left the Army right after my hitch was up. I failed those men, and that's something I'll have to live with for the rest of my life.''

''You didn't fail anyone, except your own expectations,'' she observed. ''Machines fail, and men can be their victims.'' She pressed her lips together. ''Did they ever find out why the rotor blade malfunctioned like that?''

He nodded. ''The investigation uncovered that blades of that type had a tendency to delaminate. They were literally peeling apart in layers after the helicopters had flown a certain number of hours. Since then, the company has changed the manufacturing process, taking care of the problem.''

''So, the deaths led to a greater good.'' She reached out, covering his hand with hers. ''You're blaming yourself for the role fate dealt you. Those men didn't die because of you, but in spite of what you did.''

He took her hand and clasped it firmly. ''I don't know,'' he said at length. ''Maybe I chose to see it as a personal failure because it's easier in a way than thinking it was fate. There's no way anyone can fight that.'' He clenched his free hand around a handful of sand, then slowly released the grains back to the ground. ''Then again, maybe I accept responsibility for it because I know that I'm part of the problem that goes beyond the incident.''

''I don't understand,'' she said, eyebrows furrowed in confusion.

He stared at the horizon, lost in thought. ''It doesn't matter now.'' He met her gaze, and the tenderness that flowed from it engulfed him like a soothing balm. ''All I want you to be sure of is that I won't fail *you*. Training Robertson and his gang of losers was my mistake, but I won't let them hurt you in any way. I'll get you to your uncle, then safely out again. I give you my word."

"I've never doubted you." She touched his face in a light caress. "You were doing too good a job of that all by yourself," she added with a teasing smile.

He brushed his lips across her fingertips. "Talking to you does make all this easier to bear."

"It's all right to confide in someone who cares for you."

He captured her eyes. "But you have no secrets to share, do you, honey?" he asked rhetorically. "Your life is as open as your gaze." He kissed her palm tenderly.

She smiled slowly. "There's something I can share with you. It's a side of me I want you to know. I told you once that I had a secret name. It's *dlíchíí'*, Red Warrior Girl. My uncle always said that it was a name that fit me well. I can be very stubborn, and a strong fighter when I'm trying to help someone who means a great deal to me."

"Like your uncle?"

"And you," she answered. "You still haven't told me all of your story, but I won't give up on you. The *Dinéh* teach that good and evil are blended in every human being. You've acknowledged your dark side, but I won't stop fighting until you see the good that's inside you, too."

"I want you to see the good in me," he whispered. "I need that more than you know." His mouth descended over hers slowly, devouring her with a hunger he could no longer contain. "Feel what's in my heart for you." He kissed her again, the contact as explosive as kerosene near an open flame. "Let me love you, sweetheart." He rained kisses down the side of her neck and throat.

She trembled as his hand curved around her breast. "Persuade me," she managed in a shaky voice.

He teased her lips open with the tip of his tongue, then plunged inside to take the sweetness there. With unmistakable symbolism, he told her what he wanted to do.

She shivered, the passion rising within her making her feel as if she were about to dissolve. "You're quite gifted in the art of coaxing," she whispered breathlessly.

"I haven't even begun yet," he growled. He supported her with one arm while he spread the folds of her shirt open. Unsnapping her bra in one deft motion, he lowered his mouth to her breast. The shiver that ran down her, sent a shock of pleasure all through him.

She whimpered as he guided her body. It was natural, it was good. Nothing could stand between what their souls knew to be right. She let him strip the rest of her clothing away, each touch and kiss leaving her achingly hungry. Her body arched as he began to trail moist, wet kisses down her body.

Her soft cries made his body harden into painful awareness. He needed her, but it went past the physical urge to possess her. He wanted to claim her heart and her mind as completely as he would her body.

He longed to love her in all the ways he knew a man could pleasure a woman. He grasped her hips, imprisoning them as he continued to caress her intimately. She opened to him, inviting everything, and holding nothing back. When at last she twisted and shuddered in completion, he moved up to cradle her against him.

Her eyes opened slowly, and she focused on him. She moistened the tip of her finger with her tongue, then traced the outline of his mouth. He shuddered as he tasted her, his body burning with the need to fill her body with his own.

Her smile was lazy and slumberous. "Now it's my turn."

He thought he'd burst when she began to undress him, caressing and leaving soft kisses over each place she uncovered. Her tongue was gentle as it soothed the scar on his side. He felt the love in that gesture and something dark inside him melted away. Belara continued, as merciless in her eagerness to give him pleasure as he'd been to please her. When the warmth of her breath touched him intimately, his control snapped. "Yes, honey, please." He surrendered willingly to her caress, then finally pulled her up and toward him. Holding on to her, he rolled with her until she lay beneath him. One last ragged thought urged him to be gentle as he entered her.

As her warmth enfolded him, he lost himself and then found more than he'd ever dreamed of. She was his. He felt the shock as she arched toward him and her body trembled. Her wild release hurled him to his own peak and he poured himself into her.

In the quiet aftermath, he held her, loving the feel of her against him. Her long ebony hair tumbled loose over his chest, trailing down his body. As her locks teased him with feather-light caresses, he shuddered. "I wish I could hold you for the rest of the night, but we can't stay here. We have to move on."

"I know. All's quiet now," she observed, reluctant to move away.

Suddenly a deep rumble that seemed to start off in the distance began to intensify.

He jackknifed up. "Get your clothes. Now!"

"It's just an airplane. They can't see us."

"Trust me. Do it," he said, gathering their things. "And hurry. That's no ordinary Air Force Fast Mover."

A brilliant red-yellow flash of light appeared against the dark skyline, growing to a fiery blossom a hundred or more feet high. A shock wave thumped against their bodies, followed instantly by a massive roar. The sound grew from the rage of a thunderclap to deep, guttural vibrations that made the ground shake beneath their feet. The echoes of the man-made earthquake began to fade, only to be replaced by the powerful scream of jet engines.

"Those are bomb blasts. They must have been setting up targets this afternoon," Travis shouted.

The wail increased in intensity, as if some unearthly bird of prey were about to dive at them from the clouds. A second later, a faint blue-white flame hurtled toward them across the desert floor.

Belara grabbed Travis's arm tightly, calling his attention to the approaching light. "Is it coming for us?"

Travis retrieved both their packs with one scoop of his arm, and reached for her hand. "The cellar!" he shouted, practically lifting her off her feet with one wild tug. "Quick!"

Chapter Eleven

Travis threw open the wooden cellar door. "Hurry. We've got only seconds," he said, gritting his teeth as the sound of jet engines howled above them. Bright red-yellow flashes erupted again in the distance where the other target had been set up.

She practically fell down the steps in her rush to escape. As Travis shut the door, the ground seemed to explode above them. She didn't know much about military weapons, but she was certain of one thing. Whatever was happening right outside the cellar had nothing to do with bombs. It sounded like a chain saw gone berserk. The ripping noise was moving across the ground, coming closer!

Travis pulled her into one corner just as a row of explosions hammered past the wooden door, sending splinters flying everywhere. Pushing Belara down, he covered her with his body. "Stay down! They're practicing strafing runs," he yelled over the noise. "It's automatic cannon fire."

The earth and air shuddered as the rounds streamed into the shack next to them. The oppressive buzzing made Belara's skin crawl. If death could have had a sound, that would have been it. She tried not to shudder, but failed.

When all was finally still, Travis moved away from her. "You okay?"

"That noise—" Her voice broke and she swallowed.

"I know," he answered quietly. "Even if you know you're safe from the guns, you still feel as if the rounds are ripping through you."

Belara picked up her gear, then emerged with Travis from the cellar. "I wish it was over, and we were all home safe," she said softly.

Travis didn't speak right away, he couldn't. A heart-wrenching sadness settled over him. He knew he'd never be able to hold on to her after she returned to her peaceful life. A man like him would only add confusion to the serenity that surrounded her. Eventually she'd see it and walk away from him.

"Come on. We have to get going," he said, suddenly feeling bone tired. "They're bombing other targets farther down now, hear it?" Seeing her nod, he gave her a thin smile of encouragement. "That's good for us. It'll scatter everyone behind us."

"Why did they pick this place to strafe?" Belara glanced around. "Was it just a matter of bad luck?"

"I should have taken a closer look at what they were building," he said, an apology woven into his tone. "I wasn't alert enough and that's why we were taken off guard. I bet they were setting up target frames."

"Hey, we both goofed. But even if our timing wasn't great, I don't regret any of it," she said, determined to get him to go easier on himself. "Your tenderness proved to me more than ever that I haven't overestimated the kind of man you really are."

"The true measure of a man always comes out when he's naked," he quipped.

She almost choked. "So much for helping you cheer up," she agreed.

A half hour later, from higher up on the mountainside, Travis stopped and glanced down. Belara stood beside him, following his gaze. Smoke still swirled from the wood-and-stone structure that had sheltered them, and a small fire continued to flicker where part of the farmhouse had been ignited. The center of the farmhouse now stood pockmarked and riddled with thousands of holes. Off in the distance, other tiny glowing dots sparkled on the desert floor.

"What's that piece of tattered cloth still on the roof? There's not much left, but you can still make it out."

"The pilots are supposed to make periodic gunnery runs to maintain proficiency with their aircraft cannons. They use squares like that as aiming points. That's what they were undoubtedly hammering into the building. From our vantage point on the ground, we missed it completely."

"We were right next to what they were aiming at?"

"That's about it," he grumbled, then moved into the darkness as fast as he could. "We were lucky they're such good shots. Someone will probably be coming back to check the targets and there might be others on ahead. We've got to get out of this area fast. This is going to be another really rugged hike. It's all steep slopes and rock climbs from this point until we cross over the range again."

With the elevation above seven thousand feet, it was nearly impossible to keep up the pace Travis had set. Although he continued to look behind him, his eyes flashing with concern, he never offered to slow down. She never asked, realizing that this time it was no game of wills. Her uncle's life as well as their own were at stake. Any lapse now, and their journey would either meet with failure or death.

"It'll be dawn in a few hours. We should be stopping soon."

"Can you keep on?" he asked flatly. "From here, I have no way of gauging what kind of progress the men behind us have made, and that's dangerous. We'll have to climb higher and find some clear ground before I can check back, and there isn't going to be much of that ahead. We'll have to settle for listening and staying alert to anything that seems out of place, and we ought to keep moving."

"I can keep up," she heard herself say confidently. Privately she wondered just how long she'd be able to maintain this speed. She looked at Travis in awe and with a touch of envy. There was power contained and measured in his movements, as if he'd barely taxed his reserves.

As he turned toward her in the half light, she saw his face clearly. It held lines of weariness she hadn't seen before. Her heart constricted. He appeared to be a rock, full of surety and confidence, yet beneath those layers hid a gentle and vulnerable soul.

He stopped for a moment and weighed his words carefully. "I've got our objective marked on the map. We should reach it in another two hours, but, if you'd like, we could take a shortcut. It'll be ten times rougher but a lot shorter."

"Exactly how much rougher?" she asked cautiously.

"We'll have to climb an almost vertical cliff, then hike down a ridge."

"And how much extra time will that buy us?" she asked. At the moment, she'd have signed away everything she owned for a few extra hours of sleep.

"About an hour and a half or more."

"I'll take it. Lead on."

After the first twenty minutes of hard climbing, she came to regret her decision. Some areas required that she pull herself up without the support of a firm foothold. The soreness in her muscles increased with every inch she gained up the rock face. She bit back the pain, willing it away. When they finally cleared the steepest part, she sighed with relief.

They had arrived in a small valley with gently sloping sides. The ground ahead appeared darker there, as if in perpetual shadow. They advanced quickly over the level ground. As they reached a scorched area, Travis slowed his pace and studied the ground before them. "What the heck happened here?"

The narrow box canyon seemed to have been gutted of brush and ground cover. Following an almost straight line, like an arrow pointing to the source, Belara spotted what appeared to be an aircraft wing. Her heart stopped beating. She took a few hesitant steps forward, then caught a

glimpse of the rest of the wreckage as it gleamed in the
moonlight. "No one could have survived that." Belara
stepped back as fear wrapped its icy tentacles around her.
The teachings of the *Dinéh* had been deeply ingrained into
her. There was danger in places that had seen death. "Do
you suppose someone got shot down by accident during the
practice we saw?" she asked, her voice barely audible.

"No, the wreckage would still be burning. Besides,
there's something about that model aircraft that..." His
voice trailed off as his eyes narrowed with suspicion and
curiosity. "Let's go take a closer look."

She intended to move forward, but her feet seemed to
have taken root.

Travis turned to look at her. "Come on. We have to go
across the canyon anyway."

"Yes," she replied, in total agreement. But she still
couldn't make herself go on. Death hung over the area, she
could feel it.

Travis gave her a long look. "Any corpses that might
have been there, are long gone by now," he said, wondering if perhaps that was why she was reluctant to continue.

"I realize that. But it's still a place of the dead. The
chindi..." She shrugged. "It would sound like nonsense
to you, I'm sure, but when you've grown up with those beliefs, they're real."

"You don't have to get close to the plane, but I'm going
to take a look."

"Is the knowledge you can gain from it necessary to us?"

"I won't know until I go check it out, and I really
should."

She reached back into one of the pockets of her rucksack and extracted a small object. For a moment she held
it in her hand, feeling foolish, yet compelled to offer it to
him.

He noticed her hesitation. "What's on your mind?"

She clamped her lips shut, then finally came to a decision. "If it doesn't go counter to your own beliefs, will you

take something with you? As a courtesy to me, if nothing else.''

He took the small flint points she offered and placed them in his shirt pocket. "What are they?"

"They'll guard you," she answered simply.

"The *chindi* are ghosts?" he asked.

"No, not in the way most Anglos normally mean." She noted with relief that he hadn't smiled. Some would have by now. "They're part of a belief rooted deeply in our religion. The *chindi* is that part of himself a man can't bring into universal harmony after death. Some evils just refuse to become part of the pattern. Where most powers in nature, and even the gods, can be persuaded through different means to become helpful to man, the *chindi* never can be. What I've given you is said to keep such evil at bay. Will you accept them?"

He nodded. "But if that's what you believe, shouldn't you keep them?"

"Not believing in *chindi* won't protect you from them, and you're the one who wants to go to the spot where deaths occurred. I'll go past there, but unless you see a need for me to do otherwise, I'm going to keep on walking until I get to the other side of the canyon."

"There's no need for you to approach the wreckage," he assured her. "I have to go because there's a theory I want to verify. We'll talk about it after I look over the aircraft. There's no sense in speculating until then."

Belara kept her pace brisk and did not stop until she was about fifty yards past the site of the wreck. She watched Travis, not envying him the task he'd set for himself. Had he thought her foolish? Perhaps one of the biggest problems between Anglos and Navajos was what one considered fact, the other labeled superstition. Suddenly she was acutely aware of the vast gulf that separated them.

He joined her almost ten minutes later. "It's a Mohawk all right." He took the small flint arrowheads out of his pocket and returned them to her. "I appreciate the thought behind these," he added as a gentle thanks.

She nodded and returned them to her sack. "What's so special about that particular airplane? I realize something about it concerned you, but I'm not sure why. With all the training missions flown over this area, it's surprising we haven't seen more crash sites."

"This kind of aircraft is different. It's an Army plane used only for close photo reconnaissance and electronic surveillance. Only it's sterile."

"They sterilized it?"

"No, that means they stripped it of practically everything. All that's left out there is a shell."

Belara stared off into the distance, trying to remember the details of a story she'd seen in the newspaper weeks before. "I remember reading about a crash that happened out here during maneuvers a month or so back. The two men aboard the aircraft were killed. The press was hot on the story. It was right after the FBI had come into town looking for suspected foreign agents. The reporters wanted to know more about the military exercise that had been going on, and if the two events were related. The base clamped a lid on it and the newspeople were unable to learn anything more."

He nodded. "Yeah, the articles just faded away after a few days. I wondered about it for a while. But then, like everyone else, I put it out of my mind." He rubbed his chin with one hand. "The kind of aircraft I found out there isn't normally used for training hops. My guess is that the Army's hunting for something very specific. It's possible aircraft sensors could have picked up a concentration of metal readings and the Mohawk was brought in to pinpoint the location. Now, more than ever, I believe your uncle's here on a job for the military. I don't think it was a coincidence that he chose this particular time to come onto the Range. He could have been hired to search for anything from the legendary cache of gold to lost electronic gear or experimental ordinance."

She stood up. "If that's true, everything we've encountered out here takes on new possibilities. Robertson and his men are one worry, but what about the other two? Perea identified them as the pair who tried to kidnap me, and from what I saw of them, I think he's right. Yet, I don't know anything about them. Well, except that one of them had a strange tattoo beneath his wristwatch."

"What kind of tattoo?"

"I only caught a flash of it really. It was blue and red, and there was something in the corner, maybe a star, I'm not really sure. But tattoos are a dime a dozen, though the location of this one *was* a bit unusual. It's almost as if he didn't want anyone really seeing it. Then again, that might have been a matter of personal preference. For all I know, it was something obscene."

Travis considered it for a moment. "Well, Robertson's still the most direct threat confronting either your uncle or us. We know what he wants and just how far he's prepared to go in order to get it. He's a lethal adversary. At this point, the others don't represent as great a danger."

Belara shuddered. "How much further is it to the rest spot you've got picked out? I need at least a few hours of sleep sometime soon," she admitted.

"It won't be long now. The ridge we have to follow is up ahead. After it drops off, it'll be less than half an hour."

She struggled to keep her pace from becoming sluggish, but her weariness was turning to a deadened numbness, making her stumble with increasing frequency.

"Would you like to lean on me as we walk?"

The selflessness of the gesture touched her. She knew how sore he must be by now. "No, I'm fine, just a little clumsy. How are you holding up?"

"I've had better days," he admitted, "but we should look on the bright side. I'm certain we've outdistanced Robertson and the other group, and made up almost a day's travel time. By now, we also shouldn't be too far from the depression you said indicates we're close to your uncle's ranch."

"I'll try to take a closer look at the maps after I've rested. I'm having difficulty concentrating on anything right now."

"Maybe I can rethink our stopping point. You look beat," he said, sympathy evident in his gaze.

She shook her head, then smiled wearily. "It's okay. The sun's coming over the horizon now and it'll start getting warm soon enough. It'll be better to stop then."

"I want to make it to the end of that ridge," he said, gesturing ahead, "then I'll see if I can check the area behind us. I'd like to know exactly where the others are."

They continued in silence, exhaustion beginning to sap their energy reserves. An hour later, they emerged into a high clearing. Hidden in the shade of a rock, Travis thumbed the focus ring on his field glasses. "Both groups look to have made camp," he told her. "The heat and the pace must be as draining on them as it is on us. That second group is carrying assault rifles, but what really concerns me is their tenacity trailing Robertson's group." He exhaled softly. "Well, as long as they hang back, they won't pose a problem to us. Let's take this opportunity to get some sleep."

"Let me take the first watch," Belara said, gazing at Travis thoughtfully. His eyelids were heavy and he shook his head every few minutes as if trying to keep himself alert.

"I could use it," he admitted, "but are you sure? I know you're tired, too."

"You need sleep. What I need more than anything else is rest. I can do that and still keep watch."

"Thanks," he said. "Just give me an hour. I'll be okay then," he added, stretching out in the shade of a large rock. Giving her a smile, he rolled over and closed his eyes. Seconds later his breathing evened.

Belara placed the binoculars in front of her, then leaned back against the boulder. They'd come such a long way, both as people and partners on this journey. Despite the mystery that still surrounded Travis, her feelings for him continued to grow. The knowledge that caring for him could only lead to heartbreak didn't stop her heart from yearning.

As her gaze strayed over him, she tried to concentrate on logic, desperate to send a clear warning to her heart. She could not choose a mate from outside her tribe. She had a responsibility to those still unborn. Her culture was the most special gift she could pass on to her children. Raising them in a home where beliefs were divided would undermine the very basis of what she'd be trying to impart. Comparisons between both cultures were inevitable in such situations, and in the process, emphasis on one would take precedence over the other.

She thought of her own life. If things had been different, she might have lost sight of what had become the dearest part of herself. Her father had never placed much importance on customs he didn't understand. Her mother had been forced to work hard to counter that. In the long run, she wasn't sure what choices she would have made if the situation hadn't changed. If it hadn't been for her uncle, she might have become lost between the white culture and a heritage she'd never fully known.

Hours ticked by as she continued to keep a silent vigil over Travis and the others behind them. Despite her own weariness, she was reluctant to wake Travis. She gazed at his sleeping face. The worry lines had all smoothed out and he looked blissfully at peace. Nothing could have persuaded her to do anything to pull him back to the harshness of the situation they faced.

As it was, she never had to. Travis shifted, then opened his eyes. He checked his watch and gave her a hard look. "You shouldn't have let me sleep so long."

She smiled and shrugged. "I've been keeping an eye on our friends, and they're still holed up. Do you think they've picked up our trail?"

"There's no way of telling." He stood and walked back and forth to ease stiff muscles while remaining out of the line of sight of their followers. "Get some sleep, now, and..." He gave her a sheepish grin. "Thanks for letting me take the first rest period."

Belara felt like she'd just closed her eyes, but it was mid-afternoon when Travis gently shook her awake. "We've got to get going. Robertson decided to get his boys moving again. It looks like they're going to make it up the face of that cliff."

Chapter Twelve

Belara forced herself to come fully awake. "So they did find our trail."

"I think that they must have taken the time to do more than a cursory check on your uncle's background. You'll have to eat something as we walk. I'm sorry you didn't get much of a chance to sleep."

"I'd rather lose some sleep than risk having them catch up to us."

Travis set a brisk pace, but always remained close by her side. Finally at dusk they reached the tree sprinkled northern slope of the last fragment of the San Andres chain. He pulled the binoculars from his pack. "I'll have to check on our neighbors back there," he said. "Only it's going to be difficult with so many trees and shrubs in the way. My best chance is to climb one of those boulders and see if I can spot anything from up there. It's at least fifteen feet off the ground."

"Watch your balance. The smaller one looks like it slid there recently. You can still see the trail behind it that's clear of brush."

"I'll be careful, don't worry. Here." He handed her the rifle. "If anyone closes in on us, warn them off."

She grasped the rifle in her hand and held it firmly. Her eyes were glued on the clearing below them now, bathed in moonlight. She'd hunted with her uncle before, but she'd never taken a human life. She wasn't sure she could shoot a man with intent to kill, even if it became necessary. She wouldn't hesitate to try to stop him by shooting in his direction, but she wasn't at all certain she'd ever be able to do more. Even the *possibility* of taking the life of her enemy filled her with dread. Her culture, something she could always lean on, made that normal reaction even more frightening. The teachings of the *Dinéh* were filled with warnings about such actions and the effects of the vengeful *chindis*. Many who'd returned after military service had asked that the Enemy War Chant be done over them for just that reason. She prayed that she'd never have to call upon a *hataalii* for that.

"We've got problems," Travis said from up above, interrupting her thoughts. "I don't think Robertson's group has found our trail yet, but the way they're going at it, they will. They've split up and are using flashlights to communicate back and forth in Morse code. I was able to read their signals, and I know they're looking for our footprints. That's what gave me an idea." He inched his way back down the rock slowly, then jumped the last few feet. "I want you to go on ahead." He unfolded one of the maps, then pointed to a water hole she had marked that could be found about three kilometers ahead. "We'll rendezvous here. Don't worry about me, just make the best time you can, I'll catch up. By the time I finish with these guys, they'll be so lost it'll take them hours to even find *each other* again." He gave her a wide grin.

Belara saw his eyes light up with a peculiar rush of excitement. It was either the challenge of pitting his skills against an adversary, or the false bravado of a man about to do something highly dangerous. "I'm not going anywhere without you and that's that. If you have a plan, we'll work on it together."

"We'll both be just fine, believe me. I'll be keeping them much too busy to go after you."

She said nothing, only stared at him.

Travis met Belara's gaze and challenged her with a stony one of his own. Finally he sighed and shook his head slowly. "You're not going to give up, are you?" he asked rhetorically. "Okay. Let me tell you why I've got to handle this alone. My plan is to angle between them and send each group a false message so they'll both go off in the wrong direction. Who knows? With a little luck, we'll scatter them permanently."

"Your plan sounds good, but it would work even better if I take part," she answered with a ghost of a smile.

"I *knew* you were going to say that," he muttered.

She continued, ignoring his comment. "The way you've got this set up, it's possible that when you turn to one group the ones behind you will spot the signals. We can avoid this if I create a diversion that'll distract one of the pairs while you work on the other."

Travis considered her proposal for a few moments. "Your way does leave less to chance," he conceded. "Let's do it. We'll leave our gear hidden here inside the crevice between those two boulders." He slipped off his pack. "Give me three minutes, then work your way toward the group on the left. By the way, what kind of diversion are you planning?"

"I'm going to rely on sounds to distract them. I'll be careful, so don't get too sidetracked worrying about me."

"Easier said than done. You realize that you're taking quite a chance. We'll be too far from each other for me to help if you get caught."

"I'm aware of that, but if we can pull this off, it'll give us a chance to lose them again for hours. This close to the ranch, we can use all the advantages we can get."

Emotions flickered across his eyes lighting up the dark green pools. "There are times when I could wish you had less courage." He paused, then added, "but I'd be lying if I said I couldn't use your help."

She nodded. "You've got it. Just watch out for yourself."

He gazed off into the distance and his eyes grew hard. "When this is over, and your uncle and you are both safe,

I'm going to find Robertson and settle this. He's been a thorn in my side for much too long.''

Belara kept her eyes on Travis as he jogged away. Concern for him flooded over her. After this was over, the last thing she wanted to worry about was another confrontation between the two men.

Pushing the thought from her mind, she waited for the minutes to tick by. Finally she checked her watch and started forward. It was time to do her part to support Travis's plan. Robertson's interference could cost lives unless they dealt with it now.

She crept noiselessly across the juniper and piñon covered forest. Before long, she heard the men's rough whispers up ahead. If this was their best attempt at stealth, she hoped for their sake they were never in any more danger than they were now.

She glanced around quickly, picked up a piece of dead wood, then climbed up the tallest piñon she could find. As the men approached, she methodically began to rub her piece of wood against the trunk. The noise, a dull scraping sound, echoed rhythmically in the stillness.

"What the hell is that?" one of the men demanded in a gravelly voice.

"Relax, Halliday. It's probably a mountain sheep rubbing its horns against a tree," the other suggested. "They're supposed to be in this area."

"Yeah? Well, if I do spot one, I'm taking a shot at it. I'm tired of water and dehydrated food. I could use some fresh meat. Spread out and let's go see what it is."

Belara saw a flashlight blinking off in the distance as the other team communicated mistakenly with Travis. Soon, if Travis's idea worked that pair would be moving off. Then she'd be able to stop diverting the two near her. As she glanced down from the tree, she saw the men coming straight toward her hiding place. She held her breath. She couldn't continue making the sound now, they were too close. A minute later, they stopped beneath the tree. Belara huddled into the branches, ignoring the pine needles pricking her sides and arms.

One of the men seated himself on the ground and leaned back against the trunk. "I'm tired of the desert, you know that Halliday? After this is over, I'm going to take a vacation near the ocean. Maybe even buy myself some beach-front property in Mexico.

"All of my life I've had to scrimp and save. With the money I'm going to make from my share, I'll finally get to enjoy myself. I can't even imagine what it'll be like, having all my bills paid off."

Belara saw Travis try to signal the pair beneath her, but the men were too distracted by their own musings to look his way. She waited another half minute, then decided it was time to call their attention to it. Taking a piece of bark in her hand, she flicked it as far from her as possible, in the direction of Travis's light.

The man sitting beneath the tree jumped to his feet and swirled the rifle at his hip. "What was that?"

"Probably just a rabbit, so cut the chatter." He stared into the distance. "There's a signal now." He swore. "I hope Robertson hasn't been trying to get our attention for long, otherwise he's going to be ticked off again."

There was silence for a moment as the men struggled to read the long and short flashes of light. Finally the entire message was received. "He's found Hill's trail. The guy doubled back on us again. It looks like we're finally going to get somewhere with this crazy chase."

Belara saw the men move off. As soon as they had disappeared, and she was sure they were out of hearing range, she scrambled down. She didn't know how to read Morse code, but from the conversation she'd overheard, Travis's plan had worked. They were heading in the opposite direction from where she'd last seen the other pair. She moved through the brush quickly. It was time to go to the rendezvous point.

She made good speed, but when she arrived Belara saw no sign of Travis. She'd expected to beat him back, but as she waited alone in the darkness, uneasiness crept over her like a spider's feathery light touch.

"We're going to have to stop meeting like this," he said teasingly, directly behind her.

Startled by the sound of his voice so close by, she snapped her head around to look. He emerged from the shadowed recess behind the rocks. "How did you creep up so close? I thought my senses were sharper than that."

"I was a soldier for a very long time," he said reaching for the pack. "We went through a special survival school at one point that focused on escape and evasion. I'd put that out of my mind for years. I wanted to forget it, believe me. It isn't the high point of any soldier's training. You end up learning things about yourself you'd just as soon never have known about."

"It sounds awful. What on earth did they do to you?"

He gave her a grim smile as he continued up the small slope. "They taught me how to evade capture, and how to deal with it if I was made a prisoner. That's about all I can tell you." He lapsed into a thoughtful silence. "I hope I'm wrong," he said at last, "but on this journey you may have to find out that you're capable of things you never even dreamed you could do. If so, remember, when it's over I'll be right there for you if you need a friend."

She understood what he was saying, and prayed that she'd never have to choose between their lives or someone else's. Even if she meant only to defend either herself or Travis, she'd undoubtedly hesitate before using deadly force. Those lost seconds could tip the scale against them.

Two hours later, after refilling their canteens at the water hole, Travis scanned the map before him. "There's a stretch of flat terrain a few miles from here. We'll head for that, then rest."

Belara shook her head. "That map doesn't show all the finer details," she said rubbing her shoulder absently. "That section it indicates as relatively clear doesn't actually level out until you pass a narrow ravine and several gullies that have been cut into the northern slope of the mountain. It's incredibly rugged, although only for a short stretch. Unfortunately we can't avoid it from this side. The good news, however, is that it'll take us right to my uncle's ranch."

"You lead the way. If you're confident you know where you're going, that's enough for me."

She started off briskly, eager to complete the last leg of their journey. Now she'd finally find out whether their sacrifice and efforts had been in vain. The possibility that they'd failed made a sudden tremor shoot through her. She fought to suppress her fear, and held herself in careful check. Now, more than ever, she needed to cling to the hope she'd nurtured in her heart.

"By the way, there's one possibility we haven't considered," Travis cautioned, his voice gentle. "Your uncle may have already moved on. Remember that we've been delayed by those behind us."

"If that's the case, he couldn't have had medical problems. That's all the news I need. You see, that'll mean the Blessingway Chant and his own efforts to restore his *hózhú,* all that's good and harmonious, have been successful. Yet, by coming I've honored my debt to him, and shown that my love is something he can always count on."

"Your uncle's a lucky man to have someone like you in his corner," Travis said, his voice barely audible.

"I'm in your corner, too. If you ever needed a friend, I'd be there."

"I wouldn't want you to, if it was only out of a sense of debt," he answered honestly.

"Friendship always carries obligations, and in a way, I suppose you could call them debts. But they're met easily, because your feelings for that person demand it."

Travis said nothing, his expression pensive.

"This is it," she said, interrupting his thoughts and pointing to a narrow, winding path that branched off ahead. "It's nothing more than a trail cut into the side of a canyon wall."

As they approached the entrance, Travis moved ahead and studied the path. "This isn't really that narrow. It's wide enough for a horse carrying a full load. We'll make it through just fine."

Belara touched the rock and hard-packed sand that made up the side. "The entrance has been widened recently. You can still see the spade marks. The wind and the elements would have erased these if they'd been even weeks old." Moving to one side, she allowed the faint moonlight to illuminate the ground before her. Working carefully, she bent down and felt the sand. The longer it had been since the tracks were made the harder the earth would be from dew forming on its surface. "There are tracks here where two horses came through. Unless I miss my guess, my uncle's been here."

Travis crouched beside her and studied the ground. "It may not be your uncle. Keep that in mind."

She started forward. "Who else would come this way? No army patrols go out with pack animals anymore."

"We can't afford to make assumptions. It's too dangerous," Travis said, following her. "How much farther is it from here?"

"About half an hour. By dawn we should reach the ranch house."

The tension between them grew thicker by the minute. Belara knew that Travis was worried, mostly about her. Her insistence on maintaining positive thoughts about her uncle's welfare had made him doubt that she'd be able to accept what fate might deal them. That wasn't the case at all, but she was certain it would take more than words to convince him. She couldn't blame him, not really. Navajo ways were difficult to explain and even harder for someone outside the *Dinéh* to truly understand. Still, the man *did* try and his respect was genuine.

She passed a sharp bend and stopped abruptly, staring at a barren lightning-struck pine. Its old, thick trunk had been split, the jagged halves angling toward, but not quite reaching the ground. Belara felt the blood drain from her face. She didn't want to break a taboo, particularly one that brought illness and death, but there was no way to avoid it.

"What's wrong?" he asked.

"It's a *báhádzid,* a taboo," she explained, "to walk close by a tree struck by lightning." She took a deep breath.

"Are you afraid?"

"It makes me uneasy, that's all. There are only a few *Dinéh* who can go near something like that with impunity. My uncle is one. I'm sure he would have gathered whatever sticks he could there since it's said they have special power. Then during his sweat bath, he'd use them as pokers for the fire. To the *Dinéh,* the sweat healing is a way to rid the body of whatever has contaminated it."

"How come you have to worry about that taboo, but your uncle doesn't?"

She grew quiet then added, "My uncle is...special in some ways. He trained as a *hataalii* once. But you and I are not similarly protected. We must not get any closer than is absolutely necessary."

They continued on the narrow path between cliff faces, and the sky slowly began to lighten. As the sun peeked over the horizon, Belara pointed to a small, stone ranch house barely visible near the base of the limestone canyon. "That's his old home. From the air it's all but invisible because of those stunted trees."

"That's the biggest cluster of green I've seen in quite a while. There must be a spring nearby."

"There is. It's only a small one, but it forms a pool right by the house. My uncle used to kid around, saying that it might have been primitive out here, but they always had running water."

The sun was up by the time they made their way to the front door. The wooden frame had rotted years ago, and all that really remained, were the stone walls and the opening that led inside.

Belara stepped in first and glanced around. "Uncle?" Her voice, echoing back at her, was the only answering sound. She walked to the small stone hearth and crouched before it. "He's been here." She touched a familiar small metal cup that lay on it side nearby. "Only I can't tell when."

"It wasn't too long ago, judging by the remains left in his opened ration pouches." He pointed to a small refuse pile against the stone wall.

Travis walked to the opening at the back where the rear door had once stood. "There are footprints out here, but I don't think they're fresh."

Belara joined him and crouched to examine the ground. "We've learned all that we can from the ranch house. Let's take a look inside the small sweat *hohrahn* out back, and then make a sweep around the surrounding area. If we don't find him, we'll leave. I wouldn't want any of the groups behind us to follow us here. If my uncle is in the vicinity, he doesn't need that type of trouble, even if he is okay."

They started down a path leading to the *hohrahn*. As they approached the cone-shaped structure of wood and mud, they noted that it had been recently repaired. New bark and earth covered it. "He's been here."

Travis ducked his head inside, then glanced back at her. "He built a fire in the center, but all that's left is ashes."

She nodded slowly. "He finished what he came to do. Let's search for tracks out here. If we don't find any that appear fresh, we'll leave."

She led the way farther into the narrow canyon. Water had collected here and the grasses were thick, cushioning their footsteps and obscuring their tracks. Apache plume with its bright red tendrils and yellow flowers, added a dash of color to their surroundings.

"There's no sign of him back here," Travis said, placing a gentle hand on her shoulder. "Let's go."

Belara's reply was interrupted by the racheting sound of a shell being fed into a rifle chamber.

Chapter Thirteen

"Place your weapons down on the ground slowly," a voice ordered.

Travis started to slide the rifle strap off his shoulder when Belara turned around quickly. His heart leaped to his throat. "Don't!" he warned, realizing it was already too late.

"Uncle! I recognize your voice, so you might as well come out. You probably can't see either of us very well from wherever you're hiding, or you'd have known it was me."

"Niece?" Jimmie Bowman stepped out from behind a thick juniper and gave Belara a surprised look. "Why are *you* here?"

Travis began to breathe again. "Why didn't you tell me?" he muttered to Belara. He ran an exasperated hand through his hair. "You and I are going to have to talk."

Jimmie turned to look at Travis, his gaze thoughtful. "I don't know you," he said at last, his .22 rifle starting to come back up.

"It's all right, Uncle," Belara answered. "He's a good friend. His name is Travis Hill." She told him briefly about the circumstances that had prompted her journey. "I hope you'll forgive me for violating your privacy." She held out the small amber prescription bottle she'd brought with her.

"No one else was to know about my problem." Jimmie looked first at her, then toward Travis. "Does he know all about our personal lives now?"

"I tried to prevent him from getting involved, but the only way I could convince him to cooperate with me was to tell him."

Travis glanced at the Navajo man before him. Bowman had long hair, his red headband keeping the salt-and-pepper strands away from his eyes. He was wearing brown twill pants and a pale green flannel shirt. His face was worn and wrinkled, but his eyes were black coals, alive and alert. The rifle he held was now pointed at the ground, but it wouldn't take much effort to aim the barrel back at Travis's chest. Reluctantly Travis decided to speak. "She's right. I would have done whatever I could to keep her from coming here. Even knowing her reasons, I tried my best to keep her off the Range. But she was set on coming and nothing I did or said made any difference."

Jimmie smiled grudgingly, then glanced at Belara. "I wish you had shown more faith in our ways," he admonished, taking the pills from her hand and placing them in his pants' pocket. "I'm doing just fine, as you can see. You should have listened to the man." He crouched down on his haunches, his gaze focusing on Travis. "I know you by reputation. By helping her—" he gestured to Belara "—you've proven yourself a friend to both of us. The passage to this place was difficult and dangerous. Your return will be just as hazardous, but I have one more favor to ask. Take her back to the city."

"You'll have to convince her to go yourself. I don't seem to have much luck getting her to listen to me. Of course, I could tie her up and throw her over one shoulder..."

Jimmie Bowman stared at his niece speculatively. "That's a very good idea. Do you think you could handle the extra weight? If not, I'll let you have one of my pack horses. Just tie her to the saddle—"

"Wait just one minute," Belara said crossly, folding her arms across her chest.

"I warn you, although most *Dinéh* women are very calm and pleasant to have around, she falls short of those virtues," Jimmie continued, pointedly ignoring her.

"I've found that so," Travis agreed.

"You both have a lousy sense of humor," Belara admonished quietly. "Any other time I might have indulged you, but it's much too dangerous for us to hang around here now." She gave him the details concerning the other groups. "We all have to get going. Robertson's still out there, hoping for a chance to catch up to us. We believe he's after the gold on Victorio Peak, and is determined to use you as a guide. Then there's another pair we know very little about. I haven't been able to get a good enough look to confirm it, but I think they're the same men who tried to kidnap me. Since they're also heavily armed, I'd say they're more trouble waiting to happen. They've followed Robertson's group, and us, throughout our entire journey."

Travis watched the older man and knew that Belara's words were not having any effect on him. From the way Bowman's jaw was set, he'd have bet his last cent that the man still intended to stay. "In this case she's right, sir. Robertson is bad news and he's determined to get your cooperation," he said, supporting her argument. "Don't underestimate the threat he poses to you. Robertson is relentless and smart. He's managed to stay one step behind us, despite everything Belara and I have been able to do. If he does catch up to you, he'll do whatever is necessary to force you to help him."

Bowman nodded slowly. "I hear what you're saying, now understand me. I came here to restore myself to harmony. I've achieved that and my health is as good as it ever was. I'm capable of taking care of myself until I'm ready to go back. The others may have some knowledge of the desert, but I grew up here. This is my home in more ways than one. If I choose to be, I'm more of a threat to them than they are to me."

The matter-of-fact confidence in Bowman's tone made Travis believe him. He remained silent, considering which tack to take next. Deciding, he addressed the older man again. "You've completed your personal errand here at the ranch. Why risk staying now?"

"It's what I want for myself, but you two should leave the area as quickly as possible. I know I'll be just fine, but I can't say the same for you."

"Uncle, please," Belara pleaded, trying to counter the stubbornness in his tone. "If for no other reason, come back so I won't have to worry about you."

"You have no reason to worry. My skills are more than enough to counteract the danger," he said. "Let me show you a few things. You're aware that I have two horses with me, but have either of you seen them?" He smiled, seeing the frustrated look on his niece's face and the confusion on the man's. "We're on high ground now, yet you can't see them anywhere below us. You've been to the ranch house and out the back, and still didn't see any sign of them. How do you explain that?"

Travis gave him a puzzled look. "I assume you ran them off into the desert and plan on retrieving them later."

"I wouldn't waste my energy." Bowman grinned. "There are better ways. You deal with what you see. I work with what I know. Come on. You're about to learn some of the things the mountain keeps secret."

Travis stopped in front of a steep ravine that cut across the valley and glanced around. "Where to from here?"

"You choose," Bowman said.

Travis knew he was being tested, but he'd never backed down from a challenge before and didn't intend to start now. He studied the sides of the ravine. He could see the wooden posts where a bridge had once stood. "We could climb down into the ravine, but that's a dangerous proposition. Going back up the other side would be even worse. If it was up to me, I'd travel on a parallel course until we could cross over."

Jimmie nodded slowly, then looked at his niece. "And you? What would you recommend?"

"If it was absolutely necessary to go into that ravine, I'd risk it, but it would be extremely slow going. Even then, I couldn't guarantee one of us wouldn't be injured. I'd have to agree with our friend's opinion," she said, glancing at Travis. "We should go around. That is, unless you have a way of erecting a very fast bridge."

"We don't need one." Bowman took the lead. He walked up to the steepest vertical side of the canyon then began to remove a row of thistles and weeds. "It isn't much of a path, but there's a ledge cut right into the side of the canyon. We'll have to go single file. At points, it's slow going for a horse, but it suits our needs."

Travis edged his way around carefully. The old man was as sharp as his reputation made him out to be.

The ravine rapidly became more shallow, joining a low, grassy valley encompassed by the canyon. Two horses grazed in the area ahead. "I would have never guessed this was here," Travis muttered.

"That's what I was trying to tell you. There's a big difference between reacting to what you see, and acting on what you know."

Belara gestured to a sheltered spot ahead. "It looks like you made camp there instead of at the ranch house."

"I did," Bowman answered with a grin. "I left enough of a trail at the house to be convincing in case anyone came looking for me, but this is where I've been. I told you I wanted to get back to the land. The Wind People speak more clearly out here and I can feel the power of Earth Woman beneath my feet. As one of our Holyway Chants says, in this place 'I have become again.' "

Although Bowman never looked directly at him, Travis sensed that the older man was measuring his response. "I've learned a great deal about your culture from your niece," Travis said quietly. "I may not share all your beliefs, but I sure can't argue with the results. You appear to be in perfect health."

As they entered the narrow, sequestered valley, Belara placed a hand on her uncle's arm. "I don't doubt your skills, but greed is a powerful motive. Robertson is not going to give up easily. He's willing to do whatever it takes to get you to guide him to the gold in Victorio Peak."

Jimmie Bowman laughed. "He doesn't need my help, he needs a magician. The Army searched that place inside and out for years. Even civilians came in to look. If there ever was anything there, it's long gone. The only thing they're going to find at the Peak are rocks and snakes."

"You can't hide from them forever, Uncle. When your supplies run low, they'll be waiting at the mouth of the canyon. It's true that this place is a stronghold, but it can trap you in as well as keep them out."

Bowman said nothing for a while. "You don't know if they've followed you here to the ranch," he said. A touch of uncertainty finally evidenced in his tone.

"I'm going to have to hike up to high ground and take a look around," Travis answered. "It's been a while since I've been able to check on their whereabouts." He searched the heights for a vantage point. "Can you recommend a spot where I'd have a fairly unobstructed view?"

"There's a place not too far from here that will be perfect for what you want," Bowman said. He led them across the tiny valley, then climbed up a slope adjacent to the cliff faces. "That opening several feet up from us is a mine shaft. There are a series of ladders inside that will take you to a surveillance point on top of the cliff. You'll be able to see for miles around this canyon from there."

As they entered the dark, cavernous interior, Belara noted footprints that indicated her uncle had used the mine shaft frequently as an observation post. "What have you been on the lookout for?"

He shrugged. "Almost anything," he replied, gesturing for Travis to go on up. "If you don't mind, I'll wait here. I've been out walking almost all day."

"Uncle, what are you keeping from me?" Belara demanded suspiciously.

He shrugged, but avoided the question. "Walking around the mountain has helped me remember much about my life here. It's strange how selective memories can be. Coming back has reminded me that not all my days at the ranch were pleasant. Conditions were rough, and sometimes game was scarce and we went hungry. We knew harmony and peace here, but there were times when it seemed like the mountain itself was against us. Nothing would grow and when it did it was sparse. The few head of cattle we owned would have to be killed sometimes to save them from a more lingering death by starvation.'' He shook his head slowly. ''It was good that I came. Maybe it's time I remembered things as they really were.''

She placed a hand on his arm. ''So why don't you come back with us now?'' she prodded. ''You've found what you came for, right?''

He pursed his lips tightly. ''This will be my last time here. Whatever memories I take back now will have to last me a lifetime,'' he answered quietly. ''I'll return soon enough.''

Before she could say anything more, Travis came back down the ladder. ''Robertson and his group have split up looking for our trail, and Wilson's almost found it. He's coming up the valley and moving in a line with the entrance to the canyon. He'll search until he spots the passageway. Count on it.''

Bowman straightened slightly. ''If we have to resist, this is the best possible place to do it. We can prevent them from getting closer without exposing ourselves to any danger. And it won't be a matter of hiding out here forever, either. Sooner or later, aircraft would locate us, or the patrols will come by.''

Travis weighed the alternatives. Bowman seemed to be in good shape, and Belara would be another asset, making it three against four. Yet, even though the soldier in him longed for the chance to confront his enemies, he couldn't bring himself to endanger the two with him by forcing the issue. If there was a way to avoid an all-out fight, he agreed they had to find it.

''There's still a small chance they'll miss us,'' Travis said. ''Let's see if we can help make that happen.'' He glanced at Belara. "Come and help me erase our footprints from the path leading to the ranch." Travis slipped his rifle off his shoulder and handed it to Jimmie, along with a box of shells. "Keep this, and if you see any of them coming too close to our position, fire warning shots. The sound of this will be more intimidating than rounds from your smaller caliber rifle."

"If you're going to the path by the canyon wall, it's impossible for me to cover you all the way. Remember that it winds around."

"Do what you can," Travis answered. "We'll work fast."

Travis led the way back, keeping the pace brisk. Noting Belara's silence he turned around and gave her a curious glance. "What's on your mind?"

"My uncle seems in good health, but his journey here on horseback was uneventful. He's had a chance to clear his thoughts and relax in his own way. I'm worried about how he'll do once Robertson starts putting on the pressure."

"I wouldn't underestimate your uncle's capabilities. But, you're right, we could all be in trouble. Robertson's group has got at least two semiautomatic rifles, and that's quite a bit of firepower."

"We'll hold our own. We have to," she replied resolutely.

As they crossed the ravine that led to the ranch house, Travis fought an intense feeling of foreboding. He'd only felt that way once before. It had been during a time when he'd been forced to draw on every ounce of courage he possessed just to make it. His memory drifted back to those weeks after the helicopter crash when he'd lain in the hospital. Each day, he'd prayed that the nurses would forget, but around midmorning they'd come to peel back his charred skin and soak his side in saline. No enemy's torture could have rivaled the emptiness he'd felt inside and the physical pain that had punctuated his existence. Yet as he glanced at Belara, he confronted a new fear more consuming than any he'd ever known. Losing her would send him to a different hell, one from which he'd never escape. He couldn't—no, he wouldn't—let her down. But as yet he had no idea how to keep her safe. The thought plagued him mercilessly.

It took them forty minutes at a near jog to cover the rugged terrain that lay between them and the path. As they neared their destination, Travis slowed considerably, his senses alert. He watched from behind cover for several minutes, then finally emerged.

"I think it's clear. They haven't found us yet," Travis said. "Let's see if we can make that permanent." He began pulling clumps of green thistle and placing them across the narrow passageway to obscure it. "Mix these with some dead brush and try to make it look as natural as possible," he instructed. "I'll cover up our tracks."

A branch snapped a few feet to his left. Travis spun around in a fighting stance, retrieving the remaining grenade from his jacket pocket. An instant later, his eyes locked with Robertson's. The man was standing a few feet away, a pistol in hand. "Unless you want to meet me in hell, don't even think of pulling that trigger," Travis warned. "Before your bullet finished me, I'd have the pin off."

Robertson gathered his composure, and grinned slowly. "I hope you don't expect me to believe you're willing to commit suicide just to take me with you." He laughed, and kept the .45 automatic in his hand.

"If you don't lower your gun, I'll pull the ring. I'd rather the woman and I both die right now by my hand than by yours."

Robertson's eyes narrowed. "If you pull that ring, we'll all be dead. But if you give up now, I may not kill you. My way at least gives you a chance."

"Do I *look* stupid to you? The minute you get the upper hand, you'll empty that clip into me. You'll undoubtedly keep the woman around longer, but only until she's of no further use to you. There's no way you'll leave a witness behind. If she and I are going to die, I'm going to be the one who picks the time."

Indecision shone in Robertson's eyes, but he held his ground.

Travis took a step forward. "Back up the way you came." When Robertson didn't move, he brought the grenade down and tightened his finger around the ring. "Then it's good night for all of us."

"Wait!" Halliday appeared from the shadows and yanked Robertson back. "This stinks, man. I'm not dying out here just because you two guys are nuts."

Robertson shook himself free, his gaze trained on Travis. "He's bluffing."

"You better be willing to die for that theory," Travis answered back, his voice level and calm. "Now tell me, Robertson. Do we play it out?"

Halliday grabbed Robertson by the jacket collar and hauled him back forcibly. "Sorry, Barry, but this is one lousy game." He shot Travis a venomous look. "Cool it, Hill. We're leaving, but we won't be far away. You've gained a little time, that's all."

Travis continued to step forward, his finger through the ring of the grenade, until the men were clear of the path. "Hurry back," he said as they hustled through the brush. "I promise to leave a few surprises for you on the trail." Travis grinned as he heard Robertson loudly cursing Halliday's ancestors.

Seconds later, Travis was back at the bend in the canyon path. "We've got to get out of here fast. They'll be back, although Robertson and Halliday are going to waste some time settling what just happened."

Belara nodded. "What surprises are you going to leave them?"

Travis gave her a puzzled look. "Don't you want to know if I really would have pulled the pin?"

"You would have made the right decision," she answered calmly.

He smiled, a pleasant warmth spreading over him. Her belief in him made him wish that he could be the gentle-hearted man she thought he was. But whenever he tried to look at himself through her eyes, it invariably left him even more mystified. What exactly did she see in him that he couldn't?

"I have nothing to pull surprises with," he admitted at last. "This isn't a fragmentation grenade," he said, holding it up. "It's another pepper gas grenade. The worst that would have happened to us is that we would have been deaf for a while and itched like crazy."

"How are we going to keep them from coming after us?"

"We can't, but we can keep them from getting too close. I'm a very good shot, and I guarantee, if I see them, they won't get anywhere near us." He glanced behind him. "Let's hurry. We'll need to be behind cover before Robertson gets his act together."

They'd almost reached the low valley when a hail of bullets erupted all around them. Slugs hammered into the rocky sides of the canyon. The blind firing was making their position untenable. As a shower of rock fragments sprayed over them Travis pulled Belara beneath him.

Answering fire came from the mine above them, and for a few precious minutes, they were able to move without worry. Travis turned his head and saw the puffs of dirt as slugs hit the rocks and sand near the pass. "Your uncle's good," Travis commented, wiping traces of blood from some shallow cuts on his face. "Good thing my rifle is more accurate at that range than their weapons."

Belara ran forward, bent nearly in a crouch. "We're almost at the mine."

As the cover fire from above stopped, Travis pulled her back down. "Wait until your uncle reloads, then go up the side of the canyon as fast as you can. I'll follow you."

A moment later, Jimmie peered out from above them, carefully staying in the shadows. With a new burst of fire, he guarded his niece's ascent. Travis followed quickly. "Good work, sir."

Jimmie nodded, but kept his eyes glued on the pass. "With all the gunfire going on, my animals are going to spook. I have some gear I've got to take back with me, and

I'll need to use them for that. If you two can give me some cover, I'm going to go down to round them up. There's a slope at the other end of this mine they can make, if I lead them up."

Belara shook her head. "The minute you go down there, you'll attract Robertson's fire. It's too dangerous."

Jimmie kept his eyes on the men peering out of cover and fired another round. "You two might not have had much difficulty getting here on foot, but it's been years since I've done that," he argued reluctantly. "I'm going to need those animals for the journey back. We all might, if we're going to put some fast distance between us and anyone in pursuit."

Travis nodded. "Then I'll be the one who goes. You two stay here."

"You'll need help," Jimmie protested. "There're two horses to round up and the less time you spend out there, the better it'll be." Jimmie handed Belara the rifle. "Do you remember how to shoot one of these?"

She nodded and fired a shot as she saw the men trying to advance through the narrow pass. The bullet sailed over them, hitting the top of the hillside, yards away from where they were. "Only it looks like I'm no better now than I ever was," she observed ruefully. "I think it'll make more sense for me to go. You'll at least be able to place your shots so they'll be close to where you're aiming. I won't have much luck actually scaring them off, though I might be able to annoy them." She squeezed the trigger again and the round sailed over the hillside completely.

Jimmie considered it for a moment, then glanced at Travis. "It does make more sense for my niece to go with you. She'll be able to move faster and I'll be of more use here, keeping the others off your backs."

"It's settled then," Travis answered. "How do we get the horses up here?"

"You'll have to go around the back curve of the canyon before you can even see the path I'm talking about. The slope is gradual. If you lead the animals past the rocks carefully, they'll be able to handle the climb without any problems. They've got halters on, so all you'll need is a bit of rope."

Jimmie fired two more rounds as Travis pulled what he'd be needing from his own pack. "They're still shooting blind, but they almost got one of the horses that time," Jimmie warned. "You better hurry."

"What's the fastest way down there?" Travis asked, giving Jimmie Bowman two more boxes of ammunition.

Jimmie considered it. "You could rappel down the front while I cover you. I can make sure they never have a chance to get off a shot."

"That's the game plan, then." Travis glanced at Belara. "Have you ever rappeled?"

"Not since I was a kid and my uncle took me camping."

"It'll come back to you," Jimmie assured, handing her a pair of well-worn leather gloves from his jacket pocket.

Belara retrieved the climbing rope from her pack and fastened one end around a wooden beam near the entrance to the shaft. Facing the anchor, she straddled the rope. It didn't take her long before she remembered how to position herself and the rope. Her right hand, grasping the section of rope behind her, would control her rate of descent. She'd use the length before her primarily for balance. Leaning backward against the rope, she tugged hard, testing it. "I'm ready."

Travis glanced over at her and nodded. "Okay, then." He shifted closer to the front of the mine shaft. "Be ready to move fast once we reach the bottom," he added. "Remember until we're around the bend, we're in their field of fire."

"No problem."

Jimmie thumbed four more rounds into the rifle magazine and fed one into the chamber. "Okay, here you go." Closing the bolt, he aimed and squeezed the trigger, firing another round with a loud thud.

Moving quickly, Travis jumped out of the opening and headed down, Belara at his side. She nearly matched his rate of descent, though he'd expected her to ease down more cautiously, like most beginners. Of course, gunfire was a great incentive.

Jimmie's continued cover fire managed to keep all but stray, haphazard shots from striking anywhere near them. As soon as they reached the bottom, Belara ran toward the frightened horses. Just before she reached them, a bullet ricocheted overhead and sent the gelding galloping to the other end of the small canyon.

Travis glanced back at the cave, noting that Jimmie had slowed his rate of fire.

"Do you think he's hurt?" Belara asked quickly, rushing for cover.

Travis shook his head. "I think he's conserving ammunition."

"I hope you're not trying to tell me that all we have left are the boxes you gave my uncle."

"I have two more, and that's it." He studied the spooked horse that stood, neck erect and ears pricked forward, about fifty yards away. "As soon as Robertson and the others taper off their fire, we'll make our move. I'll take the horse that's farthest from us."

Belara handed him some trail mix. "Here. This will come in handy. They like the sweet grain."

"Great idea." As it grew quiet, Travis urged her forward. "Now's our chance."

Travis headed for the gelding, but the animal laid back its ears and shied away from him. He muttered an oath. As the hail of gunfire began again across the canyon, he spurted forward, trying to grab the horse's halter. The animal's eyes grew wide, and with a terrified whinny he galloped away.

Belara ran to Travis leading the frightened mare, and handed him the rope attached to the animal's halter. "Here, take her. I'll get the gelding and follow you up."

"Leave him. He's an ornery old devil and we're not going to catch him anytime soon."

Belara held her palm open and walked up to the animal talking softly. The gelding nickered and pricked his ears forward. "You don't want to stay out here, boy. So come along and don't make us chase you." As another random shot echoed against the canyon walls, the animal shied away. Belara stood in front of him. "No! That's enough. Now let's go." With determined steps she walked up to the gelding, and looped the rope around its neck.

Travis looked at Belara and shook his head. "I'm impressed."

"You should be. I'm absolutely wonderful," she teased, short of breath as they sprinted toward the slope that lead to the mine.

"A regular renaissance woman, right? Can ride, hike, rappel and do everything else well, except maybe shoot."

Belara said nothing, only smiled.

Working quickly, they climbed back to the mine, leading the horses. As they approached the rear opening, she heard her uncle fire another shot, warning off Robertson and his men.

Her thoughts turned somber. "What in the world are we going to do when we run out of ammunition?"

Travis led the mare inside the mine. "We'll have to make sure we're out of here by then. Either that, or go steal Robertson's ammunition."

Belara followed him in, leading the gelding. "I'm sure Robertson's planning on trapping us here." She fastened both horses securely, then climbed up the ladder, ready to join her uncle. Travis was right behind her.

Jimmie looked up as they approached. "I'm glad you managed to get the horses, because we've got problems. The men are getting braver and risking an approach knowing that at this range I probably won't be able to hit them. I can't place my shots close enough to really worry them." He fired at one of the men and saw him dodge back to safety again. "Sooner or later, one of them is going to make it across. In fact, if you'll take a look through your binoculars, you'll see another about to try it again."

Travis took the rifle from Jimmie's hand. "Let me take care of this." He lay on his stomach by the opening of the mine shaft, then placed the cross hairs of his telescopic sights directly in the center of the man's chest. "Wilson my boy, you're about to get a quick lesson in Special Forces training."

Chapter Fourteen

Travis concentrated, then slowly lowered his aim to the rifle Wilson carried beneath his arm. Hitting the stock that protruded only inches behind Wilson's waist would be tricky. Yet, it would be an apt demonstration and a clear warning to him and the others.

Calculating the wind speed and the distance, he held his breath, and holding himself perfectly still, squeezed the trigger. The first bullet shattered the wooden stock of the rifle into pieces and knocked the weapon clear out of Wilson's hands. Travis zeroed in on the rifle, now on the ground, and fired again. The rifle spun in the dirt like a compass needle gone awry. By the time it stopped, the semiautomatic was nearly in two pieces.

Wilson lay flat on his stomach, hands over his head as if they could somehow deflect a bullet. Travis sent one more round mere inches from his opponent's prone body, then stopped.

After a moment's hesitation, Wilson leaped up and dived hastily behind a large boulder.

"That'll give them something to think about," Travis said with grim satisfaction.

"You certainly can shoot," Bowman observed with respect. "Sniper training?"

Travis nodded. "It seems a long time ago, but I'm finding out that I've retained all kinds of skills from my days in the Special Forces." He kept watch on the area below. As

another of the men tried to crawl forward, Travis zeroed in
on his target and sent a round to a point just in front of the
man's head. "The only shots they consider warning enough
are those that are inches from a vital organ," he commented. He pressed his lips into a tight line. "We're going
to need a new plan."

"You're able to position your shots exactly where you
want them." Jimmie gave Travis a long look. "Why don't
you shoot to kill? You must know that's what they'll do to
you at the first opportunity."

"I could have taken Wilson out with a well-placed shot,"
he conceded, "but that wouldn't have solved our problem.
Robertson already views me as a dangerous opponent. Had
I killed Wilson, he would have been convinced that it was
only a matter of time before I picked off the rest of them.
That would have forced him to throw everything he had at
us. Since, at the moment, I'm not quite sure what that in-
cludes, I didn't want to chance it."

"He won't risk killing my uncle," Belara pointed out.

"I agree, but he knows I'll do whatever is necessary to
make sure neither of you are harmed. He might decide to
manipulate the situation so I'm forced to confront him. I'm
sure he believes getting me out of the way permanently is
only going to improve his odds of catching both of you."

"He'd be right. Your fighting skills are much fresher
than mine, and your youth gives you a definite advantage," Jimmie said.

"So what next?" Belara asked.

Travis used the scope to survey the area ahead. "We'll
have to play for time. We need a very firm plan before we
can risk making an escape from this canyon. At the moment, it's our best line of defense."

Belara placed a hand on Travis's shoulder. "Let me take
the sniper position for a while. They probably won't be
trying anything soon and you need a chance to relax. I'll use
my uncle's rifle since it's easier to handle. We can save your
more lethal one for real emergencies." She placed a small

box of .22 caliber shells beside her, then lay on her stomach facing the pass.

Travis stood back out of view and stretched his muscles. "When we're really going to have problems is after it gets dark. For a while before the moon comes up, it's going to be hard to guard that pass."

"We should set up a barricade," Jimmie suggested. "There's some old barbed-wire fencing near the ranch house. We could get the rolls and tangle them across that area."

Travis nodded. "If we could also collect some tin cans, we could make trip-wire sensors. Then, even if it's cloudy, we'll hear them coming. We'll have to move in closer to that rocky ledge, though. The barricade will slow them down, but we'll need gunfire to keep them at bay. From our present position there's an entire section we can't cover."

"I know of a place that would work out for us, but it's a rough climb," Jimmie said slowly. "There's a shallow cave, not much more than a hole in the canyon wall, about a quarter of a mile east from here. It's partway up a rocky slope, right below a large stand of piñons. The route there will take you past the area where the barbed wire is. You two could drag the coils with you while I coax the horses along. By the time you finish setting up the barricade and join me, I should have managed to get the horses safely inside the cave. That's going to be the hardest part, I think. They're not going to like a space as confined as that one."

"Can we cover their eyes?" Travis asked.

"Not for very long. That'll only make them even more skittish and less surefooted."

"Is there another vantage point we could use that'd be easier on the animals?" Travis asked.

The older man considered it. "Not that I know of," he said at last. "That particular cave is ideal for us. We'll be able to guard the pass in relative safety, protected by the rock sides, and completely out of sight." He paused for a moment. "I know the two horses I've brought along. As long as one of us holds on to their reins, I think they'll be able to handle it. What we can't do is leave them tied up. If we do, they'll probably try to bolt and end up injuring themselves."

"When should we leave our position here?" Belara asked. "If we wait too long we'll lose the light and our advantage guarding the pass. But if we try to move now and we're detected, we won't be in a position to fire at them and stop them from coming through."

"I've already considered that," Travis said. "You two are going to have to go ahead and start setting up the barricade. I'll cover you from here. Then, after nightfall, I'll come join you."

Jimmie pursed his lips. "You won't be able to find your way there easily after dark...I will. It makes more sense for both of you to go on ahead. I'll bring the horses along after you're in position, and join you." He took a deep breath and let it out slowly.

Belara's eyes narrowed as she studied him closely. "Are you all right?" she asked gently.

"I'm not ill, but I am tired. These men who've followed you bring disruption and evil with them. I have to work very hard not to let them destroy the harmony I've found within myself. Unless I'm successful, even the white doctor's medicine you brought me won't work for long."

"I understand what you're saying," Travis mentioned, "but don't discount the value of the pills. They might help you get through a time when there is nothing but inharmony around you."

Jimmie nodded slowly. "You've made a good point. Now please stop worrying. If I need them, I'll use them. I'm not about to jeopardize all our lives by allowing myself to become incapacitated." He took his rifle from Belara's hand. "The sun will set soon. You better get ready to go. I'll meet with you later."

Travis peered through his binoculars. "I don't see any sign of Robertson or the others. I think they've decided to come up with another plan. After what happened to them last time, I doubt they'll come out into the open before nightfall.''

"If they do, I'll be here. Once I fire a few rounds, they'll probably back off again until it's completely dark. They won't know you're no longer here with me," Jimmie said, turning to Travis, "and they're not about to risk having you use them for target practice."

Travis switched rifles with him. "You keep mine. I'll take the .22 with me. Your niece and I will be closer to the pass, and this will be very accurate at that range."

"Once you're in position, fire two shots in rapid succession. I'll recognize the sound of my rifle. Its high-pitched crack is very distinctive when compared to the sound of the weapons the others have. Then I'll ride out one of the horses and lead the other."

"We'll keep them busy until you reach us," Travis said. "They won't even have a chance to notice your approach."

"Before you go," Jimmie said slowly, "I'd like to ask the gods to bless both of you." He glanced at Travis, waiting for his response.

"We can use all the help we can get," Travis said quietly. "I'd consider it an honor to be included in your prayers."

Jimmie nodded, and began the *hozonji,* the Song of Blessing, in a low tone. Opening a small pouch, he took some of the pollen inside, placed it on the tip of his tongue and the top of his head. Then, with a loud invocation, he tossed the rest toward the heavens. "The gods have been appeased," he assured them with a smile. "All will be well," he said. Then he returned to his position by the front of the mine shaft.

Travis glanced at Belara. "This has got to be fast," he warned. "Even more so than anything we've done so far. To make sure we aren't spotted, we'll have to go down into the canyon, right through the ravine, then climb up through thick brush. There's no telling how long it'll take us to find the cave, particularly in the half light."

"We better get started then," Belara said strapping on her pack.

Travis gave her a long look. "Remember that we're a team. If you're in trouble or need to slow down, tell me. This is no time for games. The stakes are too high."

"I'll keep up," she assured. "And if I can't, go on without me and I'll join you as soon as I can. That barricade needs to be set up."

"No, we'll stay together." As they began scrambling down the slope at the rear of the mine shaft, Travis took the lead.

"You said this was a partnership. Teammates take advantage of each other's strengths to minimize weaknesses," she countered, brushing away strands of hair the breeze tossed against her face. "If you can get there faster, then you should. But I plan to keep up. You're not going to be able to jog your way across this mess of bramble. The land itself will dictate how fast we can go."

"You're right about that," Travis replied in a whisper. They entered the winding canyon and began to work their way toward the ranch house. The ground was loose and sandy, making walking difficult. Down in the low area it was almost pitch-black.

"At some point, the stream must have run through here. It's too deep to account for any other way," Travis commented softly.

As they hurried along, trying to stay well within the shadows, Travis listened for signs that would indicate what Robertson and the others were doing. No shots had been fired for quite a while. Then again, it wasn't completely dark yet.

Belara glanced behind her, then gasped as she saw the dense cloud of smoke beginning to obscure the rising moon. "Surely they aren't thinking of burning us out of here. The grasses aren't dry enough to catch."

"I hadn't expected this," Travis said, his hand clenched in white-knuckled tightness around the .22 rifle. "No, they're not trying to drive us out. They've thrown some brush into the path and set fire to it. They're hoping to hide their passage into the canyon behind clouds of smoke.''

"My uncle won't be able to see them, so they'll get through. They'll head straight for the mine and cross the ravine on their way." She met his eyes, her stomach knotting painfully. "With all the brush that's down in here, they'll be right on top of us before we can spot them."

His eyes were alive with determination. "Don't count us out yet," he said, his voice as cold as ice. "There're a few tricks in my bag still. Let's hurry."

Belara glanced back and saw the billowing white smoke thickening in the pass. Slowly the breeze that had been barely noticeable before began to pick up. In a matter of a few minutes, strong gusts flew through the canyon, lifting the cloud of smoke and funneling it back through the pass to the other side. To enter the small, stone clearing now would leave the intruders completely in the open, exposed by the full moon.

Travis glanced toward the cloudless sky in surprise, then looked at her. "Winds like that usually precede a storm, but there's no weather front around. And it's not moving in a circular motion, like a dust devil. Where did that come from?"

"My uncle," she whispered in awe. "His father was a powerful *hataalii,* a medicine man, who taught him many things. He always did say my uncle was quite gifted, and it was a shame that he chose a different path."

Travis stared at her, then back at the spot where Jimmie Bowman lay in his hiding place. He wasn't sure what to believe. He would have felt more comfortable perhaps attributing the whole thing to coincidence. Yet that wind *had* come up at just the right time.

"Let's not waste the Wind People's gift to us," she said with a ghost of a smile. "The coils of barbed wire we came for are straight ahead. I can see one now. Let's pick up what we need and get going."

"If you can get the empty ration cans your uncle left behind, pick them up, too. I can make good use of them."

The grayness of dusk finally metamorphosed into velvet darkness as they continued toward the pass. Faint rays of starlight probed the dark recesses of the earth, providing only enough illumination to make their passage possible. Travis and Belara approached their destination carefully. There was no sign of the intruders, and a steady breeze continued to blow away the smoke from the smoldering brush.

"The smoke is going to be more of an advantage to us than it ever was to them," Travis observed. "They'll have to stay well back in order to breathe, and in the meantime, it'll shield us as we set up the barricade."

They worked quickly. Belara placed a few pebbles in each of the cans they'd gathered at the ranch house while Travis positioned the barbed wire in large, closely spaced coils. The gloves Travis had taken from his pack tore as they became tangled in the sharp, rusty prongs, and he had to finish the job using the ones Jimmie Bowman had loaned Belara.

Together they positioned the cans so they dangled from the wire like bells. An intruder would find it impossible to tamper with the wire without rattling one or more of the cans.

As shots rang out from the mine behind them, Travis gave her a quick half smile. "Your uncle's making sure we're not disturbed. Now it's our turn to find that cave and give him some cover fire."

The rugged hillside seemed filled with pockets of loose rock that made footing precarious. By the time they finally reached the cave, Travis noted that the last of the smoke had cleared. Moonlight streamed into the pass from almost directly overhead, making even shadows impossible. Travis lay in the cavernous opening, shielded by the darkness. "Your uncle was right. From here it'll be easy to zero in on targets."

"With that barricade in place, they're not going to be able to do much to us. Those rolls are so tightly coiled that cutting through them would take hours and they won't risk standing in the open that long. If they try, a few rounds should convince them they're making a mistake."

Travis held his binoculars steady and scoured the area behind them. "I can't see any signs of your uncle. Maybe I should go back and make sure he's okay."

Belara shook her head. "No, not yet. Even though he's leading the horses, he'll know how to blend in with the shadows. We used to play games of hide and seek when I was younger, and no matter how hard I tried, I was never able to find him. Sometimes he'd be standing only a few yards from me, and I'd still miss him."

Travis thought back to the unexpected winds that had come to their aid. "I don't doubt that he's a very complex man, but remember as long as we have Robertson's men to contend with, none of us can stand completely alone. Your uncle is going to need our help now more than ever. Don't rob him of that by seeing too much in him."

"Seeing too much in whom?" A voice came from behind one of the large boulders that covered the slope.

Travis jumped, his rifle automatically swinging in the direction of the sound. "Halt!"

"It's just me, son," Jimmie assured him. "The horses are getting a little nervous so, if you don't mind, we're coming up to join you. I just thought I'd let you know I'm here."

Travis found his voice. "Yeah, sure, come up." Bowman certainly had an edge on anyone Travis had seen when it came to moving silently.

Jimmie led the horses inside, then handed the reins to his niece. "Before you ask, I'm doing very well. It's all a matter of pacing." He saw the look on Travis's face and began to smile. "You've made the same mistake my niece has. To see someone clearly and judge what they're capable of, you first have to get your own preconceptions out of the way." He crouched by the opening, and glanced outside. "We'll need a new plan soon," he warned, trading Travis's rifle and ammunition for his own weapon.

"I've been studying the layout of the canyon, trying to come up with one, but so far, I don't like the choices we have." Travis gestured toward the ravine. "It's possible to use the ropes and climb out of the gorge at night, only if we do, we won't be able to take the horses. Without them, we'd have to force ourselves to maintain a very fast pace. It's a foregone conclusion that Robertson and his men will be right behind ready to hunt us down," Travis cautioned.

Jimmie nodded. "You're right. Finding a straggler wouldn't be hard for a good tracker, either, and they must have someone in their group who's very skilled if they've trailed you."

Belara smiled, hidden in the shadows. "That's probably the understatement of the year. He did everything possible to throw them off our trail."

"I can believe that," Jimmie replied. "You see, I haven't underestimated you," he added.

"The military will be making flights over this area, sooner or later. We could build a bonfire and get their attention," Belara suggested, looking up.

"It would work, but there's another danger," Jimmie answered her. "These men who've followed you would realize that their time had run out. They've expended a great deal of energy to get this far, so I don't think they'll just give up and leave, military planes overhead or not. It's more likely that they'd rush our position in a last-ditch effort, and then there would be some killings."

Belara sighed softly. "You're probably right."

Jimmie took the reins from her hand, then gestured to the front of the cave where Travis was standing, keeping watch. "Why don't you take over for him? The man needs a break."

"I'm all right," Travis assured.

"No doubt," Jimmie agreed. "And we want to make sure you stay that way."

Travis grinned. The man had a will of iron that could rival his own. He was beginning to see where Belara's tenacity had come from. "I think I'm really in trouble now. All

I need is two of the world's most stubborn people ganging up on me.''

Belara laughed softly. "I'm so glad you're aware of your limitations. By the way, we do have one option you haven't mentioned. We could shoot our way out of this canyon, and then make a run for it.''

"We're outnumbered," Jimmie answered from the darkness. "If it comes to that, we'll handle it, but let's not make that alternative really high on the list. We just haven't come up with the right—''

"We've got trouble," Belara interrupted. A second later, one of the cans rattled as the wire blocking the path began to shake.

Chapter Fifteen

Belara sighted carefully and squeezed the trigger as Travis dived to the ground beside her, rifle in hand. "For someone who can't shoot," he whispered, "that was remarkable. You hit right where Halliday was going so he had to back off."

"Just lucky," she said, squeezing off another shot. This one impacted directly above Wilson's head showering him with rock chips. He quickly backed out of sight. "I'm having all sorts of luck today."

Travis gave her a long sideways glance, then looked back at the barricade. "Robertson's a fool if he thinks he can go through that barbed wire with his bare hands." He watched, conserving his ammunition. "Here comes Perea to see if he can help. He's about to learn that his skin isn't any tougher than anyone else's."

Jimmie crouched beside them on one knee, squinting to see. "They certainly are persistent. If we allow them to stay there, eventually they'll manage to work that barbed wire loose."

"You're right. It's time to send them packing," Travis said.

"I'll do it," Belara suggested. With two well-placed shots that struck only inches from each man, she sent them scurrying back down the pass behind cover.

Jimmie touched her on the shoulder. "When did you acquire so much skill? You've never been able to hit your target as long as I've known you."

"I dislike shooting," she answered honestly. "Trying your patience by never showing much aptitude seemed the best way to avoid it."

"Not to mention making sure you were the one to round up the horses," her uncle muttered.

Trying to suppress a smile, she handed her uncle the rifle, then backed away from the opening. "It's your turn."

She heard the men mumbling to one another as she stood in the shadows, grinning. She couldn't help but wonder how her uncle felt knowing that he'd underestimated her as well.

As her gaze drifted over the horses, her eyes fastened on the heavy saddlebags that had been secured to the lead horse. Her uncle had always traveled light. The weight and shape of the bulging leather pouches filled her with curiosity. She knew of his personal reasons for coming to the Range, but was it possible Travis and Robertson had been right? The others were occupied, at least for now. It was time to find out once and for all if her uncle was out here doing a job for the military.

She again considered asking him directly. But if he *was* working for the Army, he probably wouldn't tell her. She'd have to find out on her own. The time for secrets was over. They were all out here, risking their lives. Noiselessly she approached the gelding's side.

She patted the animal's neck, then began searching through the contents of the saddlebags. The small metal disk she found first looked oddly familiar. A moment later she discovered a folded handle and a battery and realized that she'd found the main components of a metal detector. As she glanced toward the men, she saw her uncle's gaze rested on her.

"Why must you suddenly show so little respect for the property of others?" he asked, his voice hard. "What exactly are you searching for, niece?"

Belara squared her shoulders. "It's time to put an end to secrets, Uncle. You came here for more than personal reasons. I've heard others claim the Army hired you to do or find something. This metal detector in your bags seems to confirm it. Don't you think we deserve to know the truth?"

"If what the men shooting at us want is to go after the gold in Victorio Peak, that has nothing to do with my mission."

"Okay, I'll accept that, but there are two others out there, also armed. They are still a mystery. All we know for sure about them is that they're probably the same men who attacked me before I came looking for you, and that, if so, one of them has some kind of tattoo on his wrist," she said, explaining the events behind that knowledge briefly. "Until we know who they are and what they want, we have to assume they pose a very real threat. This man and I—" she gestured toward Travis "—have risked our lives willingly to get here to help you. We deserve your complete trust."

Jimmie considered Belara's words for a few moments. Finally he glanced up. "You've made your point, niece, and I agree. The information won't do you much good, but there's no reason to keep it from either of you." He sat near the entrance, facing the pass, and relieved Travis from his post as sentinel. "The Army contacted me because of my knowledge of this area. About six weeks ago, an older model Soviet photo reconnaissance satellite of the Cosmos series malfunctioned. The mechanism deployed a film capsule at the wrong time. Tracking equipment narrowed the probable touchdown point to the area surrounding Victorio Peak. The Soviet government, in the new spirit of *glasnost,* notified us through secure diplomatic channels. They would like the capsule back and our government agreed to conduct a search for it. There was an intensive, classified search just after the device was supposed to have landed, but nothing was found. They sent aircraft with electronic sensors out, but the mountainous terrain is filled with downdrafts this time of year. It made low-level reconnaissance extremely hazardous. One of the search planes crashed and two Army crewmen were killed."

"We came upon the crash site on our way here," Travis said. "I wondered about that, once I realized what type of aircraft that was."

"The crash created all kinds of problems for the Army, which was responsible for the search efforts," Jimmie explained. "The flurry of activity surrounding the search and the subsequent accident, attracted the press like bees to honey. Base officials were ordered to do whatever was necessary to suppress the real story. They stonewalled, claiming it was all a routine exercise, and slowly it blew over. By that time, though, they were afraid to do anything that would alert the press and rekindle public interest. Although the search had to be continued, they were determined to keep it low-key. They'd already tried the high-tech approach, so they decided to do something different. That's where I came into the picture."

"I imagine you jumped at the chance to return to the ranch," Belara observed.

"Yes, I did. I was also eager to do the job. I knew I could find the canister, given enough time, and I figured it would be a fairly pleasant task for me. I never expected to encounter any trouble. Both governments were cooperating on the search, and the press didn't know anything about it."

"Wait a minute. If you're out here on a job for them, you must have a field radio. We could use it to call for help," Travis said.

Jimmie gave them an apologetic look. "I didn't bring one because I figured the Army would be the ones doing all the calling. I'd never be able to get anything done then. That's the same reason why I don't have a telephone at home." He glanced at Belara. "Tell me more about the tattoo you saw on the man. Maybe that'll give us a clue."

Belara shrugged. "I've told you all I remember. I think it has a little red star in the corner, outlined in gold, but I only caught a flash of it, so I wouldn't swear to it."

"The Russians are the ones most noted for red stars outlined in gold," Travis observed.

"Yes, but that doesn't make any sense. They've been in on the details of the official mission right from the start. They wouldn't launch a covert operation at the same time, that would only complicate something they want to keep as simple as possible." He gave his niece a curious glance. "You remember seeing colors. Think back and try to tell me about shape."

She closed her eyes and tried to imagine it. "I can see only one small section and it seemed rectangular, or maybe square."

"Like a flag?"

"Maybe," she answered with a helpless shrug. "I can't tell you any more." As Belara started to say more, the whine of ricocheting bullets filled the sky above them. Several rounds hammered into the canyon walls, deflecting and continuing in an erratic path through the piñons.

Travis dived for the ground, then joined Jimmie at the opening. "Where are they?"

"I can't see them," Jimmie answered, holding his rifle steady and searching the area with the scope. As the flash of a muzzle sparked against the night, he sighted in.

Travis placed a hand on the older man's shoulder. "No, don't return fire. They're just working off a little steam. It's nuisance sniping. They can't hope to hit anything from where they're at except by accident. They're too far behind the barricade. Let's not waste our ammo."

Another hail of bullets slammed into the rocks around them, forcing their heads down. "Hold on to the horses," Jimmie warned. "They're going to get nervous."

Belara stood in the shadows at the back. "They already are. I've bribed them with a bit more grain, but it's not going to work for long."

"It better, because we won't be able to get out of here anytime soon. I have a feeling they're going to keep this up," Travis called back.

"What do they think they're going to accomplish?" Belara asked sarcastically. "Sooner or later, they'll run out of ammunition, too."

"We have no way of knowing how much they brought with them," Travis countered. "My guess is they're hoping to force us to give up. Our water isn't going to last long if we can't replenish it."

The hours of night passed, and the random gunfire continued to keep them pinned to the ground and wide-awake. The horses pawed at the ground restlessly, becoming increasingly hard to handle. Slowly the sky began to lighten as dawn grew near.

"Maybe the time has come to strike a compromise with them," Jimmie said at last. "We do have some leverage. They probably want me to lead them to all the mine shafts and cave openings around the Peak where gold could be hidden. Without my help, they could be out there for months, and never be sure they hadn't missed half of them. I can agree to take them wherever they want, if they'll let you two go."

"There's no way I'm going to go anywhere without you," Belara countered staunchly. "We escape together, or not at all."

Travis nodded. "I agree with her. You'd be signing your own death warrant. Once they finished looking, successfully or not, they'd kill you. Then, they'd come after us."

"You'd still gain some time," Jimmie countered.

"I don't care," Belara answered, her hands tight around the reins that held each of the horses. "We can't allow them to lower us to the point where we're willing to barter your life for ours."

Travis glanced at Jimmie. "Your niece is right. This is a time when we need to stand together."

Jimmie nodded in assent, then moved back to take his turn at calming the horses. As he took the reins, several more rounds exploded against the rock face not far from the entrance. "We'll have to come up with something soon. I'm not sure how much more of this the animals will take."

Travis reached for his binoculars, and carefully focused on the activity below. "We're going to have to use up more of our ammunition to warn them off. Since we have more .22 shells than ammo for my rifle, I'll use yours," he said, glancing at Jimmie for permission.

Belara lay on her stomach and peered toward the path. "What on earth are they doing?"

"They've decided to gamble on a new idea. They're carving handholds in the side of the cliff so they can climb up and go over the wire," Travis said. He took a deep breath, his finger settling securely on the trigger.

For a moment he sighted in on Perea's chest. The temptation to meet his adversary's offensive with all his lethal knowledge and training was great. Had it only been him out here, he might have accepted the challenge. He was tired of having to hold back.

"Your aim is sure. Perhaps it is time to make each shot count," Jimmie said quietly, as if reading Travis's thoughts.

"I am capable of killing a man," Travis said in a deadly quiet voice. "Yet at this stage, I believe it would only make things rougher on both you and your niece. Something happens to a man when he faces an adversary in an all-or-nothing situation. Things would get out of control very fast, believe me."

"I've seen combat. I know what you're referring to," Jimmie answered.

"I'm not sure I do," Belara ventured.

"The heat of battle can distort things. Winning, not survival, is all that counts. It's what drives you. That rush can help a man when he has to fight, but it can also turn on him. It can take over and control him until he loses sight of himself," Travis said, his voice barely audible. "As long as they're not a direct threat, I won't use deadly force. What I might unleash will be far worse than what we're facing. I won't be part of the problem again."

Belara noted his tone. It was as if Travis was arguing with himself, not them. "What do you mean 'again'?"

He shook his head. "This isn't the time." He squeezed the trigger slowly. It would be one hell of a shot from here, particularly with a .22. He'd have to hit just above the handhold, and hope to discourage them from using it.

The shot cracked through the clear morning air, dropping a yard in elevation, but hitting its mark. He heard the man yelp and jump away, falling behind the barricade. "That should stop them for now. But my guess is that they'll just wait a while, then try again."

Belara remained on her stomach and surveyed the area below with Travis's binoculars. "I've got more bad news. The two men that have been trailing Robertson's group and us are now standing near the rise at the far end of the canyon." She handed Travis the field glasses. "You can make them out clearly in the morning light."

Travis studied the distant pair. "They're not coming up, at least. They're just camped there," he observed. "I think they're waiting to see what happens before they make their move." He shook his head. "I don't like this at all."

A burst of gunfire erupted again, forcing them to keep their heads down until the barrage ended. Belara was the first to glance up, moments after it was silent. "We've got to find out the status of Robertson's ammo. That'll tell us something about his plans, and give us some idea of what action to take."

"There's only one way to do that," Travis replied slowly.

"Right, and I'm the logical one to go and infiltrate their camp," Jimmie said staunchly. "If I get caught, I can go back to my original idea and try to negotiate for your freedom."

"That's not a good plan," Travis countered. "Remember your own words? You have to pace what you do. A mission like this one will require speed and endurance. You can't go into it depending on what you'll do when you fail.

"One of the biggest problems will be going over the barricade we set up. There's only one way to do it without alerting Robertson. You'd have to drop down off the ledge using a rope, and swing over to the other cliff side. At best, it'll be tricky. At worst, they'll spot you and use you for target practice."

"Then that leaves me," Belara answered. "If anyone gets used for target practice, I'm the smallest and most difficult to hit. Besides, since you're the best shot, you could provide cover for me."

"Wrong," Travis argued. "They'll be in a great position to aim at you, but I won't be able to hit them from this angle. The only way I can effectively cover you is if they come through the pass and approach the barricade again." He met Belara's gaze, then shrugged as if implying that circumstances had already decided the matter for them. "Logically I'm the one who should go. I can move faster and if one of the men spots me, I might be able to neutralize him before he could act. If not, I can still make it difficult for them. They'll be so worried about finding me to prevent me from ambushing them, their attention will be diverted away from you. Should it come to that, you two could even use the opportunity to make your escape. I could join you later."

"No. You can't go," Belara argued. "Robertson or Wilson would kill you without any hesitation. At least I can play for time."

"I disagree. If you're caught they'll use you as a hostage and get the rest of us anyway. If I get caught, it's a loss of one, not three."

"Acceptable losses?" Jimmie muttered.

Travis nodded. "Precisely."

"This might sound terribly reasonable to both of you, but your plan stinks," Belara said, glaring at Travis.

"Do you have a better one?"

She looked away, searching her brain.

Travis handed her his rifle. "Take over for me. I'm going to try to get some sleep. We'll take turns resting during the day, then I'll make my move soon after sunset, before the moon comes up. That will give me the advantage of being able to blend into the shadows."

Belara glanced at Travis as he curled up in the darkest corner of the shallow cave. The gunfire had stopped and for the moment the desert was silent. Even the birds had flown away, searching for haven elsewhere. Not wanting to disturb Travis, her uncle and she refrained from speaking until his breathing evened, signifying he'd fallen asleep.

As the horses relaxed, Jimmie hobbled them. Then he silently moved toward her. "The man has a great deal of courage."

"He'll need more than that to stay alive, but I don't know how to help him."

"You could stop letting him see that you fear for his safety," Jimmie answered simply. "That can undermine his self-confidence."

She nodded. "You're right, but it's difficult. I care what happens to him. He's shown both of us a great deal of loyalty. He's here because I came."

"I know, and you came because of me. We're all linked in this, but you can't assume responsibility for the decisions he made any more than I can for yours. What we *can* do is use the knowledge of the *Dinéh* to compel the spirits to help him. We can add to his strength by calling on powers he knows nothing about. Our songs and rituals have allowed us to survive and become the largest tribe in the nation. Don't underestimate their value."

"I've seen you do many things that I've never been able to explain, but I'm not like you. I feel more comfortable taking direct action."

"Action takes many forms. Your unwillingness to recognize more than one kind is the reason your prayers fail," Jimmie admonished softly.

Many hours later, after the sun began to sink over the horizon, Travis stirred. This was the end of his second shift and he'd been able to get more sleep than he'd expected. The day had been uneventful, with neither side doing much more than keeping watch.

Jimmie watched him pensively. "You slept some today, but you didn't rest much."

"It's time for me to get ready," Travis said, studying the fading light outside the cave. "If I'm not back within two hours, assume I've been caught. Providing you haven't made your escape by then, your best bet will be to build a large fire. Hopefully the ammunition will last until Range security comes by to check."

"Which of the rifles do you want to take with you?" Belara asked.

"Neither. It wouldn't do me much good down there to have one. I'd be outgunned and chances are I won't be able to find a solid defensive position. You two can at least hold your own using them from up here. I'll be far better off taking a knife and relying on stealth."

"I'll keep watch. If anyone comes into view while you're crossing over, I'll fire," Belara assured him. "If I'm not in a position to hit anything, at least I can make them worry. Between my uncle and I, you'll have as much support as possible."

"Wish me luck," Travis said, going toward the cave entrance.

"We'll do more than that," Jimmie answered. "We'll work to see that you have it."

Travis moved out of the cave in a crouch, calling upon all his training and experience. He knew he needed to concentrate solely on the task ahead, but wrenching Belara from his thoughts wasn't easy. The concern in her eyes had filled him with intense emotions. He figured his chances of returning in one piece were fifty-fifty at best. Yet even if he did get caught, he was fairly certain he'd achieve some success. It was possible he'd be able to slow Robertson and his men down long enough to give Jimmie and Belara a chance to escape. Still, he couldn't help but wonder if he'd be in any shape afterward to join them.

When he reached the pass, Travis felt the hairs at the back of his neck stand on end. He knew Belara and Jimmie could probably see him by now against the cliff side, but Robertson was the one who concerned him most. He searched the shadows for his enemies. If the men discovered him this close to their position, they'd blow him away for sure. One thing weighed in his favor: they wouldn't be expecting him to come across. Putting the threat of danger out of his mind, he forced a piton into a horizontal crack in the rock, and secured it.

He swung around and reached the other side moments later. In a low crouch, knife in hand, he slipped into the brush. Travis moved cautiously toward the area he suspected the men would use as a campsite. He felt the coolness of the rocks as he crept around them, drawing closer to the low voices just ahead. So far, so good. He didn't want to get caught, just eavesdrop and take a good look at their supplies.

Peering around the base of a boulder at the circle of rocks ahead, Travis confirmed the location of Robertson's camp. Robertson was there, and all his men were accounted for, sitting comfortably in the shadows. Travis narrowed his eyes as he studied the one closest to him. All he could see was the man's back, but there was something peculiar about him. He seemed too still and his posture was unnaturally rigid. Travis shifted a little to his left, angling for a better look. Suddenly he knew he'd walked into a trap.

Chapter Sixteen

Belara used the hunting scope mounted on Travis's rifle. With its extra-light-gathering power, she could study the area below. "I've lost sight of him," she said. "I'm going down the slope where I can see through the pass and try to monitor his progress."

"You'll only make yourself a target in the moonlight. Don't give the man something else to worry about."

"I won't," Belara replied, giving her uncle the rifle. "My skills are better than that. You should know, you taught me."

Jimmie stared at his niece silently for a moment, then nodded. "You have a point. Do what you have to."

Belara moved quickly, careful to stay in the shadows or behind cover. Brush was scarce in spots, forcing her to change directions often and work hard to remain inconspicuous. Finally she reached a position above the cave where both the angle and altitude gave her a full view of the pass. Through the binoculars, she could see Robertson's camp clearly.

She checked the gathering around Robertson's campsite and saw the four men sitting with their backs to the rocks. Their rifles lay beside them. From the looks of it, they were taking a break.

Travis had to be around there somewhere. She searched the immediate area with methodical precision and finally spotted a flicker of movement. Travis was on his stomach, crawling toward the group. A line of low rocks hid him from their view. Relief flooded over her, then instantly vanished as she glimpsed something in the bushes behind him.

Desperately she tried to focus on the form, but all she could make out were shadows. Something was stalking Travis, and she was too far away to warn him! Her skin went clammy as fear plowed through her.

She shifted the binoculars back to the men at the camp. All four were there. It didn't make sense, unless the pair who'd been far behind had managed to sneak up on Robertson. If that was the case, then Travis was about to get caught in the middle with no chance of escape!

Belara struggled to identify the vague, outlined form behind Travis and saw a flash of metal in the glow of the moon. Whoever was there had drawn his knife.

Travis needed help and fast, but from this distant observation point there was little she could do. Her chances of hitting a target from here were virtually nil. It was far more likely that a wild shot would alert Robertson and the others and place Travis in even greater danger.

Ignoring caution, Belara moved quickly back to the cave. As she approached, she saw the surprised look on her uncle's face. "I'm going after our friend," she said, explaining the situation. "The moment he defends himself, he'll alert Robertson and the others. Alone, he doesn't stand a chance."

"What can you possibly do?"

"I can create a diversion and distract the other men so that he will have an opportunity to get away. Maybe you can go where I just was and cover me using his rifle. I'll take your .22 with me."

"And how will you escape once their attention is focused on what you're doing?" Jimmie countered, shaking his head. "It's a foolhardy plan."

"I'll get away, don't worry. I'll buy him a few minutes, and then he'll find a way to do the same for me. We've worked well as partners before. I can't desert him now, Uncle."

"Then I should go with you," Jimmie said flatly.

"No, Uncle, I need you up here. Once they start firing on my position, you'll have to give me some cover until he can help me. There's an area above the cave that'll give you an ample view of Robertson's camp. You'll have to position yourself there once I clear the barricade." She glanced at the horses. "I think the animals will be fine, since any return fire shouldn't be aimed at the cave."

Jimmie's eyes focused on her. "You care deeply for this man," he said thoughtfully. "You've made a good choice."

"He's been a loyal friend to both of us," she defended. "You've always taught me to honor those obligations. Don't start seeing more than that in our relationship. He's not Navajo, and when I choose a husband, it'll be someone from our tribe."

"Not if you've already fallen in love. You won't adapt to the demands of a relationship if your heart isn't in it. You're too much of a free spirit, niece. You've never been one to tolerate a situation that goes against what you really want."

She placed the equipment she'd need into the pockets of her webbed belt. "I can't think about this now, Uncle. There's another job I've got to do. Too much is going on in the present for me to think about the future."

"You're right." Jimmie lay by the opening of the cave. "I'll be here until you clear the barricade, then I'll climb up above and watch over you." He paused. "And I'll sing a *hozonji* to the Slayer, the war god. He'll help you complete your task."

Belara tried to suppress the fear she felt as she left the safety of the cave. Moving quickly, she padded quietly across the canyon toward the pass. She'd almost reached the barricade when the moon came out from behind a cloud, outlining her clearly. Belara sprinted toward the rope Travis had left dangling from the piton. Where were Robertson and his men? They could have picked her off easily.

Brushing that thought aside, she looped the sling of the rifle over her head and across her chest. Belara stared at the thirty-foot drop that lay below her, swallowing convulsively. This was no time to lose her nerve. Concentrating on what she hoped to accomplish, she grasped the rope and stepped off the edge.

Belara began to swing to and fro, stretching her body upward toward the shelf on the other side. Her feet touched the narrow walkway an instant later, then slid off in a shower of loose stones. She tumbled off the shelf, and like the pendulum of a clock swung backward to where she'd started. Dangling in midair, her grip on the rope still firm, she choked back a sob of frustration. Damn Travis for making it look so easy!

She began to swing her body again, determined to make it. This time, she bent her body sharply at the waist angling her legs up like a child on a swing. A few long seconds later, she cleared the barricade and landed firmly on her buttocks with a loud slap.

Still struggling to catch her breath, she dived into the bushes, certain that gunfire was about to sweep the entire rocky path. Instead, everything remained calm. The hum of insects continued uninterrupted. Her skin prickled with alarm. Something was very wrong.

She worked her way toward Robertson's camp slowly and cautiously. Knowing they would be less likely to expect anyone to approach from the opposite side, she angled around. The brush was thick, making her flanking movement difficult, but providing her with cover.

As she passed the circle of rocks, she glanced at the seated figures and realized what Robertson had done. The fourth man was no man at all, but rather a dummy made out of carefully stuffed clothing. Suddenly the sound of a struggle erupted on the other side of the camp. Wilson appeared, then Travis came out of nowhere, tackling him. Travis pulled Wilson to his feet in front of the others.

She saw the knife in Travis's hand, then an instant later it was at Wilson's throat. "The rest of you get back, or

Wilson will be the first to go," Travis said, his tone icy and deadly.

Robertson laughed, his weapon pointed at Wilson's chest. "Don't you know I'd shoot right through my old buddy to get you, Hill? Now drop that knife and kick it away from you."

"Yeah, somehow I think you would," Travis observed without any particular emphasis. Without taking his eyes off Robertson, Travis released his grip on Wilson.

Wilson spun away, gasping for air, but his gaze was fastened on Robertson. Halliday stood well back, his rifle pointed at Travis. He looked at Wilson, then Robertson.

Travis set the knife down, then kicked it aside. "So now what? You want a one-on-one, or is murdering an unarmed man more your speed?"

Noiselessly, Belara pulled her rifle free. All she'd need was one clear shot. She sighted in, but from her angle and position the men were too close together, almost lined up with each other.

"I had you figured out right all along," Robertson boasted, ignoring Travis's challenge. "I knew you'd try something like this. You're the type who just has to try to be a hero."

"Well, if you've got to go, you might as well do it with style," Travis countered in a quiet voice.

"We'll try to oblige," Robertson said.

Belara tensed, then took aim at Robertson's back. As she began to squeeze the trigger, Robertson bent over to get the knife Travis had dropped. Belara released the trigger instantly. Another second and she would have shot Travis by mistake. Her mind recoiled at the thought and she swallowed back the bitter liquid in her throat.

Trying to recapture her courage, she watched as Robertson gestured to Wilson and Halliday. "Tie him up."

Halliday slung his weapon over his shoulder, and moved to help his companion.

Wilson came up from behind and grabbed one of Travis's arms as Robertson turned away. Reacting instantly,

Travis rammed the elbow of his other arm into the man's stomach. As Wilson doubled over, he brought the back of his fist up, slamming it against Wilson's nose. Halliday jumped back, scrambling to bring his rifle to bear. Perea moved aside, simultaneously reaching for his sidearm.

Robertson spun around and thumbed back the hammer of his gun. The ominous click reverberated around them. "You move another muscle, Hill, and you're a dead man. I'm not ready to kill you yet, but you're making it really easy for me to change my mind."

Wilson staggered back, blood pouring down his face. "You gonna pay for thid. You dthestroyed myd dose!"

"I think you need a speech therapist," Travis replied evenly.

Wilson reached for a small camp shovel, but Robertson pushed him back. "You can have him *after* I'm through with him," he snapped.

"He id no use," Wilson protested. "Shood him."

"No," Robertson replied. "I want to use him as bait to get the others. If it doesn't work, then he's history." Robertson moved behind Travis and forced him at gunpoint to return to their camp. "You're a real pain, Hill."

"I try to be."

"Just keep your hands locked behind your head, and don't give me any more reasons than I already have to kill you."

"All this for some gold that doesn't even exist. Face it, Robertson, you and your buddies are on a wild-goose chase. If there had been gold there, the Army would have found it years ago."

Robertson laughed heartily. "Is that what you think I'm after? I figured you were smarter than that. I'm not looking for gold. Never was. I'm interested in something much more valuable than that."

"There's nothing else out here except used ordinance. Don't tell me you're into metal salvage," Travis answered.

"Not quite." As they reached the camp, Robertson sat down on a rock facing Travis.

"Why don't you enlighten me," Travis baited as he started to sit on the ground.

"Freeze." Robertson's voice was deadly as he pointed his .45 pistol at Travis again. "You just stand there like a good boy and don't even twitch. I'm losing my patience with you."

"So, are you at least going to tell me what's out here that's worth your life?"

"I see no reason not to, I'm talking to a dead man. As soon as we get the old man or the woman down here, you're of no further use to us." He gave Travis a mirthless grin. "I think it's only fitting that you should know what you walked into. The stakes have been much higher than you ever suspected." He leaned back against his pack, but kept his gun aimed steadily at Travis. "You heard that there was a crash out here, not too long ago, didn't you?"

"Yeah, but so what? There're a half dozen or more plane crashes somewhere in New Mexico every year. If you're thinking about retrieving any electronic equipment from that airplane, forget it. Everything's been cleaned out. All that's left is a hunk of scrap metal."

Robertson clenched his jaw tightly. "I couldn't care less about the plane. My brother died aboard that hunk of junk. He told me all about the search the military was conducting the day before the crash. There's some kind of capsule of Soviet satellite film out here somewhere. It's top-secret stuff that's worth lots of money to the government. We're going to find it and make them pay through the nose."

"Your brother died serving his country. It seems to me you should show a little more respect for what he was trying to do."

"Raymond lost his *life* looking for that thing, and do you know what the military sent my family? A flag and a letter of condolence. He didn't even get a decent funeral. They wanted to avoid 'publicity.'" He curled his lips in disgust. "My brother was barely thirty and he died for nothing. The military owed him and his family more than just a letter saying how sorry they were. That's when I decided my friends and I should go find the capsule. Once we have it, we'll tell the Army I found it on my land near the Lincoln National Forest. Then I'll give them a choice: either they pay the price I'm asking, or the television networks get something to liven up the six o'clock news.''

''I hate to put a damper on things, but how do you plan to get Bowman down here? He's no fool. He barely knows me. He's not about to give himself up for my sake,'' Travis commented casually.

''I'll provide him with some incentive. I've been told I've got a creative side to my nature, Hill. I plan to use it to get what I want. Unfortunately it's going to be at your expense.'' His smile was mirthless and deadly. ''Don't worry. It shouldn't take too long. Bowman knows that sooner or later he has to come out anyway. If he has a soft heart, he'll join us in no time.''

Belara remained hidden in the shadows, listening. Robertson's tone made her shiver with revulsion and fear. She had to get Travis out of there now. Yet, if she shot directly at any of the men, they'd turn on her and Travis with a vengeance, concluding their own lives were at stake. The chances of Travis or her surviving a close-range battle against high-powered weapons were slim. There had to be another way to create the diversion she needed to help Travis.

A desperate idea flashed into her head. Out in the desert, water spelled life. She had to find their canteens. If she shot holes in those, they'd be forced to try to save as much of their supply as they could. That would divert their attention away from Travis and minimize the armed response against her.

Quietly she edged farther around the perimeter of the camp and located their gear. Their supplies were in four piles, including their canteens. Picking a spot where she was protected by some boulders, she began to shoot carefully at the water containers.

At the sound of the gunshots, Robertson and the others dived to the ground. Travis spun loose and scrambled away from the men as fast as he could. Belara smiled, in spite of the gravity of the situation, as she caught a glimpse of the rifle Travis now held in his hand. Next she fired a few rounds right over the heads of Robertson's men. Slipping in a new clip, Belara moved to a new position and shot more holes in their canteens. The men who were scrambling to retrieve their water had to dive for cover again.

Seconds later Travis reached her. "What are you doing here? You could have been killed!" His whispered words were darkly heated.

"Yes, but I was more afraid of what they'd do to you," she answered, struggling to sound calm.

Her simple candor melted away his anger. He swore under his breath, then reached for her hand. "Honey..." As gunfire from Robertson's group began to thump all around them, he pulled her down into the shelter of the rocks. "Go back. I'll hold them off."

"No," she answered simply. Positioning herself in good cover beside him, she began to fire back helping Travis keep the men pinned down. "We'll go back together. We can do it in increments. I'll keep them ducking while you go to a new hiding spot, then you shoot, covering me. Fair enough?"

"All right," Travis conceded. Belara's plan was safer for both of them, and since Robertson's men wouldn't be able to follow them far without canteens, there was no real reason why he needed to remain out here. The sooner Belara and her uncle were ready to start back, the safer they'd all be.

"You go first," Belara suggested. "You pick the spot, and I'll join you. You're more experienced at picking firing positions." She gave him a hesitant half smile.

"Finally a compliment." He smiled encouragingly at her. "At the moment, it doesn't make me feel any better." He handed her the semiautomatic rifle. "With this one all you have to do is pull the trigger, there's no bolt action to work.

Use it, I'll take yours. When you hear me fire, then come toward me."

"I'll be ready," she said, handing him her extra clip and a small box of .22 shells.

"Okay. Cover me," he said. He kept his head down and dodged quickly out among the rocks.

The military-style weapon he'd given her was easy to fire. Belara's biggest problem was not knowing how many rounds remained in the clip. She placed her shots carefully, pinning Robertson and the others farther down the hillside. Moments later, she heard the light crack of the .22 rifle behind her. Belara ran toward Travis's position as fast as she could, arriving at his side in seconds. They repeated the procedure twice more, gaining confidence with each successful attempt.

"The next lap is the pass," he said. "We'll have to swing across the barricade on the rope just like we did on the way here. This time, I want you to go first. Take the .22 with you because it has a sling. As soon as you're over, take a position behind the barricade, and cover me. We'll be out in the open as we're crossing, so whoever's providing cover has to force Robertson's group to keep their heads down."

As soon as Travis gave the signal, Belara ran down the narrow trail leading to the pass. Before she could reach the narrow cleft in the rocks, she saw her uncle's outline. He was standing behind two large boulders, the horses off to one side. He held the reins in his free hand, and Travis's rifle in the other.

"How..." she blurted then stopped.

"They were so worried about you two that they weren't paying attention to anything else. I knew it was time to take advantage of the situation. By the time shooting broke out, I had already worked one side of the barricade free. I swung it aside and led the animals quickly through the pass. I had to leave the pack saddle and most of the equipment, but this way we'll be on horseback while they're on foot. We'll make better time." He glanced behind her. "Where's our friend?"

"Waiting for covering fire," Belara answered. "Bullets are really flying back there."

Making sure they aimed high, Belara and Jimmie each fired several shots. Jimmie spotted movement first, and cautiously switched his aim toward the advancing figure. Recognizing Travis a second later, he lowered his rifle.

Travis ran up and stared at Jimmie in surprise. "I thought I heard *two* guns firing. How did you get past the barricade with the horses?" He looked at Jimmie, then shook his head. "Never mind. We'll get to that later. Right now, we've got to get moving before they regroup and advance up that slope."

Jimmie mounted the gelding. "Let me lead the way. I know the quickest way back to Range headquarters."

"We'll be right behind you," Travis answered, then glanced at Belara. "I haven't ridden bareback before. Do you want to ride in front and take the reins?"

She shook her head. "If you're in front, you'll have the mane to hang on to if you need it. An inexperienced rider can slide off the back very easily."

With a quick nod, Travis swung up onto the horse's back, then took the two rifles from her. Belara followed him a second later. "Ready," she said, after using the sling to settle the .22 on her back.

As they urged the horses farther down the mountain, Travis heard the whine of bullets hammering into the pass above them. Robertson's men were probably spraying the opening, thinking they were heading back to the cave. For the first time in a long while, he felt they might have a future to think about.

They came to a stop in front of a deep, dry arroyo with steeply sloped sides. "We'll have quite a scramble to the bottom," Jimmie said. "Don't worry about the horses, they can handle it."

"I'm not worried about the horses, I'm worried about us," Belara protested. "You've got a saddle to hang on to. We're riding double, bareback."

"Then get off the horse and give me the reins. I'll lead your mount in with me. You two can slide down. It won't be comfortable, but you won't break anything important." He grinned. "You can mount up again at the bottom."

"It's a good twelve feet, nearly straight down," she protested.

Travis took her hand and urged her down to the ground. "Come on. It isn't going to get any shallower by just staring at it."

Side by side, they made their slide to the bottom, keeping their weapons in front of them. Belara and Travis hurried to their feet to get out of Jimmie's way.

"This arroyo will lead down and around the Peak and out of the area completely," he said after rejoining them. "It's the safest way to go because they won't be able to see us. They'll eventually track us to this point but to follow us they'll have to come down here. The horses should manage quite easily, but if you'll notice, the bottom is very sandy here and walking is going to wear our pursuers out. If they decide to climb in and then back out, they'll be expending even more of their energy and time. We'll outdistance them easily."

Travis remounted the horse and gave Belara a hand up. "Robertson's not about to give up, and neither are the others. Don't underestimate the threat they still pose to us. Even without the rifle I stole, they've got plenty of lethal firepower. The rifle Perea has, for instance, is a heavy-barreled Remington, the kind snipers and SWAT teams use. Providing he has the skill to use it, he should be able to hit a target at almost a thousand yards. He hasn't used it yet. Perhaps he didn't bring much ammunition for it. But if he thinks we're getting away, count on his trying it. We've got to move at top speed, even if it means pushing the horses and ourselves to the limit."

They began loping through the sandy wash as quickly as they dared, maneuvering the tight corners carefully. Travis shifted uncomfortably as Belara's breasts rubbed against him in rhythm with the movement of the horse.

Trying to keep his mind alert to the dangers they still faced, he shifted his attention to Jimmie. They couldn't afford to tax his strength too much. If he became ill now, it might cost them their lives.

"Don't worry," Belara said, noticing he was watching her uncle. "Sitting on a horse for hours on end comes easy to him. He's been riding ever since he was a kid. It's his favorite pastime."

Jimmie guided his horse through an almost ninety-degree turn with an ease that neither Travis nor Belara could match. Belara's legs gripped the horse tightly as she fought to stay on without pulling Travis off balance. Instinctively Travis reached back, grabbing her thigh and steadying her with his hand. "Are you okay?" he asked gently.

"No problem," she answered, winding her arms tighter around him.

He felt the warmth and strength of her as she responded to his touch. For a moment he imagined what it would feel like to have her beautiful thighs wrapped around him. He shifted awkwardly, hoping no one else would notice his arousal in the darkness. Damnation, fate was certainly having a laugh on him. It was asking too much of a man to ignore the way Belara's softness brushed over him intimately from behind, yet that's exactly what he had to do.

"When in blazes are we going to get there?" Belara muttered to herself.

Travis smiled, suspecting the reason for her sudden impatience and irritability.

After a rough ten-minute ride, Jimmie slowed his mount. "We're almost to the end of the main wash," he said. "It's much simpler to get out than it was to get in, so you won't have to worry about that."

Travis could see the sides of the arroyo becoming lower, then finally merging with the large salt flats ahead. "I'll be glad to reach an area where we'll have more room to maneuver in case of an emergency. Tactically speaking, this isn't the ideal location for us."

"I know, but it was the fastest escape route I could think of." Jimmie glanced back at them. "How are you two doing?"

"We're fine. Just keep leading the way," Travis answered. He watched Jimmie carefully, but the older man seemed better off than he felt himself at the moment. His whole body seemed to have turned to fire. He almost groaned when Belara shifted against him.

Jimmie slowed his horse's pace. "The worst of it is behind us. There's no way they're going to catch up to us now." He patted his horse's neck. "Come on, old Bill. I know you still have quite a few miles in you."

Suddenly Jimmie saw his horse's ears prick forward and he felt the animal tense beneath him. "Something's up ahead," he warned, reining his horse to a quick stop.

Chapter Seventeen

Spotting moving shadows on the side of the wash, Travis pulled his own mount to an abrupt halt. The horse nearly reared. "Get down! Someone's—"

Before he could finish the sentence, bullets began to thud into the low sand and dirt walls around them. Travis followed Belara, jumping off the horse and ducking into a hollowed-out section of the arroyo wall. As he swung his rifle around, Belara grabbed the horse's reins tightly.

"Robertson couldn't have managed to get ahead of us!" Belara protested.

"It must be the other pair," Travis replied. "It looks like they cut across the countryside in order to ambush us here."

Bullets peppered the area in front of them, but hidden down in the arroyo and behind the small bend, they remained protected. Travis held his fire and checked the clip on the rifle he'd taken from Robertson. "I'm going to save these ten rounds for as long as I can. If they want us, they'll have to advance, and I intend to be ready."

"Robertson is going to hear the shots echoing down the canyon and figure out where we've gone," Jimmie warned. "When he gets here, we'll be caught between the two groups."

"From their position, I'd guess that these two guys have decided no one's leaving this area. Robertson's arrival might work to our benefit, as strange as that sounds. Once they're busy shooting it out with each other, we might get a chance to duck out of here. In the dark, no one's going to be sure who's firing at whom."

"I wonder if this pair wants me, too," Jimmie mused as the shooting started again, this time hitting the top of the arroyo above them.

"By the way, Robertson and his men weren't after gold," Travis told him. "They wanted the film canister, and thought you were their best chance of finding it."

"These two jokers are probably thinking along the same lines," Jimmie observed. "It looks like even if you two hadn't come along, I wouldn't have been able to spend the three weeks I wanted up here."

"What if we go back the way we came?" Belara suggested. "Once we're out of rifle range, we could get back on the horses and ride in a new direction."

"That would be great *if* we could get out of the canyon with the horses. But the places I remember seeing behind us were far too steep for that." Travis looked at Jimmie. "Am I right?"

Jimmie nodded. "Coming down back there was possible for the horses, but climbing back out is beyond their ability. The sides are too high."

"That sure narrows down our options. If all we did was retreat, we'd be closely followed by these two. And, to make things worse, we'd run into Robertson's people again," Belara commented.

"Right now we have to figure out a way to gain ground, not lose it." Travis leaned out around the bend to take a look, and was forced back by a hail of bullets.

Time dragged by. The men before them made one attempt to approach, but Travis's deadly aim sent them scurrying back. The stalemate continued.

"I better make sure they're still there," Travis said, after a ten-minute lull in the shooting. He took his tattered glove out of a jacket pocket, placed it on a stick, then held it out slowly as if he was reaching around the corner. A burst of rounds greeted it quickly. He pulled back the stick, noting the tips of two glove fingers were shorter than they had been before. "Well, they're still there."

As soon as it was quiet again, Travis checked behind them with the binoculars. "It looks like Robertson and the others are catching up. There's a small cloud of dust in the air about a quarter of a mile back down the arroyo."

"If we're going to make a move, we better make it now. If we get pinned here for any length of time we'll risk running out of ammunition," Belara said.

Travis pulled the pepper gas grenade from his pocket. It wasn't much, but it would have to do. "I've come up with a plan. I'm going to sneak back down the arroyo, climb out, and work my way around behind them. As soon as Robertson's closer, I'll throw this right in front of the two men who are blocking our way. The flash in the darkness should blind them temporarily and the gas will irritate their eyes further and give you more of a head start. You two take the opportunity to ride out of here as fast as you can. They'll be forced to deal with Robertson's group, too, before going after us." Travis checked Belara's watch, then adjusted his own to read the same. "In exactly six minutes, I'll set it off. Just make sure you don't look up. And remember to turn the horses away, too."

"How will you get away?"

"If need be, I'll shoot a few rounds to pin them down while you go by. Then, I'll meet you where the arroyo dumps out into the salt flats."

Belara gave Travis a worried look. "Splitting up isn't a good idea. We're going to need all of each of our skills to survive out here."

"We don't have a choice," he answered simply. "Ride like the wind, and I'll see you at the mouth of the arroyo," he said, looking at her as if memorizing her face.

Belara's stomach was in a knot as he moved off behind them and merged with the darkness in the wash. She'd never been one to believe in revenge, but if anything happened to him . . .

"He'll be all right, niece," Jimmie said, as if reading her thoughts.

Belara started to answer, but her throat felt too achingly tight to produce words.

The minutes passed slowly, with an occasional shot reminding them that the men were still out there above the arroyo, blocking their way. Belara mounted her horse and held the skittish animal against the sides of the dry arroyo, out of danger. Her uncle's horse responded to barely discernible cues and stood rock still. Belara felt the tension all through her body as they hunched down and waited for the grenade blast.

"Robertson's almost here. It won't be long before we'll have to fire to keep him back," Jimmie warned.

Belara felt her heart hammering against her sides. Time was running out. Just then a loud thud and a flash of light flooded the sky. "That's it! Go!" she said, and urged the animal for all the speed it could give.

Her uncle's horse, despite a heavier load, took the lead. She heard gunfire erupting directly behind her, and knew Robertson had begun his attack. Before the pair blocking their escape route could clear their vision, they managed to run past them. A burst of shots struck the ground well behind them as their attackers fired blindly at the sound of the horses' hooves.

Her uncle, settled low on his mount, looked back, checking for her. She gave him a nod. His face was drawn as fatigue and exertion took their toll. They'd have to stop soon to rest, but they'd need to get well away first and then find a secure place to hole up.

Reaching the bottom of the slope, Belara slowed her horse and looked around. Travis was nowhere to be found. Clutching the reins in a white-knuckled grip, she whirled the horse around frantically. Dread, numbing and total, filled her. She saw the alarm in her uncle's features, and thought for one terror-filled moment that she was going to be sick. The possibility that Travis had been wounded or perhaps worse was unbearable.

Suddenly Travis burst out of a cluster of thick brush, running low to the ground. "You went even faster than I expected. Good thing you decided to wait."

She fought the impulse to slide off the horse and run into his arms. "I thought..." Her voice cracked. Embarrassed, she averted her gaze.

Travis placed his hand over hers and gave it a gentle squeeze. "Didn't mean to worry anyone, but it's crazy back there. I used up all the ammo from the rifle I stole from Robertson, then I field stripped it and scattered the parts so it'll be useless to them. Robertson and his men have run into the same ambush we just escaped. His group outnumbers the other two, but the new players are much better armed. I think I heard an automatic weapon open up as you rode by." Moving quickly, he hoisted himself up onto the horse, behind Belara.

At first, he hadn't thought about it, but as they loped off, he realized sitting behind her was even worse than sitting in front. She seemed to fit right into the cradle of his thighs. When she moved with the horse, her buttocks would graze against him. He began to sweat despite the cool night air.

The knowledge that they were depending totally on each other for their survival gave him the strength to bring his thinking back under control. "I've always felt responsible for everyone who was with me," he said in a voice that was only loud enough for her to hear. "Around you and your uncle, I'm just part of a three-way partnership. That's a new feeling, and a good one," he admitted.

She smiled, but said nothing.

They rode hard for more than an hour. "We'll have to watch out for my uncle," Belara said quietly. "I don't think he's feeling well." She urged her horse forward until they were almost alongside him.

Travis saw that Jimmie Bowman was bent over in his saddle, his hands barely gripping the reins. "We need to stop," Travis said in a loud voice. He saw the sharp glance Jimmie Bowman gave him and knew the man would not permit any allowances to be made on his behalf. "This horse has been carrying a double load," Travis said, thinking quickly. "It's all lathered up. It won't last if we keep pushing it."

Jimmie straightened up, and nodded. "There's a small mesa ahead. It's got a clear view of everything around it. No one can sneak up on us there."

"How far?"

"Thirty minutes," Jimmie answered in a weary tone. "Follow me." Jimmie pressed his mount to a fast lope, trying to get all the speed the animal was capable of giving him without jeopardizing its endurance.

They stayed together as they crossed into a dried-up salt marsh. It took closer to an hour, but finally they arrived at the base of a butte. "From the top we'll be able to see for miles," Jimmie assured them as they climbed up the rocky slope. "Since the others are on foot, they'll have a good day's travel before they ever reach us. Best of all, we'll be able to see them coming long before they get here."

"That's if they haven't wiped each other out back there," Travis commented, realizing he could no longer hear the gunfire in the distance.

When they reached the crest, they stopped their weary animals and dismounted. Belara went to her uncle's side. "I know you're not feeling well, Uncle. Is it your heart?"

Jimmie shook his head. "I'm feeling a bit weak because I haven't eaten since yesterday afternoon. Moving at this pace without nourishment is difficult."

Belara's shoulders slumped as she realized that she'd never even bothered to think of food. She looked at Travis, who shrugged. "I don't have anything on me except some dried fruit in my jacket pocket." He took out three small boxes of raisins and handed one to each of them. "We left our backpacks and provisions in the cave." He glanced at Jimmie. "Did you bring any supplies in your saddle-bags?"

"Just the bare minimum," he admitted. "When I saw the chance to escape, I took it immediately. I gathered up a few things that were necessary, like water and some quick-

energy foods, but avoided loading up the horses. I figure
we could live off the land for the day or so it would take u
to get off the Range." He gave her a shaky smile. "Don'
worry. All I need is some food, then I'll be fine. I can hel
you look around later, after I rest for a bit." He fished
plastic bag full of trail mix out of his pocket and con
sumed the rations hungrily.

Belara watched him lay down beside a large boulder, the
close his eyes, the box of raisins still in his hand. He looke
drawn and exhausted in the glow of the moon, now almos
setting in the west. She kicked herself mentally for no
having been more alert. Her stomach grumbled noisily an
she realized that she, too, hadn't eaten since noon the pre
vious day. Dawn was almost upon them, and she shivere
in the gentle breeze that blew from the west. Soon it woul
be hot. They'd all need to eat and rest, or the heat woul
sap their remaining energy.

Belara sat down beside her uncle and opened her con
tainer of raisins. Savoring the pleasant taste, she ate then
carefully, one at a time. Five minutes later she was asleep.

When she awoke, it was hot. Looking up, Belara wa
surprised to find the sun directly overhead. She had slep
for hours! Looking over to her uncle, she saw he was sti
asleep. She watched him and noticed his sleep was restless
but he appeared to be breathing normally.

Quietly, she walked toward Travis. He was giving th
horses some water out of a plastic bag he held in his hands
Seeing her approach, he managed a weary smile. "Hell
there. How's your uncle doing?"

"You heard him earlier, he said it wasn't his heart. Bu
I'm not sure that he'd admit it, if it was," she said, he
voice low.

"Do you still have his pills?"

"The first thing I did when we caught up to him was giv
him the bottle. I hope he brought them along." She glance
back at her uncle's still figure. "I'm going to check. I can
stand the suspense. If he didn't, we're going to be in trou
ble. I know a few herbs that might help him, but it'll b

difficult to find them even in daylight." She took a deep breath, then let it out again.

Belara opened one of the saddlebags and reached down into it. She could feel her uncle's prayer stick nestled inside. Not wanting to damage it, she gently lifted the wooden *kaytahn* out, then searched for the pills again. Her fingertips brushed a tiny bottle somewhere below a small tin can.

She chuckled softly. "I think he brought his coffee. He always did have a weakness for it." She pulled out the metal container, then the bottle. "His medication is here," she said, relieved. As she started to return everything to the saddlebags, the smooth, gray metal container caught her attention. "This isn't a coffee can. What is it?"

Travis stared at the object, shaking his head. "I don't believe that wily old fox!"

"What's this strange lettering?" She stared at it for a moment, then slowly recognition dawned over her. "He had the film canister all along!" Belara stared at Travis in shock. As she turned her head to look at her uncle, she saw him propped up on one elbow looking at her.

"Don't you dare lecture me," she said, challenging him with a bold stare. "I just wanted to make sure you'd brought your pills in case you needed them. I had no idea I'd also find this." She held up the can.

Jimmie stared at her solemnly. "Did I forget to mention that I'd already found the satellite film?"

Travis's expression didn't alter. "You gave us the distinct impression that we'd interrupted your search."

"You interrupted my visit to the ranch," he corrected, giving them both an innocent look. "You must have misunderstood." He watched one stony glare, then another. "Okay, okay. I found it by accident a few days before you two came. It had landed safely, thanks to a small parachute, right near the base of the spring that runs by the ranch. Only it had rolled beneath an overhang in the small canyon, making it impossible for sensors to spot it from the air. I almost walked past it myself."

He met Travis's gaze with a steady one of his own. "Ever since you told me about the second group, I've suspected that they could be the foreign agents the FBI had warned the base about. At the time I first learned about them, the only evidence was based on an informant's report. Now it seems that information could have been accurate."

"If the tattoo is really what it appears to be, it suggests that they're Russians, and that makes no sense," Belara insisted. "Something else you said a few days ago," she reminded Travis, "makes me think there's another possibility. Didn't Sy tell you about two hunters? These could be the very same men. We have as much evidence to believe they're after the gold as for anything else. But either way they're a problem and we have to avoid them at all costs."

"Yes," Travis conceded, "but if they're trained agents not prospectors, then they'll be far more dangerous than Robertson ever was."

"Well, with any luck, we won't see them again. The military will have to worry about it, not us."

Jimmie looked at Travis. "If anything happens that prevents me from delivering the canister, you'll have to complete the task. It should be taken directly to the Base Commander. He'll know what to do with it."

"Nothing's going to happen to you," Belara said flatly. "We're in this together and we're going to watch out for each other." She noted with relief that her uncle looked less exhausted. Yet it was undeniable that the constant danger was wearing them all down. "We have to find some food. We should save the prepared stuff for eating while on the move."

Travis stood up. "If you can keep a lookout, I'll take care of that." He was tired and needed the activity to sharpen his senses.

"Wouldn't you prefer to get some sleep?" she suggested.

He shook his head. "Not yet. Food's more important right now."

Belara picked up the rifle to hand him, but Travis shook his head. "I don't want to use that. It'll telegraph our whereabouts. I haven't heard gunfire all day."

"If you're going to rely solely on plants, I think my niece should go with you. She'll make your search easier and faster."

"I saw banana yucca not too far from here. There's mesquite, too, I think," she said.

"I can get the mesquite." He glanced at Jimmie, handing him the field glasses. "Can you keep watch for us?"

He nodded, then watched them go off. The young needed help sometimes to see what was right in front of their faces. He smiled. He'd do that much for them.

Belara bent over the pointed leaves of a yucca plant and pulled several seed pods from its center. "This will help out. It's savory when roasted, and can give Uncle more of his energy back." She began to fill her jacket pockets.

"Mesquite is farther down the slope. I'll be back in a bit."

"Bring the pods. We can eat the dough between the seeds as well if it's not too dry."

Once her pockets were full, Belara started down the slope. Travis met her halfway, his hands filled with green, beanlike pods.

"I've been thinking about our predicament," she said. "Once we get a bit farther away from the others, we should start a fire and signal the military. Do you agree?"

"Definitely, but first we'll have to make sure we know exactly where the others are. If we miscalculate, it'll put us in immediate danger. We could be dead before the military even looks this way. The Army concentrates on trying to keep people from coming in here. They're not going to be watching as closely for people who are trying to get out."

Travis slowed his strides then finally stopped yards away from the top of the butte. Placing the pods on the ground, he glanced up at her. "Would you sit down for a minute? There's something I want to talk to you about. I should have told you this before, but the right moment never seemed to come up." He pressed his lips together, struggling with what he knew must be said. "When you left the cave and risked your life to come after me, I knew that I couldn't let you go on believing a lie. You've seen far too much in me, Belara." His voice was strained. "Your life wasn't worth mine. You're a sweet, gentle person. You deserve someone far better than I am."

She sat down on the ground, then looked up at him. "You've kept things back that I need to know before I can understand you. Please talk to me. There's nothing you can't tell me. I won't judge or condemn you."

"Don't make any promises until you hear what I have to say." He sat across from her, but did not meet her eyes. "I hadn't wanted to tell you because I was vain enough to want you to continue seeing me in the best possible light. Your belief in me meant more than you'll ever know. But it's time you knew the truth and started seeing me as I am."

His eyes took on an unfocused, faraway quality. "When I was in the Special Forces, I took pride in knowing I was part of an elite group. We were the men who could be counted on when the going got tough. Later, when I became an instructor, I tried to instill that pride in my men. I taught them never to accept second best, or take a back seat to anyone. I pushed them hard, and never let up on them. Consequently, whenever we had competitive exercises between the units, my soldiers always came in first."

His voice grew somber. "The day of the crash, we'd already completed the exercise once. Our time was good enough to put us in second place, but I felt they hadn't done their best. I got the men assembled again and I let them know in no uncertain terms that they'd botched it. I knew that they were tired after three days of constant maneuvers and insufficient sleep, but I raked them over the coals. Finally they came up to me as a unit and asked for permission to repeat the exercise. I agreed. I saw nothing wrong with pushing them to be the best. Only, as it turned out, everything about that decision was wrong."

"It was your job to make them into good soldiers. You had to encourage them to try again."

"You don't understand. It went way beyond that. I *drove* them to do that because I couldn't stop pushing or curb my need to be number one." He finally met her eyes. "I'm still that way. You'd think after the price others already paid for it, I'd have no trouble controlling it. Yet, I do. Even out here, I've pushed you and myself to the limit." His voice dropped even more. "That need to win, to neutralize the opponent, can turn deadly. It's taken everything I've got to keep holding back and not try to finish this with Robertson once and for all, regardless of the cost."

"But you've done it. If you've pushed us it's because you're working very hard to keep all of us alive. There's a big difference between men like the ones behind us and someone like you. They thrive on violence. You use it to get attention as well as for self-preservation. Every man has the right to defend himself and those he cares about. That's the same kind of loyalty that keeps families strong. What you've seen isn't a failing in yourself. It's a mark of your humanity and shows that you're the kind and caring man I've always know you were."

It took several minutes for her words to sink in. The rejection he'd expected had turned into the most loving of all declarations. She was telling him that she accepted him just as he was. In her eyes, he was the man he'd always wanted to be. His fear of lacking some mysterious dimension that others more noble had was groundless. In light of her belief in him, he found he could also believe in himself.

Travis stood and pulled her into his arms. "Sweetheart, I don't ever want to lose you."

She buried her head against his chest, wishing that what he asked were possible. "I care for you more than you'll ever know. You'll always have my friendship, but there can't be anything more. In the long run, things wouldn't work out for us." Belara moved away, though doing so was tearing her heart. "The way of the *Dinéh* is precious to me. I don't want the family I'll have someday to grow up knowing and being more comfortable in your world than in mine. Many in our tribe have lost sight of their heritage by adopting the white culture as their own. It surrounds them, I know, and that makes it difficult. It's easier to blend than to hold on to what they have. I want more than that for myself and my future family. My mother was caught between two worlds and it ended disastrously. I don't want to repeat her mistakes.''

"Oh, honey, you won't!" Frustrated by his inability to find the right words to explain how he felt, he drew her to him. Wanting them to remain together didn't mean she'd have to sacrifice part of her heritage. He had to make her see all the understanding and support that were his to give, were hers for the taking. "Feel what I do for you," he said in a raw voice. "Help me show you what's in my heart." He tilted her chin up and had started to lower his mouth to hers when he heard footsteps.

A second later Jimmie came into view. "I used your binoculars to look over the trail we left last night. There's one man on foot coming straight for us and he sure seems in a hurry.''

Chapter Eighteen

Travis followed Jimmie back to the summit. He could still feel the warm imprint of Belara's body against his own. With a soldier's discipline, he forced himself to put that memory aside and concentrate on the threat now facing them.

Jimmie handed Travis the binoculars as they reached the top. "You can barely make him out to the left of the rise."

"Thanks." Travis studied the distant figure, apparently running. He'd seen enough men engaged in evasion and escape maneuvers to recognize the tactics. Whatever had happened at the pass had left at least one man being pursued by others, and he was doing his best to throw them off the trail.

"I've checked the horses carefully, and they still haven't recovered from that long ride last night," Jimmie warned, his gaze resting on the animals. "With the limited water we could spare them, they aren't going to be able to carry us very far in this heat before they give out. If we wait until tonight when it's cooler, there's a good chance we can ride them and be back to civilization by tomorrow morning."

Travis considered the matter, his forehead furrowed in thought. "Then we'll have to stay for a few more hours. At least we have a better chance of defending ourselves up here than out on the flats. If something prevents us from riding out once darkness falls, we'll go ahead and start a large bonfire. The light and flames are bound to attract any aircraft that flies overhead."

"I think that's the best plan," Jimmie agreed, eating some of the food Belara brought to him. Staying low, he studied the man approaching through the rifle scope. "I think he's tracking us. His path follows ours too closely to be coincidental. Of course, in the daylight he couldn't possibly miss the trail the horses left behind."

Travis moved in beside him. "If he is trailing us, then he's leading whoever's after him directly to us, too. Have you caught a glimpse of anyone else yet?"

"No," Jimmie answered, "but from the way he keeps looking back and the behavior of the birds in that dried-out salt marsh, I think they'll be coming into view soon."

Travis kept his eyes fastened on the area Jimmie had pointed out and within five minutes two faint dots appeared. "They're moving faster than the man they're after and gaining on him. I'll try to warn the first guy off if he gets close to the base of this mesa." He met Belara's eyes with a steady gaze. "But if he keeps on coming, I won't give him a second chance. We don't have enough ammunition left for that."

She nodded. "I understand."

Travis touched her lightly on the shoulder, then took over the watch. "Start gathering some brush. We'll have to light that bonfire right after it gets dark. From the looks of it, we're going to have too much company to be able to ride out of here tonight."

As the first man came closer to their position it was obvious that fear had replaced caution. He was no longer attempting to throw his pursuers off by zigzagging. He was running as fast as he could straight toward them. Finally Travis was able to make out his features. "Robertson's the one being chased."

Belara stopped clearing brush away from the area that would surround their bonfire. "So the pair who tried to ambush us must have wiped out his group," she said.

"Not necessarily," Jimmie cautioned. "This man is full of tricks. We can't trust him."

Belara stood by the low, wide stack of brush she'd accumulated. "This should make a fire that's big enough to be seen for miles."

"Make sure you wait until it's completely dark before lighting it. We have a limited amount of brush we can gather up here and we shouldn't waste any of it," Jimmie said.

Time dragged by as Travis monitored Robertson's approach carefully. "He's at the base of the mesa," he said at last. "I can't let him get any closer." He took careful aim. "Stop right there, Robertson. I've got you in my sights," he shouted.

The man stopped abruptly. "I'm coming up, Hill," he yelled back hoarsely, out of breath. "I don't have a chance if I stay down here."

"You don't have a chance if you try to climb up," Travis responded.

Robertson stood rock still, his chest heaving, then finally answered. "Unless I join with you, they'll kill me anyway." He opened his jacket. "I'm unarmed, Hill, so go ahead and shoot me if you want to kill a man in cold blood."

Travis swore softly, then handed Jimmie the rifle. "I'm going down. For now at least, he's alone. If this is a trick, he's going to have to face the consequences without any help from his buddies. Keep the cross hairs on him. In the meantime, let me borrow your knife. I lost mine when I infiltrated their camp and I'm not going down there empty-handed."

Belara placed her hand on his arm, trying to stop him. "Don't go. You're assuming that you can handle him in a hand-to-hand situation, but you've underestimated him before. What makes you think you're not doing it again?"

Travis gave her a look that suggested he was running low on patience. "I fought him that way before and won." Seeing the worried look on her face, he gave a quirky half grin. "I keep telling you I'm a nasty son of a gun. You just never believe me."

Belara watched him pick his way down the slope. "Can we cover him from here?" she asked her uncle quickly.

"No problem. But this is his fight. We shouldn't interfere unless it's absolutely necessary. You have to honor his right to face his enemy. To rob him of that is to strip him of his self-respect."

Belara held her uncle's .22 caliber rifle in her hands. "If it gets out of hand, I'm going to put a stop to it. I'd rather have him safe than worry about his pride."

Jimmie sighed. "You have a lot to learn about men, niece."

She sighted on Robertson and waited, ignoring her uncle's muttering about her stubbornness.

Travis scrambled down the hillside, knife in hand. "Stay right there," he ordered. "And don't get any stupid ideas. If I don't kill you myself, my friends up at the top will drop you in your tracks."

"If we stay here we're both dead. Let's go up to your camp."

Travis saw caked blood intermingled with the sweat on Robertson's side. It had permeated the fabric of his shirt, making it cling to his body like a second skin. "Where are the men who were with you?"

Robertson's hands clenched at his sides. "All dead," he said, his voice bitter. "The two waiting for us didn't hesitate to kill to get what they wanted. Now they're after all of us. And they've got quality training. They're *good*, Hill. You're going to need the information I have, and I'll only trade it in exchange for the chance to join up with you."

Travis studied the man before him, trying to make up his mind. Robertson's blood loss must have been considerable, judging from the amount on his clothes. He was surprised to see him still standing. "All right. You can come up, but lock your hands behind your head."

"Give me a break, Hill. There's a bullet inches from my shoulder blade. I tore up my T-shirt and made it into a bandage to stop the blood. It isn't going to kill me, but my shoulder and back feel like they're on fire.''

"Then hold your hands as high as you can. I want them where I can see them.'' Travis looked into the man's eyes, searching for any sign that he was being tricked, but all he saw reflected there were fear and defeat. "There's something I want to make very clear to you. The people waiting at the top are far more important to me than you'll ever be, no matter what information you can provide. Keep that in mind as you climb up.''

Robertson, obviously exhausted, staggered a few times, but made it to the summit on his own. Wearily, he sat down across from Jimmie and Belara. He stared out toward the horizon, watching the darkening sky.

"Start talking,'' Travis ordered, exchanging Jimmie's knife for his own rifle. "I want to know exactly what's going on and who those men are.''

"We'd seen those two paralleling our course right from the start,'' Robertson began. "They were the same pair who tried to kidnap you on the road that day,'' he said, looking at Belara, "but that was the only thing we knew about them. We watched them, sure, but we didn't worry. We'd run them off before, so we figured we wouldn't have any trouble handling them. When we lost track of them about a day and a half ago, we were too occupied with you three to think much about it. It was the ambush that took us off guard. From what they told Perea and me after they captured us, they thought either my people or you three had the canister. When they'd seen you and then us heading back, they'd decided to cut us off. They were after the film and were prepared to get it at any cost.''

"How did you get captured?'' Jimmie asked. "It was four against two. Surely you wouldn't have let either of those men sneak up on you from behind.''

"After you got past them, they were determined to dispense with us as quickly as possible. They opened up with automatic weapons. We knew that we wouldn't leave that arroyo alive unless we found a way to kill them. When we tried to outflank them, we walked right into a trap. They pretended to retreat, and as we advanced they seemed able to appear out of nowhere. Their training and tactics were top-notch. They killed Wilson right away, and took Halliday, Perea and I prisoner when we bunched up in the wrong spot."

"Why? If they wanted to question you, they wouldn't have needed three of you. One, or at most two, would have been enough," Travis prodded.

"Yeah, that's why we had some hope that they'd let us go. Then, they started by asking Halliday about the canister. When Halliday played dumb, they shot and killed him. They left Perea and me tied up and let us sweat it out for a while."

"Did they talk to each other at all?" Belara asked.

Robertson nodded. "They sure did, but it wasn't in English. Perea thought it was Russian or something like that. The strange thing was that when they actually started questioning us, they spoke perfect English. One of the men even had a trace of a Spanish accent, and believe me, if he was Hispanic, I'm Santa Claus."

"What did they want to know?" Jimmie urged, exchanging concerned glances with Travis and Belara.

"They asked us if we knew whether you were working independently or for the government. They also wanted to know if we'd found anything with Soviet markings. We told them we hadn't, but they still searched through everything we owned. Then they decided to separate us. They left me tied up while they worked on Perea. After a while I heard a shot and I knew they were coming for me next. Only I'd worked the ropes loose by then with a key I had in my pocket. I took off through the brush without looking back. When I finally broke out into the open just one shot was fired—the one that hit me. I think they wanted me alive. They weren't convinced we'd told them the truth and really didn't know where the satellite film packet was."

"You got off lucky. Two inches lower and you'd have been dead instantly," Travis said.

"Lucky?" Robertson shuddered. "You don't know how many times I almost gave up. It was a real fight not to let myself pass out, but I knew if I did I'd be finished for sure. As long as I had a breath, there was no way I was going to make it easy for them." He met Travis's gaze with a steady one of his own. "You're more of a match for them, Hill. Remember the old saying, 'my enemy's enemy is my friend.' You're going to need all the help you can get against that pair, and I'd like to fight on your side. They killed my friends, and it's payback time."

Travis's face hardened. "A full-scale firefight is the last thing we need," he answered. "We're almost out of ammunition."

Suddenly Jimmie rose to one knee and fastened his sights on a moving shadow below. The figure was barely discernible in the gathering twilight. He fired one round as a warning, then shouted the alarm to the others. "Find cover. We've got company!" A shot rang out from below, and Jimmie flattened.

"Wait a second," Robertson protested, ducking onto his belly.

"Just stay down!" Travis barked.

Crawling on his stomach, Travis moved rapidly to the rim of the slope. To his surprise, two well-placed shots sent dust and dirt flying over him as soon as he reached the edge. Quickly he shifted back out of their field of fire.

"I was about to tell you—" Robertson yelled, "—one of those guys is a marksman, as good as you are, if not better. And he has some kind of starlight scope on his rifle."

Jimmie, now well away from the edge, reached down and pressed his hand against his calf. Blood was trickling through his fingers.

Belara's eyes widened. "You've been shot." She crawled to his side and helped him slide back farther. "Let me take a look."

"Leave it. The bullet went right through the muscle, not bone. I'm okay."

Belara tore off her shirtsleeve, and used it as a bandage. "This will do for now."

Jimmie nodded. "I can crawl or drag myself around, just don't expect me to do any running," he said, glancing at Travis.

Travis started to answer when a bullet struck a rock just a few inches from Belara's head. Travis dived across and pushed her completely to the ground. "Don't get up, even in a crouch. These guys mean business."

A steady and accurate flow of bullets kept them close to the ground as they pulled back. The shots were well placed. Some hit near enough to draw blood when rock fragments flew in all directions.

"I've seen these two work, and unless we do something fast, we won't last long," Robertson warned. "They'll cover each other's advances so well that we won't be able to defend ourselves effectively."

Jimmie crawled up next to Travis. "I've got an idea. Having a starlight scope doesn't make them invincible. Maybe we can overload it. That brush sitting back there can be put to good use now, and I can move around enough to light it. A bright fire is going to render the scope useless if we're in line with the flames."

Robertson reached into his shirt pocket, pulled out a lighter, and handed it to Jimmie. "This will help get that pile of brush burning fast."

"We're going to need more than a fire to turn the odds in our favor," Travis added thoughtfully. "We have seven rounds, and only one is for the high-powered rifle. If these guys are as sharp as we think, they'll probably wait until it's completely dark, then go on the offensive. We've got to make our move now, while we still can."

"What we really need to do is get our hands on their guns and ammunition," Belara said.

"I agree. It's risky, but it's our only chance." Travis gestured for Robertson and Belara to join him at Jimmie's side. Using his index finger, he drew a rough map on the sandy soil. "The three of us—" he nodded to Robertson

nd Belara "—will go down the back side of the mesa and
vork our way in close to the men. By the time they begin
heir attack, we should be in position. You, sir—" he
ooked at Jimmie "—will light the bonfire then. That
hould blind their scope, maybe even burn it out. Robert-
on, with that wound, you're not likely to be able to move
quietly, so you'll have to be our decoy. Make lots of noise
nd draw their attention, then get down under cover.
They'll have some doubts about what we're up to by that
ime because no one's going to be returning their fire right
way. With no real targets except you, they may hesitate to
ontinue their attack. Try to keep their attention focused on
vhat you're doing, at least until you can get help from up
ere."

Travis glanced at Jimmie. "We'll be leaving both rifles
vith you since you're going to be the only one in position
o cover all of us."

"Good. That's something I'll be able to do well, despite
ay injured leg."

Travis reached out and touched Belara's arm. "You and
, meanwhile, are going to sneak over to where they've left
heir extra gear. You'll go in from behind and get what you
an. I'll come in from the front, grab a weapon, and make
ure they never get near you. If I get the chance, I'll try to
ut them out of action. If not, we'll cover each other and
.obertson until we make it make to the top. By then, maybe
ae military will have spotted the fire and we won't have to
old out for too much longer."

"Hill, your plan is damned dangerous," Robertson
auttered. "We could all end up dead."

"That's been a possibility all along," Travis answered
omberly. "If you have any other ideas, speak up now."

Robertson said nothing, his lips pursed into a tight line.
We sure can't hold them off with seven rounds until the
avalry arrives—*if* they arrive." His shoulders slumped.
It's your way, I guess."

Travis handed Jimmie the remaining shells for the rifles.
Keep a sharp lookout, sir, and if you see them get too

close, go ahead and shoot. Otherwise try to save the ammo
as long as you can."

"It's a good plan," Jimmie agreed. "When I don't shoo
back, they'll start to wonder. Then when I light the fire
they'll realize it'll be only a matter of time before Rang
security is all over this place. Maybe that'll force them to
make a mistake we can take advantage of."

Travis's admiration for Jimmie Bowman grew. The
courage and poise he displayed now made him realize jus
how badly they'd all underestimated his strength. "That'
what I'm hoping for. Is there anything we can do for yo
before we leave?"

"Watch out for my niece as best you can," Jimmie said
handing Travis his hunting knife. Travis said nothing, bu
nodded silently.

As he moved away, Travis heard the soft *hozonji* bein
sung behind them. For a moment, he thought he felt th
power of the song, then he shook his head. This was a tim
for him to rely solely on logic and reason. Bowman wa
helping all of them with the knowledge he possessed. It wa
now time for him to do the same.

Travis watched Belara start quietly down the norther
side of the butte. Hers was the longest distance to trave
She'd have to move fast and silently in order for their pla
to work. After she left, restlessness gnawed at him. It wa
difficult waiting, knowing that Belara was out there alone
with only her stalking skills to protect her.

The realization caused his normally rock-solid hands t
shake, and it took a moment for him to calm down agair
Then it was his turn. In the silence, the sound of every ste
he took was magnified by his imagination, and he wor
dered how he managed to avoid detection. His trainin
prevailed as he moved from bush to rock quickly and qu
etly, and reached the area he had selected for himself. It wa
pitch-black now, and somewhere to his left Belara waite
along with him. Travis wondered if she was thinking o
him, but quickly wished the opposite. Survival was all h

wanted for her now, and that would take complete concentration.

In spite of his combat experience, he was startled when a sudden burst of automatic weapons fire broke the silence. The attack was beginning. Travis watched from hiding as the man with the assault rifle sprinted toward the mesa, firing from the hip. He stopped after about fifty feet and hid behind a bush. The other man, the sniper, then fired several shots at the ridge. Travis watched with a mixture of relief and apprehension as the men followed exactly the type of plan he'd predicted.

Travis moved forward silently, his destination fixed firmly in his mind. His timing had to be perfect. There was no room for mistakes. He'd have to reach the men's supplies, arm himself, and get into position quickly. Belara's life was hanging in the balance.

Chapter Nineteen

Belara was crouching behind a boulder when the first shot rang out. Even though she was about fifty yards behind the gunman, she ducked involuntarily as a powerful, deep-throated burst of gunfire shattered the night. A heartbeat later, several more rounds whined through the air from an area less than ten yards to her right. Guided by the muzzle flash, she crawled toward her enemy's position.

Belara edged forward cautiously, straining to see through the darkness. Finally she caught a flicker of movement. Robertson was in position, and he'd have to make his move soon. She held her breath waiting for the blaze that would ruin the starlight scope. Seconds later, light flooded the small plateau. She heard Robertson's loud, rustling footsteps and a dull thud as he pretended to fall heavily into the brush. The gunman ahead of her turned his head, shifting his rifle barrel as he did. Focusing on the area of the sound, he fired twice.

Making use of the diversion, Belara eased around, positioning herself closer to the rifleman and the gear strewn behind him. From her new vantage point, she could see the dark outline of their second adversary near the bottom of the mesa. As the sniper provided his partner with cover fire, she noticed the pattern of his shots had become more random. Forced to look in the direction of the flames, he'd lost the advantage of the starlight scope and thus his accuracy.

Belara took a deep breath and steadied herself. Her enemy's night vision was undoubtedly lost for the moment. It was time to press her advantage. Trying to ignore her fear, she moved toward the men's packs. A half-open pouch containing several clips of ammunition lay out on the ground. Silently she took it with her. As she crept toward a rifle resting against some brush, she realized that the gunman had stopped firing. Belara stole a glance at him and saw him in a half crouch, releasing a spent clip.

Fear engulfed her as the man's gaze shifted toward his ammunition pouch and discovered her standing there. For a second, neither of them moved. She had the ammunition, but no gun. He had a gun, but no ammunition. Recovering from his surprise, the man lunged toward her, and Belara started to run.

TRAVIS WAS ALREADY MOVING to tackle the gunman before he could reach Belara when, suddenly, a burst of automatic weapon fire swept the brush near Robertson's position, and then ripped past him. Travis dived to the ground, unscathed, and saw the second man running in his direction, firing from the hip. Alerted by the absence of cover fire, the man had stopped his advance and was returning to help his partner.

Travis rolled to his left, drawing his knife as he moved. He crouched behind a rock, ready to spring when the man stopped to reload.

As the man discarded an empty clip, Travis jumped out from cover and was upon him. The man dropped his assault rifle and reached for the pistol at his waist. In an instant, Travis kicked the weapon out of his grasp. Countering with lightning-fast reflexes, the man ducked and came back with a long-bladed boot knife secure in his hand.

Travis saw the deadly look in his opponent's eyes and knew it would be a fight to the finish. Only skill and luck could help him now.

"Who are you?" Travis said, his body poised.

"The man who's going to kill you. Robertson and the others were amateurs, now you're up against a pro. You're not going to walk away from this."

"Don't bet the farm on that," Travis growled, evading and parrying his enemy's move.

They moved in a tight circle, each searching for weakness in his opponent's defenses. Travis heard the sounds of a struggle down the hill, and for a brief moment, worry about Belara disrupted his concentration. In that split second, his enemy struck.

Bringing his leg up, the man caught Travis firmly in the stomach and knocked him back. While Travis tried to recapture his balance, his opponent lunged, keeping the blade in line with Travis's chest.

Travis twisted away quickly and managed to land a blow to the back of his opponent's head with the butt of his knife. The man slumped to the ground, unconscious.

Travis picked up the man's .45 caliber pistol as Robertson came rushing up.

"I'll hold him," Robertson yelled, moving toward the discarded assault rifle. "You go on."

"He's out of ammo," Travis shouted back as he ran toward where Belara had been. "Just find his knife."

As Jimmie fired off two rounds, which passed well over Travis's head, Travis realized Bowman was doing what he could to protect Belara. Somewhere ahead, in the dark, he could hear the sounds of a struggle. As he approached the clearing, he saw Belara fighting to keep the ammo pouch from a man twice her size. Despite the delay, she'd held her own.

"Freeze!" Travis shouted, then fired a round into the ground beside the man, hoping to disrupt his concentration.

Their enemy reacted with the instincts of a professional soldier. With one massive effort, he yanked the strap of the ammo pouch Belara still clung to and threw her into Travis's line of fire. Belara tumbled to the ground in front of Travis, ammunition flying in every direction.

As the man retrieved one of the clips, Travis tried to shoot, but nothing happened. His pistol was jammed.

His adversary quickly swung the loaded weapon around and pointed the muzzle toward Belara, who was just rising to her knees.

Before he could fire, Travis made a move toward the rifle, and it swung back toward him.

"No, Travis, don't!" she yelled, knowing he intended to draw the gunfire to himself.

A heartbeat later, the man gasped and dropped his rifle. The handle of a knife, buried to the hilt, protruded from his chest. His hand curled around the grip, then fell away, as his lifeless body crumpled to the ground.

"Sorry I took so long," Robertson said, stepping into view. His face was white and drawn from the pain the knife throw had cost him. "I tied up the other guy with his belt and came down to help as soon as I could. Only I had to get close enough to make sure I'd hit him."

"I never thought I'd see the day when I was glad to see you," Travis muttered, "but thanks." He remembered Belara's words about the teachings of the *Dinéh*. Everything existed in two parts and understanding the balance between good and evil was the way to "walk in beauty." There'd been a time when he'd chafed for the opportunity to confront Robertson. Yet in the end, what he'd seen as evil had accomplished good.

"This was payback time, Hill," he muttered. "You don't have to thank me."

Travis offered Belara a hand up. "Hear it?" he asked, looking up into the night sky.

"Aircraft overhead." Belara felt her spirits soar. "We might be taking the short route out of here after all."

Robertson started toward the top of the butte. "I'm going to see if your uncle needs any help keeping that fire going."

IT WAS NEARLY dawn by the time the fire died down completely. "Do you think they could have missed it?" Belara asked, concerned.

"Not on your life," Jimmie answered, keeping his rifle pointed at their captive. "They saw it. That's why the pilot came around and circled once before leaving. They'll be dispatching helicopters to investigate." Jimmie studied the man Travis had captured. He sat on the ground, hands and feet tied, his face set rigidly. "I still don't know how *he* fits in."

Belara walked behind their prisoner and, staying a discreet distance away, studied the mark on his hand. The man's watch had slipped forward, completely revealing it. "What is that tattoo?"

The man didn't answer.

"Surely it can't hurt to tell us," she said quietly. "That gold star looks like part of the Russian emblem. Are you working for them?"

"Never," the man answered in perfect English.

"But that does look a great deal like the Soviet flag," she insisted.

"Only to an ignorant American," he answered flatly.

Travis came around. "You're from one of the satellite countries, aren't you? But what's your angle? Why were you trying to steal the capsule from the Soviets and the U.S.?"

The man's face remained impassive and he said nothing.

"We're not going to get any answers from him," Travis muttered, then stood.

Shaking her head, Belara walked to the rim of the mesa and stared pensively into the distance. Travis joined her a moment later. "I almost lost you," she whispered, a lump in her throat. "You were ready to give up your life for mine," her voice trembled with emotion.

Travis pulled her into the shadows of a large boulder, well away from the others. "Don't you understand yet?" he whispered, tenderly brushing a few wisps of hair away from her face. "I couldn't have let anything happen to you. I love you, sweetheart, and in loving you I've found myself.

"If you decide to walk away from me, I won't stop you. I couldn't live with the knowledge that your feelings for me were mingled with regret. That's not the kind of love I have to offer you." His voice shook slightly. "Letting you go would be the hardest thing I've ever done, but you'd never be far from me. I'd carry you in my heart for as long as I live."

She placed her hands against Travis's chest, struggling to hold back her tears. "I've been wrong about many things," she managed. "I told you that I wanted only the best for my children, that your culture couldn't give them what mine could. That's why I was determined to find a mate from my tribe. But I forgot that nobility and courage aren't restricted to a race. Your world and mine both have things worth treasuring and sharing. Our children will grow up knowing the best of both, and enjoy the abundance of the gifts of love."

"Honey..." Emotions too powerful to contain flooded through him. "Whole. That's how you make me feel."

"And you make me feel loved."

He tilted her face up and kissed her. Her lips opened beneath his and what he'd meant as a tender caress turned fierce.

"Hey, you two," Jimmie yelled to them. "Better bring those horses. There's choppers coming. My guess is that they'll be here in ten minutes."

Travis groaned. "Just what we need, more company," he said, muttering to himself.

They went to retrieve the animals, who were feeding on some brush near the rim of the butte. As the helicopters approached, Belara gave him a worried look. "Are you going to be all right?"

He nodded. "There was a time when that sound would have made me break out in a cold sweat. Now, it only means we're safe. The past is finally behind me."

Twenty minutes later, after the others were all safely inside the helicopter, an airman approached Travis and Belara. "It'll be a few days before we can get a trailer out here for the horses," he said.

"I thought we'd ride them out," Travis said, glancing at Belara and seeing her eager nod. "You've brought enough water to tide them over and, with your emergency rations, we'll be just fine." Travis handed the airman the keys to his Jeep, and gave him directions to its hiding place. "I'd appreciate it if someone could go get this for me before it gets strafed or bombed. It'll be hard to spot, but it's there."

"You've both served your country well. We owe you a big thanks for what you've done," the soldier answered. "We'll be glad to take care of that little detail for you."

An MP approached them. "The prisoner has been secured on board and we're about to take off. Is there anything else you need?"

"Yes, I have a question," Belara said. "We know what Robertson was doing and why, but we're still not sure how the other two men were involved. Can you tell us anything about them?"

"They're Azerbaijanis. Our information led us to believe they were in Mexico and had not crossed to our side of the border yet. We suspect that they wanted the film canister to gain concessions in negotiations for their Republic. They've been seeking autonomy from the Soviet central government for some time now."

Belara and Travis watched the two men board. Sunrise lit the landscape with its array of gold and orange hues as the helicopter lifted off the mesa. Standing behind Belara, Travis gently drew her against the hard contours of his body.

"It's finally finished," she said, her body relaxing into his as the helicopter faded from view.

"No, my love," he said, caressing her and bringing one hand down to rest on her stomach. "Our future is just beginning and we have lots yet to do."